Praise for the *New York Times* bestselling
CITY SPIES series

"Ingeniously plotted, and a grin-inducing delight."
　—People.com on *City Spies*

"A well-paced story laced with suspense, wit, and entertaining dialogue. . . . Laying the groundwork for a new series, this brisk adventure features mysteries, intrigues, and five clever young heroes."
　—*Booklist* on *City Spies*

"Combining their skills in areas like math, hacking, and sneaking around, the prodigies traverse the Western hemisphere looking for clues. The thriller is well paced, the characters animated, and the adventure engaging. A winner."
　—*Kirkus Reviews* on *Golden Gate*

ALSO BY JAMES PONTI

The Framed! series
Framed!
Vanished!
Trapped!

The Dead City trilogy
Dead City
Blue Moon
Dark Days

The City Spies series
City Spies
Golden Gate
Forbidden City

BOOK 2

CITY SPIES

GOLDEN GATE

BY JAMES PONTI

ALADDIN
New York London Toronto Sydney New Delhi

This book is a work of fiction. Any references to historical events, real people, or real places are used fictitiously. Other names, characters, places, and events are products of the author's imagination, and any resemblance to actual events or places or persons, living or dead, is entirely coincidental.

❦ALADDIN
An imprint of Simon & Schuster Children's Publishing Division
1230 Avenue of the Americas, New York, New York 10020
First Aladdin paperback edition January 2022
Text copyright © 2021 by James Ponti
Cover illustration copyright © 2021 by Yaoyao Ma Van As
Also available in an Aladdin hardcover edition.
All rights reserved, including the right of reproduction in whole or in part in any form.
ALADDIN and related logo are registered trademarks of Simon & Schuster, Inc.
For information about special discounts for bulk purchases, please contact Simon & Schuster Special Sales at 1-866-506-1949 or business@simonandschuster.com.
The Simon & Schuster Speakers Bureau can bring authors to your live event. For more information or to book an event contact the Simon & Schuster Speakers Bureau at 1-866-248-3049 or visit our website at www.simonspeakers.com.
Book designed by Tiara Iandiorio
The illustrations for this book were rendered digitally.
The text of this book was set in Sabon LT Std.
Manufactured in the United States of America 1221 OFF
10 9 8 7 6 5 4 3 2 1
The Library of Congress has cataloged the hardcover edition as follows:
ISBN 978-1-5344-1494-5 (hc)
ISBN 978-1-5344-1495-2 (pbk)
ISBN 978-1-5344-1496-9 (ebook)

FOR MY BROTHERS,
CAREY AND TERRY,
WHO'VE BEEN PART
OF THE ADVENTURES
EVER SINCE THE
BEGINNING

The *Sylvia Earle*, North Sea

IT WAS JUST AFTER DAWN, SO THE BLACK-clad hijackers were barely visible as they moved with military precision across the deck of the marine research vessel *Sylvia Earle*. There were seven of them, and they wore special nonslip tactical shoes that gripped the damp metal surface, and balaclava ski masks that concealed their identities and shielded them from the cold ocean air. Virtually all of the ship's passengers and crew were still asleep, so the intruders faced no resistance as they stormed the bridge and caught the duty officer by surprise.

1

No alarm was sounded.

No desperate call for help was transmitted over the radio.

That meant the best hope to save the *Sylvia Earle* was one deck below, only half awake and yawning as she groggily looked for her best friend. There was no precision in her movements, and her pajamas were comfortable, not tactical: neon blue sweatpants, a Ravenclaw T-shirt, and wool socks decorated with cartoon narwhals. According to the ship's manifest, her name was Christina Diaz, but that was just a cover identity created by the British Secret Intelligence Service. Among her fellow MI6 agents, she was Brooklyn.

She was also twelve years old.

Brooklyn had been awakened not by the arrival of the hijackers, but rather the endless snoring of two of her cabinmates. She turned on a small reading light above her bed to see if the same fate had befallen her friend Sydney, only to find Sydney's bunk empty. At first, she assumed her fellow spy was down the hall using the restroom, or the "head" as they called it on the ship. But when Sydney didn't return after a while and the snoring got louder, Brooklyn decided to look for her.

She silently lowered herself from the upper bunk and

slipped out the door into the passageway. She was on her way to the galley to see if Sydney was raiding the freezer for ice cream when a man's voice came over the loudspeaker. That was the first sign of trouble. There weren't supposed to be any men on the *Sylvia Earle*. The ship was carrying sixteen students, seven crew members, three scientists, and a documentary filmmaker on a weeklong trip meant to inspire girls to pursue careers in the sciences. Everyone on board was female . . . until now.

Someone had crashed the party.

"Attention! Attention!" He had a mild Scandinavian accent and spoke in a chilling monotone. "I am sorry to wake you, but we have taken control of the ship. Everybody must immediately come up to the main deck in a calm, orderly manner. If you obey our instructions, nobody will get hurt. But if you disobey, then you will be responsible for what happens next."

Just like that, Brooklyn was wide awake and fully alert as she raced toward her cabin. MI6 had placed her and Sydney on the trip specifically to protect two girls: Judy Somersby, whose mother was a high-ranking member of Parliament, and Alice Hawthorne, who, despite being thirteen years old, was officially *Lady* Alice Hawthorne, daughter of the Duke of Covington. She was thirty-second in line for the throne, and for anyone who didn't know that, she managed to work it into conversation with astonishing frequency.

"Get up, now!" Brooklyn commanded as she flung open the door.

The room was cramped—two sets of bunk beds with a narrow space barely shoulder-wide between them. Alice and Judy were on the bottom bunks, and when they failed to respond quickly enough, Brooklyn reached down, grabbed both sets of covers, and yanked them away like a magician.

"I said, get up!"

"I beg your pardon," Alice exclaimed. "You can't speak to me that way. I'll have you know—"

"What?" Brooklyn interrupted. "That you're thirty-second in line for the throne? If you don't listen to me, there's a decent chance everyone from thirty-three on down is going to move up a spot."

Still sleepy, Judy sat up and mumbled, "What are you going on about?"

"Pirates have seized the boat," Brooklyn said. "I think they're coming for the two of you."

"Pirates?" Judy gave her a confused look. "You mean with peg legs and parrots?"

"Yes, and a crocodile with a loud clock in its stomach," Brooklyn replied sarcastically. "This isn't a storybook. These are actual twenty-first-century criminals at sea. And you two are the most valuable treasure on this boat."

There was a commotion in the passageway, and they could hear one of the hijackers yelling at everyone to get up to the main deck.

"Is this some sort of prank?" asked Alice. "Because it's not funny at all."

"Apple jack!" blurted Brooklyn.

"What?" Judy asked, still confused.

"Apple jack," Brooklyn replied, although this time with less certainty. "That is the code, isn't it? Didn't your parents tell you about 'apple jack'?"

MI6 had given this emergency code to the parents of both girls with the instructions that if someone used the term, they were supposed to follow that person's directions without question. Neither Alice nor Judy had taken it very seriously, and if at all, they expected it to come from someone in authority wearing a uniform, not a twelve-year-old girl in Harry Potter jammies. But that's because they had no way of knowing that perhaps the biggest secret in the British Secret Intelligence Service was an experimental team of five young agents aged twelve to fifteen who called themselves the City Spies. Their success relied heavily on the fact that their mere existence seemed unimaginable. Nobody ever saw them coming. And even if they did, who'd believe it?

"Yes, but . . . ," sputtered Alice.

Just then a massive man filled the doorway. He was so big, his muscles had muscles. "Everybody to the main deck," he snarled, his yellowed teeth visible through the opening in his ski mask. "You don't have time to put on the makeup."

He was menacing. But while Alice and Judy were properly terrified, Brooklyn seemed more . . . *annoyed*.

"What's that supposed to mean?" she asked.

He was only expecting shrieks and screams, so her question caught him off guard. "What do you say?"

"That crack about makeup," she replied. "You think because we're girls all we care about is our appearance? Is that it? That's really sexist."

"Get to the top of the boat, now!" he bellowed. To punctuate his point, he stepped through the doorway so that he loomed over the foot of each bed.

Which was exactly where Brooklyn wanted him.

She put her arms on the upper bunks to brace herself. Then, like a gymnast using parallel bars, she swung up the lower half of her body and executed a perfect scissor kick to the underside of his jaw. He froze momentarily before collapsing into a heap.

Brooklyn turned to the girls. "So are you coming or what?" she asked. "Because there's going to be more of him, and, at the moment, there's only one of me."

The two of them looked at the behemoth on the floor and then the slender girl who'd put him there.

"We're coming with you!" they said in unison as they scrambled to their feet.

"Grab your shoes," Brooklyn said as she jammed on a pair of sneakers. "There's climbing involved."

"Climbing what?" Alice asked, alarmed, but Brooklyn was already out the door.

The passageway was pure pandemonium. The alarm system blared and emergency lights flashed. Their shipmates headed toward the stairwell while Mr. Creepy kept talking over the loudspeaker. Brooklyn ignored it all and focused on going in the opposite direction with Alice and Judy right behind her. All the while, she kept an eye out for Sydney, who should've come straight to their cabin at the first sign of trouble. Brooklyn couldn't imagine where she was and that had her worried.

"Where are we going?" Alice demanded.

"I'm not going to say it out loud because I don't want anyone else to hear," Brooklyn said. "Just stay with me."

She turned back and saw that the hijacker had regained consciousness and was now emerging from the cabin. He rubbed his tender jaw as he scanned the passageway, looking for them. When he spied Brooklyn, his eyes filled with rage.

"You!" he roared as he lumbered toward them, swatting people out of his way like a movie monster. "I want you!"

"Pick up the pace," Brooklyn urgently told the others. "We've got company."

They hurried into a room marked WET LAB and closed the metal door behind them. The lab was filled with display tables, scientific equipment, and shallow saltwater tanks that held the marine specimens they'd studied during the week. Brooklyn checked for a lock on the door, but there wasn't one.

"What do we do?" asked Judy.

"Hide," said Brooklyn. "Let me deal with him."

"How?" asked Alice.

"I don't know yet," Brooklyn replied as she scanned a table, looking for anything that might fend him off. "We considered a lot of variables when we planned this op, but unfortunately didn't come up with any specific contingencies for neutralizing a humongous hijacker with really bad teeth."

"*We?*" said Alice, confused.

"*Op?*" added Judy, equally befuddled.

Brooklyn ignored them and turned off the overhead so that now the only light was coming from the aquariums built into the wall. This gave the room a hazy blue look, while the gentle movement of the water in the aquariums cast ghostly shadows across everything.

Brooklyn kept looking until she heard the door opening. That's when she dived behind a table and tried to remain perfectly still. She hoped they were lucky enough that he hadn't been able to tell which room they'd entered.

"Come out, come out, wherever you are," he said as he hit a switch and the fluorescent lights hissed to life. "I know you're in here."

So much for luck.

He wanted her scared, so Brooklyn decided to be brave. She came out from behind the desk and stood tall. All the while, she kept her right hand behind her back so that he couldn't see what she'd found.

"You lucky punch me the first time," he said as he pulled off his ski mask. "Because the balaclava blocked my vision. But not again."

"Sucker punch," she corrected.

"What?"

"You said 'lucky' punch, but the term is 'sucker' punch," she said. "English is a confusing language. What do you normally speak? Swedish? Norwegian?"

The man growled, and Brooklyn decided to stop correcting his grammar and asking questions. Instead, she surveyed the situation, just as she'd been trained to do. He was big, but he had an unsteady look about him. With his mask off, she could see the swelling on his jaw. She felt certain she'd given him a concussion. That was his weakness. She couldn't outmuscle him, but maybe she could outsmart him.

"You should leave right now," she suggested, still holding her hand behind her back. "Don't make me hurt you again."

"What do you have?" he challenged. "Some kind of weapon?"

"Better than that." She pulled out her hand and held it up in a fist in front of her face to reveal that she was now . . . wearing a bright yellow rubber glove. She'd grabbed it from the table right before hiding. The reveal was dramatic but not even a little bit intimidating.

"A rubber glove?" He let out a booming laugh. "What

are you going to do? Wash the dishes like a good girl?"

She shook her head in disappointment. "Again with the sexist comments," she said. "Don't you ever learn?"

He moved toward her, but with lightning speed she grabbed something from a display tank and threw it at him. He reflexively caught it right before it hit his face and smiled for an instant, thinking that he'd foiled her pathetic attempt. Then he let out a yelp of pain.

"Wh-wh-what?" he stammered, confused by what was happening.

"You already feel it, don't you?" she said with a confident smile. "That's a flower sea urchin. It's got a pretty name, but what it does to your body is downright ugly."

He looked at the spiny sea creature in his hand. It was globular, about four inches wide, with tiny pink petals that resembled flowers. He dropped it to the floor, but it was too late. His palm was already beginning to swell.

"That tingling in your hand," she continued, "that's caused by the poison on the petals. Pretty soon it will reach your bloodstream and that's when the real trouble starts."

He looked at her with fear in his eyes.

"First, your fingers will start feeling numb and then

your lips," she said. "Once it affects your tongue, you won't be able to scream for help."

He went to say something but realized he could barely use his mouth.

"So the question you have to ask yourself is this," Brooklyn continued. "Do you want to keep chasing us until the poison overwhelms your entire body? Or do you want to leave us alone and drink the antidote that will save your life? It's totally your choice."

He tried to answer but the best he could do was *"Amp-li-dope."*

She shook her head. "I'm sorry. I can't understand what you're saying."

"Amp-li-dope!" he pleaded.

"I still can't understand, but I'm guessing it's probably antidote," she answered. "That would be the wise choice."

He nodded frantically.

"It's in the first aid kit in the back of the closet." She pointed at a walk-in storage room that held lab samples and scientific supplies. "It's the yellow bottle labeled 'antitoxin.'"

He staggered over and stepped in to look for the antidote. He was still looking when Brooklyn shut the door behind him and closed the latch, trapping him inside. He pounded on the door, but there was nothing he could do to get out. He called for help, but his muffled pleas were completely unintelligible.

The others came out from their hiding places. "That's the first aid cabinet," Judy said, pointing toward a metal wall unit with a red cross on its door.

Brooklyn shrugged. "Yeah, but there's no way to lock him up over there."

"So you're just going to let him die?" Alice asked, incredulous.

"Of course not," Brooklyn answered as she carefully picked up the sea creature from the floor. "Flower sea urchins can be lethal, but this specimen is way too small. The effects should wear off in about fifteen minutes. You would've known that if you'd paid attention during the lab session yesterday. I think you were moving around the room trying to find a spot where you could get bars on your mobile, which is pretty funny considering we're in the middle of the North Sea, where the number of cell towers is exactly zero." She gently placed the urchin back in the display tank.

Alice looked at her curiously. "Who are you again?"

"I'm the girl you haven't paid attention to for the five days we've been sharing a room," Brooklyn responded as she yanked off the rubber glove and dropped it on the table. "Now, let's keep moving."

She led them to the corner of the lab, where she opened a hatch to reveal a ladder that accessed the engine deck below.

"We're going down there?" asked Judy.

"Yep," Brooklyn said. "We found the perfect hiding spot."

"There you go with 'we' again," said Judy. "Who's 'we' and why were you planning?"

"MI6 received intel about a possible threat that simultaneously targeted Parliament *and* the royal family," said Brooklyn. "They assumed it would take place in London, at Westminster or Buckingham Palace, but then someone saw that the two of you were going to be on this trip and decided to put some assets on board just in case."

"*You* are an MI6 asset?" asked Alice, disbelieving.

"We're not going to worry about what I am," said Brooklyn. "We're just going down this ladder before anyone else comes through that door."

In fact, there were three MI6 agents on board. Sydney and Brooklyn had been assigned to protect Alice and Judy, while an adult had been placed among the ship's crew and tasked with combating any possible hijackers.

In keeping with their top-secret status within the Intelligence Service, Sydney and Brooklyn had no idea who the agent was, and the agent had no idea that Sydney and Brooklyn were any different from the other bright students interested in marine biology.

"This is disgusting," said Alice as they reached the bottom of the ladder. "What's that smell?"

"That smell's going to save your life," said Brooklyn, raising her voice to be heard over the generators that provided electricity for the ship. "It's a mix of saltwater, diesel fuel, and lubricating oil. It's the guts of the boat, and it leads us to the stern thruster machine room."

"Was that something else I missed when we were supposed to be paying attention?" asked Judy with her customary snarky attitude.

"No," said Brooklyn. "Nobody knows anything about it, which is why it's such an excellent hiding place."

Deep in the bowels of the ship, they reached a crowded room filled with machinery. A giant metal shaft ran through the middle of it all, connecting the engine room to the propeller. Because the ship was anchored, the shaft was motionless. Above it was a platform large enough for both girls to hide.

"No one's going to find you up there," Brooklyn said,

pointing to the platform. "Climb up and wait. Don't move until I come for you or somebody else tells you 'apple jack.'"

Alice took a whiff of the sour smell and was about to make a comment when Brooklyn cut her off.

"And so help me, if you complain about anything, I'm going to lead them right to you. Got it?"

Alice nodded. "Got it."

"Aren't you hiding with us?" asked Judy.

Brooklyn shook her head. "No. I've got to make sure a distress signal's been sent. You two will be safe here."

Alice looked at her. "Thank you, um—" Her words trailed off and it was obvious that she didn't know Brooklyn's name.

"Really?" Brooklyn said, incredulous. "We spent five days together in a tiny cabin and you still don't know my name?"

"I get it," Alice said. "I'm a total spoiled toff. But I'd like to make up for that. Tell me your name and I promise I won't forget it. Ever."

Brooklyn went to answer, but then she caught herself. "Actually, it's better that you don't know," she said. "Because when this is all over and people ask you how you survived, it's best if you don't mention me at all."

Sydney

IN HER THREE YEARS WITH MI6, SYDNEY had already dangled upside down from a cliff, broken through the ice of a frozen pond, burned off her eyebrows on more than one occasion, and raced along the top of a rapidly moving Indonesian passenger train while carrying an explosive device of her own making. One time she even eluded the Albanian secret police by hiding in a sewage pipe. An active sewage pipe.

But of all the difficult, dangerous, and terribly malodorous aspects of the job, for Sydney the absolute worst was the fact that she couldn't tell anyone about it. The trains, the eyebrows, the sewage pipes all had to remain confidential. Only the team could know what they'd done. No one else.

It was not insignificant that the first word in "secret agent" was "secret."

And this week on the *Sylvia Earle*, keeping that secret had proven particularly frustrating. Surrounded by amazing scientists she wanted to impress, and more than a few full-of-themselves girls she would've liked to knock down a peg or two, Sydney couldn't say a single word about the things that made her life truly spectacular. Instead, her job required her to anonymously disappear into the background.

She'd done a good job of it too. So good that during the entire hijacking, no one but Brooklyn even noticed she was missing. She wasn't with the girls corralled on the main deck, nor was she one of the ones the intruders discovered hiding in the laundry room. She was nowhere to be found, because while the *Sylvia Earle* was under siege, Sydney was underwater.

Twelve meters to be exact.

She'd snuck off the ship for some unauthorized scuba diving, hoping to clear her head. Something had been troubling her for weeks, and she couldn't quite put her finger on it. Lately, she hadn't felt right about her role on the team, and whenever Sydney needed to straighten out her thinking, her first instinct was always to look toward the ocean.

She grew up near the beach in Australia and felt most at home when she was in the water, whether that was surfing, swimming, or diving. She was a certified scuba instructor and had trained at the elite Royal Navy diving school. That meant she knew how to do everything from open-ocean rescues to underwater demolitions. It also meant she knew better than to go scuba diving all alone in the middle of the night. But for Sydney, knowing what was right didn't always mean doing what was right.

According to her most recent MI6 evaluation, she was "practically allergic to following the rules." Still, it was rare for her to break so many at one time. At the moment she was in violation of at least six:

> Breaking into the dive locker
> "Borrowing" diving gear without
>   permission
> Going into the water without adult
>   supervision
> Going into the water without sufficient
>   daylight

> Scuba diving without a partner
>
> And most seriously, going off-grid
>
> during an MI6 mission

This last one was made even worse by the fact that Sydney was the alpha, which meant she was in charge of the mission while they were in the field. Her rationalization for such bad decision-making was that after five days at sea with no trouble in sight, she felt certain the operation was a dud.

MI6 had it right from the start, she told herself as she suited up in the dive room. *London's a much more likely target than a research ship traveling through the Shetlands.*

Besides, she couldn't stop thinking about the phytoplankton.

During one of their labs, the chief scientist taught them about bioluminescent phytoplankton: microscopic marine organisms that glowed in the dark. To demonstrate this phenomenon, she turned out the lights and held up a beaker of water containing some specimens.

When she shook the beaker and it transformed into a swirl of magical blue light, Sydney was mesmerized. When the marine biologist further explained that the sample had just been collected from the waters where the *Sylvia Earle* was anchored, Sydney began planning.

Still, it was more dream than scheme until the snoring woke her in the middle of the night. Lady Hawthorne and Judy Somersby snored so much and so loudly, she'd nicknamed them Lady Nosehorn and Judy Bumblebee. Normally she wanted to pummel them with their pillows when they disrupted her sleep, but this time she took it as a lucky break. It was almost four o'clock, and she figured she had just enough time to go for a dive and get back on the ship before anyone woke up.

For thirty minutes the plan worked perfectly as she glided through the water and created a ribbon of light in her wake. The problems that had been nagging at her now seemed distant. And the fact that she was breaking the rules gave her rebel heart a thrill. She was relaxed and exhilarated all at once.

Then she heard the motor.

It was much too small to be the engine of the *Sylvia Earle*, but the high-pitched whine was unmistakable. There was another boat in the water, and judging by the sound, it was moving fast.

From this depth, it looked like little more than an inkblot flickering above. When it stopped alongside the *Sylvia Earle*, adrenaline flooded Sydney's system.

She had to get back as quickly as possibly, but she had to be careful. If she moved too fast, it could cause serious health problems that would make the situation worse.

Halfway to the surface she needed to make a five-minute decompression stop so her body could adjust to the changing water pressure and expel the dissolved gases that had accumulated in her bloodstream.

While she waited, she heard the engine come to life again and looked up to see that the second boat was now moving around to the back of the *Sylvia Earle*. She was now close enough to make out the outline and could tell that it was a Zodiac, a high-speed, high-performance inflatable that carried up to a dozen people. The Royal Marines used them for commando raids, although she felt fairly certain there were no Royal Marines on this vessel.

She checked her dive watch and saw that she had to wait another four minutes, thirteen seconds. Rather than get angry with herself for winding up in this situation, she tried to use the time to develop a strategy. She ran through the plan they'd devised at the start of the mission. It was solid, and although Brooklyn was still new to MI6, she'd already proven that she was an excellent operative. Sydney was confident she'd be able to get Alice and Judy to the hiding spot in the stern thruster machine room. That meant the two of them should be safe for the time being.

What would Mother do? she asked herself.

Mother was the MI6 agent in charge of their team. He had little sayings he called Motherisms, designed to help them remember the keys to spycraft. She tried to think of a relevant one and came up with *Anything that you think is wrong, is something that can make you strong.* It was a reminder that she needed to turn negatives into positives, weaknesses into strengths.

She was out of position, which was a negative. But she was also someplace where nobody would ever suspect her to be, which could be a huge positive. She had the element of surprise on her side.

Fifteen seconds.

That's close enough, she thought as she furiously started kicking her fins and raced to the surface.

First, she checked to see if there was anyone on board the Zodiac, and once she saw it was clear, she swam over to it and pulled herself up to peek over the gunwale. That's when she saw the brown wooden box with rope handles and really began to panic.

"*Blimey!*" she exclaimed, recognizing it from her training. "This is bad news."

The box was a British Army munitions container that held PE4—military-grade plastic explosives. More troubling, the lid was off, and she could see that it was empty. She had to assume the contents had been weaponized and placed somewhere on the *Sylvia Earle*.

Staying calm was getting harder to do.

She looked to see if there was a radio so she could call for help, but all she found was a small yellow walkie-talkie. She turned it on, making sure to keep the volume low. No one spoke at first, but then she heard an exchange.

"Have you found them?" a voice asked impatiently.

"No," came the reluctant answer. "Their cabin's empty."

"And Karl?"

The was a brief pause before, "No sign of him either."

The first speaker made a frustrated noise and barked, "Find them now!"

Sydney didn't know who Karl was, but she assumed the other people they were looking for were Alice and Judy, which meant Brooklyn had done her job. *That's my girl*, she thought, happy for the news. *Now it's my turn. What do I do?* she asked herself as she returned her focus to the explosives. *How can I help?*

Another Motherism came to her. *When there's a doubt, just figure it out.*

Figuring it out meant figuring out where the bomb was. She thought she should be able to do that. Not only did she have extensive explosives training, but she'd also studied detailed diagrams of the *Sylvia Earle* when she and Brooklyn were first given the assignment.

If I were a villain, where would I put a bomb? she asked herself. *The bridge? The engine room? One of the cabins?*

Then she considered the fact that the Zodiac had momentarily stopped alongside the *Sylvia Earle*. *They wouldn't put it on board the ship,* she thought with a smile of realization. *Someone might find that. They'd attach it to the outside.*

Sydney pulled the diving mask back down over her face and quietly slipped into the water. It was time to work.

21 Minutes, 13 Seconds

MAIN DECK–RV SYLVIA EARLE

EMIL BLIX HAD NEVER KIDNAPPED ANY-
one before, and his lack of experience was beginning to
show. It had started off well enough with the storming
of the bridge, but since then, things had gone steadily
downhill. First, it took much longer than expected to get
everybody up to the main deck. Then one of his henchmen disappeared after pleading over the walkie-talkie
for something that sounded like "amp-li-dope." But
most importantly, his men couldn't find the two people
he'd come to kidnap.

"Where are they?" he demanded as he held up photographs of Alice and Judy. He was talking to a dozen girls huddled together on the ship's marine mammal observation platform. This was where they'd been a day earlier, eyes wide with amazement, watching a pod of orcas swimming off the starboard bow. Now their eyes were filled with fear as Blix paced back and forth in front of them.

It was just after six, and the early morning air was cold and damp. A fourteen-year-old named Ashlee tried to sound brave as she said, "We don't know. We were all asleep. Nobody saw them."

"One of you must know!" he seethed. He'd taken off his ski mask once their phones had been confiscated, and they could see that his cheeks were flush with anger. "If you don't tell me, things are going to turn out very bad!"

This threat had the dual distinction of being both ominous and truthful. The explosive device he'd attached to the hull of the ship was set to go off in twenty-one minutes, thirteen seconds. Emil Blix was running out of time.

Brooklyn surveyed the scene from a hiding spot behind a metal staircase leading from the main deck up to the pilothouse. She was crouched down low, watching it unfold through the opening between two steps. None of the ship's crew or scientists were among those on the observation platform, and she assumed that meant the adults were being held somewhere more secure. But Sydney wasn't with them either.

Where are you, Syd? she wondered. *What are you up to?*

EXTERIOR HULL–*RV* SYLVIA EARLE

Sydney's head was filled with numbers and she was trying to keep them straight. The first was sixty-five. That was the length in meters of the *Sylvia Earle*. She knew that because she'd learned everything she could about the ship while she was preparing for the mission. Sixty-five meters didn't seem very long when you were looking at a schematic on a computer screen. After all, one lap in an Olympic-size pool is only fifty. But it sure felt long as she swam alongside the ship looking for an explosive device. Her progress was slowed because she had to check above and below the waterline, contend with the ocean current, and, unlike Olympic swimmers, carry a load of heavy scuba gear designed for safety, not speed.

The second number was fifty. That's where the needle

pointed on her air pressure gauge. It was marked in red because once you reached it, you were supposed to end your dive. At best, she had about fifteen minutes of air left in her tank, but that was only if she kept her breathing calm and level. As the adrenaline raced through her body, she was undoubtedly taking deeper breaths and depleting what little air she had remaining.

She located the bomb toward the rear of the ship. It was about a meter below the waterline and attached to the steel hull by a magnetic device known as a "limpet mine." She'd learned about them at the Royal Navy diving school. One troubling detail she remembered was that they were sometimes set to automatically explode if anyone tried to tamper with them.

More troubling, though, was the location of the mine. Limpets weren't designed to blow up ships or sink them like torpedoes. They were meant to disable them. When this one exploded, either by remote detonation or timer, it would blow a hole in the hull, and water would begin rushing in. When the Coast Guard and Navy arrived on the scene, rescuers would be busy evacuating passengers and trying to salvage the ship, giving the intruders extra time to make their getaway.

But the location of this mine created an additional

danger. As Sydney swept the beam of her dive light across the hull, she could see the side thruster used to stabilize the ship. It was just a few meters away. That meant the mine was attached to the outside of the stern thruster machine room.

If Brooklyn had followed the plan, then Judy and Alice were right in the heart of the blast zone.

MAIN DECK—RV SYLVIA EARLE

Brooklyn knew there was a third MI6 agent somewhere on the ship, but she didn't know who it was. She and Sydney had tried to figure that out during the trip, and after leaning toward one of the scientists for a few days, they'd settled on Hannah Delapp as their prime candidate. Hannah was the second mate, and they suspected her because she was the newest member of the crew, having just joined for this sailing. Her primary job was to watch the bridge on the overnight shift, but during the afternoon, when she should've been sleeping, she was often up and about keeping an eye on things.

"Total spy," Sydney had declared knowingly.

Hannah would've been on duty when the ship was seized, which meant the hijackers might have overwhelmed her before she could send a distress signal. Brooklyn had to assume that no one onshore knew they were in danger. As much as she wanted to find Sydney, her top priority was activating the Ship Security Alert System. The SSAS worked like a silent alarm in a bank. If Brooklyn could trigger it, no one would hear anything on board the *Sylvia Earle*, but warning bells would sound back on the mainland and help would immediately be rushed to their location.

The problem was that the button for the SSAS was on the bridge, and Brooklyn didn't know how to get there without being seen by the hijackers. She needed to create a massive diversion to distract them long enough for her to sprint up the stairs and into the room before anyone realized what was happening.

The best idea she could think of was to activate the giant A-frame crane on the fantail of the ship. It was designed to lift boats and buoys out of the ocean, but maybe she could use it to lure the intruders out of position. If she could just get it to start moving, then the hijackers would have to investigate, and that might buy her all the time she needed. She was trying to figure out how to operate it remotely when she felt a hand on her shoulder.

A very large hand.

She turned to see that her old friend Mr. Amplidope had managed to break out of the closet in the wet lab. His jaw was swollen, there were red blotches all over his face, and his lips were bloated and purple. Despite this, Brooklyn acted like they were long lost friends.

"Hey, look at you," she said with a smile. "You're recovering nicely. Did you find the antitoxin?"

He didn't answer so much as he growled while he put a tight grip on her shoulder and moved her out from behind the stairs. Brooklyn's mind raced as she tried to come up with anything remotely resembling a plan as he led her over to Blix.

She came up empty.

"Karl, where have you been?" Blix asked angrily. "I've been trying to reach you. . . ." His words trailed off when he noticed the man's injuries. "What happened to your face?"

Karl tried to answer, but his tongue and lips weren't completely functional yet so "flower sea urchin" came out "*flabber bee gerkin.*" Rather than try again, he simply pointed at the pictures of Alice and Judy in Blix's hand and then at Brooklyn.

Even without words, the message was loud and clear.

Blix turned to her and said, "You know where they are." He flashed a sinister smile and added, "How lovely."

Brooklyn tried to talk her way out of the situation. "Well, actually, I only know—"

Karl was having none of it. He reached over and covered her mouth with his huge left paw and managed to say something resembling, "She knows."

"Excellent," Blix said with an evil rasp. "Take me to them. Now."

"I—I—I ca-can't," she stammered.

Blix stepped closer and tilted his head down so that they were practically nose-to-nose. "Oh, but you will."

She tried to think of a Motherism that would help, but she couldn't come up with a single one. The best she could do was try to stall. And the best way to stall was to stop thinking like a spy and start acting like a twelve-year-old. Fake tears began welling up in her eyes.

"If I take you to them, Alice and Judy will see me," Brooklyn blubbered. "So will they." She nodded toward the other girls. "Everyone will know that I helped you. Do you know how powerful their families are? Judy's mom's an MP. Alice is a member of the royal family. They'll ruin my life. I'll get kicked out of school. Everything will go bad."

Blix chuckled. "That's not my problem."

Brooklyn wiped some tears from her cheeks and looked away to compose herself. That's when she remembered the tour the captain gave them just after they'd set sail from Aberdeen harbor. The inkling of a plan came to her. "I *can't* take you to them," she said, her emotion calming. Then she turned back and whispered, "But I *can* show you where they are."

"What do you mean?" he asked.

"There's a detailed map of the ship. Take me to that and I can point out exactly where they're hiding. That way Judy and Alice won't see me and nobody has to know that I helped."

"You're not really in a position to—"

Brooklyn cut him off. "Do you want to find them or not?"

Blix wasn't in the mood to be told what to do by a twelve-year-old. But he didn't have any time to waste. There were less than seventeen minutes left before the bomb was set to explode, and for his plan to work he needed Alice and Judy on the Zodiac before that happened.

"Fine," he said. "Where's the map?"

Now it was Brooklyn's turn to smile, although she fought the urge. "It's up in the pilothouse . . . on the bridge." It turned out she didn't need the crane at all. *She* was her own massive distraction.

EXTERIOR HULL—RV SYLVIA EARLE

Unlike the bombs in action movies, which came with nice, easy-to-read digital displays that told everyone exactly how much time they had, the limpet mine gave Sydney no indication as to when it was set to explode. She assumed the intruders would not have it go off while they were still on board, so she felt she should be safe until she heard the whine of the Zodiac's motor. Well, maybe "safe" wasn't the right word, but that's what she was telling herself.

She did know, however, that there were only a few minutes of air left in her tank. The needle on her pressure gauge was now well into the red on the dial. She tried to take slow, shallow breaths as she studied the mine.

During her training, she'd worked with limpets that had been manufactured for the military, but this one looked more like it was built in someone's garage. That was good and bad. Good because that meant it might have some sort of defect she could exploit. Bad because that meant it might go off accidentally.

It resembled a metal bowl with two long fingers that stretched out along the hull. The magnets were clamped on the fingers, and she was studying one when she heard an ominous sound. It was a clicking noise in her regulator. She'd never heard it before, but she knew what it meant.

She was out of air.

4.

Boom

UMBRA WAS A GLOBAL CRIME SYNDICATE motivated entirely by money. Even the decision to kidnap Alice and Judy was based on profit, not politics. The organization didn't have an opinion on the British monarchy and didn't care what party Judy's mother represented in Parliament. It was interested solely in the fact that their families would have the means and the willingness to pay a large ransom for their return.

Blix had jumped at the opportunity to carry out the operation. Up until that point, he'd worked primarily as a smuggler carrying stolen merchandise between ports on the North Sea. This was his chance to show the higher-ups in the organization that he was capable of more.

This was a test . . . and he was failing miserably.

He now realized that he should've brought more men. There were seven on the Zodiac, but four were occupied guarding the hostages, two with each group, and another was on the bridge monitoring all communication. That left him only Karl, whose unexplained disappearance had put them behind schedule.

Blix hoped that Brooklyn was the solution to his problems. If she could direct them to Alice and Judy, then they could get back on track. As he led her up to the bridge, he was surprised to see Karl following them. "Where are you going?"

"With you," mumbled Karl.

"Why?"

He nodded toward Brooklyn. "She's tricky."

"She's *twelve*," Blix sniped. "I think I've got it under control. Why don't you help watch the hostages? Your face should frighten them nicely."

Chastened, Karl nodded and went back to the marine mammal observation deck while Blix and Brooklyn went up the stairs.

"Did you do that to his face?" Blix asked, more intrigued than angry.

"I don't know what you're talking about," Brooklyn answered unconvincingly.

Blix laughed. "How very interesting."

Brooklyn studied him as they walked, looking for any details she could later pass on to MI6. He had black hair and a thick beard. There was a jagged scar behind his ear, and she noticed two tattoos: a blue-and-red wolf on the side of his neck and a cluster of three stars on the back of his left hand.

"How'd you know I was twelve?" she asked. "Do you have full biographical rundowns for everybody on board the ship?"

"No," he said. "I have three teenage daughters. I know what twelve-year-old girls look like." He stopped for a moment before adding, "And I know exactly how tricky they can be."

This surprised Brooklyn. She never thought of terror-ists as having children. "You've got kids?"

He didn't respond, so she just kept talking. "That must make for interesting dinner conversation. 'How was school today?' 'Okay, I got a good grade on my book report, but I bombed my math test. How was work?'

'Really good. I hijacked a ship and terrorized a bunch of girls. Can you pass the potatoes?'"

"My daughters are top students," he said proudly. "They don't *bomb* tests."

"No?" asked Brooklyn. "What about you? What do you bomb?"

He gave her a dirty look but didn't answer, and when they reached the top of the stairs, Brooklyn noticed him check his watch. It was the third time she'd seen him do it, and it reminded her of a Motherism: *Look for a crack, then give it a whack.* The idea was to find your adversary's weakness, no matter how small, and use it as a point of attack. Maybe the watch was the crack.

"What's wrong?" she asked. "Running out of time?"

He ignored her question, and they entered a narrow hallway that led to the bridge.

"That's it, isn't it?" she continued pressing. "It's taken too long to find Alice and Judy, and it's messed up your schedule."

Again he ignored the question, although Brooklyn could see his neck muscles tighten. She was onto something. She'd found the crack, so she kept whacking.

"You know, I'm sure the Navy and the Coast Guard track all the ships in British waters, which means there's probably some group on the way to rescue us right now. If you're still on the boat when they arrive, it'll go badly. If I were you, I'd make a run for it, while there's still time. You'd hate for your daughters to have to visit you in prison."

He turned slowly and seemed to grow more menacing as he did. "I have bad news for you. Nobody is coming to your rescue. By the time the Coast Guard and Navy figure out something's wrong, I'll be long gone. Your fate is up to me alone. So, if *I* were *you*, I'd keep quiet."

His eyes were a piercing shade of blue, and she knew he was serious. She responded not with words, but just a nod.

"Smart decision," he said as they resumed.

Just before they reached the bridge, they passed the chart room, which held the maps, tables, and instruments necessary to navigate the high seas. At the moment, it also held all the adults on the trip. There were eleven in total: seven crew members, three scientists, and a documentary filmmaker. Brooklyn did a quick count and saw they were all in there. That meant whichever one of them was secretly an MI6 agent had been captured. Two of Blix's men guarded the door. Each gave Brooklyn the evil eye as they passed.

"Where are you taking her?" demanded one of the women. "She's just a kid."

It was Virginia Wescott, a documentary filmmaker with the BBC. She'd come along to shoot footage for a film she was making about women in the sciences. Brooklyn had enjoyed hanging out with her and learning about her computer editing programs.

"It's okay," Brooklyn responded, trying to ease her concern. "I'll be fine."

Brooklyn and Blix entered the bridge, the nerve center for every aspect of the *Sylvia Earle*. It was spotless and modern, with wraparound windows that provided a view of everything in front of and on both sides of the ship. There was a massive console filled with dials, monitors, throttles, and buttons. There were two tall chairs—one for any officer who was on duty and the other reserved exclusively for the captain. Except now it was occupied by one of Blix's henchmen.

"You're not supposed to sit there," Brooklyn said defiantly. "That's just for the captain."

The man chuckled and slid back into the seat, filling as much of it as he could. "I guess that means I'm the captain now."

Brooklyn scanned the console and quickly spotted

the SSAS button, which was hidden in plain sight in the middle of the bottom row. It was unmarked and unre-markable, no different from any of the other buttons so that no criminal or hijacker would be able to spot and disconnect it. She only knew its location because she learned it during her preparation for the mission.

Unfortunately, there was nearly ten feet between the map on the wall and the console. Brooklyn had to fig-ure out how to get to the button and push it without anybody noticing. Once again, she decided to act like a twelve-year-old instead of a spy.

She darted across the room and grabbed the hand-set for the ship's radio. "Mayday! Mayday!" she said breathlessly into the microphone. "This is the research vessel *Sylvia Earle*! We've been hijacked!"

Blix just stood there and shook his head.

"Impulsive, like my daughters," Blix said. "Go ahead, call for help. It won't do any good because I disconnected the radio. Like I told you, no one is coming to rescue you."

Brooklyn knew the radio would be dead, but she had to play the part. She sighed heavily and sagged in defeat. As she did, her hand dropped down to her side, and she slyly pressed the SSAS button.

Help was on the way.

She knew the protocol step-by-step. The alarm would sound first at the nearest Coast Guard station. They would immediately send a rescue helicopter and notify the Secret Intelligence Service. The moment MI6 got word, they'd alert the Royal Navy and a team of commandos with the Special Boat Service would be deployed. The problem was that the *Sylvia Earle* was in a remote location, and it was going to take time for anyone to arrive.

"Playtime is over," said Blix. "Show me where they are."

The map of the ship was divided into six framed diagrams on the wall. She walked up to the layout for the main deck and pointed to the forecastle anchor room, an off-limits area she knew about because it was one of the rooms she and Sydney had considered using to hide Judy and Alice.

"They're in there," she said. "Both of them."

"They better be," he said.

He turned to the henchman in the captain's chair and said, "Jakob, hurry up and go to the anchor room. Get the girls and bring them straight to the Zodiac."

The man rushed out the door, and Blix turned to Brooklyn. "You come with me."

"How can you do this?" she asked. "You've got daughters of your own."

"None of you are going to get hurt," he said.

"What about Judy and Alice?" asked Brooklyn. "Aren't they going to get hurt?"

"Not if their parents pay their ransoms." He smiled and pointed toward the chart room. "Now, you get in there."

Blix opened the door to the chart room and signaled Brooklyn to get in. Frida Hovland, the captain of the ship, moved toward him. "I demand you return control of the ship to me."

Blix laughed. "You are in no position to demand anything."

She got angry, and then something very unexpected happened. They started arguing in *Norwegian*. Brooklyn had no idea what they were saying, and it didn't seem like anyone in the room did, but it was heated and continued for a few exchanges until they were interrupted by a desperate call over Blix's walkie-talkie. "Danger! Danger! You have trouble!"

Blix keyed his walkie-talkie and asked, "What sort of trouble?"

"A Coast Guard helicopter has just been sent out of

Sumburgh, and Special Boat Service is on the way."

"How?" he demanded. "Who alerted them?"

"An SSAS signal from the ship."

Blix tried to run through everything in his head. He didn't know how this could have happened, but then the hint of an idea came to him. He looked right at Brooklyn, and the anger in his eyes made her flinch. He stepped toward her, but someone stepped between them. It was Virginia Wescott, the documentary filmmaker.

"Don't you have better things to do?" Wescott said coolly.

Before he could react, they were interrupted by the sound of a loud explosion.

BOOM!

5

Chaos

BROOKLYN COULDN'T TELL IF THE BOMB actually caused the ship to move or if it was just her imagination. It felt like it did, but that might've been all the people crowded around her moving in reaction to the blast. She also couldn't tell where the explosion took place. It could've been anywhere on the ship: the engine, the main deck, or worst of all, the stern thruster machine room. Was it possible that instead of hiding Alice and Judy somewhere safe, she'd endangered them?

She was worried about that. She was also worried about her friend.

Where are you, Sydney? Brooklyn wondered. *Why haven't you shown up yet?*

She wasn't the only one with questions. Emil Blix was on the walkie-talkie demanding to know what was happening.

"What was that?" he yelled into the radio. "Who detonated that charge?"

There was no response, which only infuriated him more. Everything was going wrong. He couldn't find the girls he was supposed to kidnap. The British military was racing to the scene. And now there was an unplanned explosion. He'd completely lost control of his hijacking.

"I want answers!" he bellowed.

Tentatively, a voice chimed in with a reply. "Boss."

"Who is this?"

"Jakob."

It was the man he'd sent from the bridge to get Alice and Judy.

"I don't know about the blast," he continued. "But I do know those girls aren't in the anchor room. I'm there right now, and there's no sign of them."

Blix spun around and stared right at Brooklyn, his face flushed with anger. She moved back and pressed herself against a wall.

Blix glared at her and took heavy breaths, his nostrils flared. He looked like he was about to say something when:

BOOM!

Another blast rocked the *Sylvia Earle*, and Brooklyn wondered if it were somehow the British military. It had been only a few minutes since she pushed the SSAS button. Could they have already arrived on the scene? Were they setting off explosions to disrupt the hijacking?

"What is going on?" Blix yelled into his radio.

None of his men replied, but the captain got right in his face and thundered at him in Norwegian. *"Gå av båten min! Nå!"*

Brooklyn expected him to lash back, but he didn't. Blix had no idea how things had gone so wrong, but he knew there was no saving his mission. It was a lost cause. Instead of arguing with the captain, he calmly called into his walkie-talkie, "Abort mission. Abort mission. The Zodiac leaves in ninety seconds."

He gave one last look at Brooklyn, wondering if she had somehow caused everything to unravel, and then he hurried away toward the fantail of the ship, and his escape.

The captain turned to the members of her crew. "Emergency stations. Check first on the passengers, get lifeboats and life jackets ready, then see if there is damage to the ship."

"What can we do?" asked one of the scientists.

"Look for the girls," said the captain. "Get them all together in the muster station next to the lifeboats."

"They're on the marine mammal observation platform," Brooklyn said. "I just saw them there."

Everyone sprung into action, but Brooklyn hesitated for a moment. She wanted to check on Alice and Judy, but she needed to make sure the threat was over. That it was okay to get them.

She stepped onto the bridge and surveyed the pandemonium through the giant window overlooking the ship. At first glance it seemed like everyone on the platform was safe. They were shaken, but it didn't appear that any of them were hurt. She quickly scanned the group again, hoping to see Sydney, but there was no sign of her.

The captain took the handset for the intercom to address the whole ship. "This is Captain Hovland. The hijackers have left the ship. I need everyone on the main deck at your lifeguard station so that we can make sure we are all accounted for, and be ready in case we have to evacuate the ship."

The hijackers haven't actually left yet, Brooklyn thought.

She headed toward the back of the ship so that she could see Blix and his men leave, but a hand reached out for her. It was the captain. Up until this point the captain had been friendly, if still a little stiff. She had tried to project a "one of the girls" vibe for most of the trip. But now she was much more gruff.

"Where are you going?" she asked.

"I want to make sure that those men are actually leaving," answered Brooklyn. "And I want to look for my friend."

"It's not safe," Hovland replied curtly. "Go to the lifeboat station. Your friend will be there."

"But I—"

"No buts," said the captain, who signaled her second mate, Hannah Delapp. "Take her with you."

"Aye, Captain," said the woman who Brooklyn and Sydney thought might be an MI6 spy.

"I'm really worried about my friend," Brooklyn said as they exited the bridge. "Can't I just go look for her? I'll be right back."

"You heard the captain," replied Delapp. "Your friend will be fine."

Brooklyn thought it was time to appeal to her agent-to-agent. She looked to make sure no one else could hear and said, "Apple jack."

"What?" asked the woman.

Brooklyn repeated the mission's emergency code. "Apple jack."

"I don't understand," said the woman. "Is that some American phrase?"

Either she wasn't the spy or she was an amazing actor, because her face indicated no recognition of the phrase.

"Never mind," Brooklyn said.

When she left Alice and Judy in the stern thruster machine room, Brooklyn told them not to leave unless she came to get them or somebody told them "apple jack." She didn't know if they'd follow that directive or not, but she couldn't get away now without causing suspicion, so she went with Delapp down to the main deck where everyone was gathering by the lifeboats. Two of the scientists were giving out life jackets, and one of them handed one to Brooklyn.

"Put this on," she instructed.

Brooklyn slipped the jacket on and continued scanning faces, looking for Sydney, Alice, and Judy. The longer she went without seeing them, the more concerned she was. On the bright side, there didn't seem to be any serious damage to the ship. It wasn't listing at all. There weren't any signs of it sinking.

She wanted to slip away in the confusion, but truthfully, there wasn't any. The crew was handling the situation with great efficiency.

"Look!" cried one of the girls as she pointed out over the water. "Helicopter."

A red-and-white Coast Guard chopper was headed right toward them, and they all let out a cheer.

Despite everyone else's relief at the sign of rescue, Brooklyn was still concerned. It had been at least ten minutes since the explosions, and there was still no sign of any of her cabinmates.

She was just about to make a run for the stairs when she saw them emerge from a doorway. Alice and Judy came out first, and behind them was Sydney, who'd shed her wet suit and was now wearing baggy sweats and a long-sleeve T-shirt.

Brooklyn let out a huge sigh and smiled as she headed right to them.

"Look who I found hiding out," Sydney said with a wink.

"I was so worried about you," answered Brooklyn as she wrapped her up in a hug.

"No need to worry," Sydney said. Then she whispered, "Nice work by you."

Brooklyn didn't respond right away. She just squeezed tight. But when she finally did let go, she had a question for Sydney.

"Why's your hair wet?"

Sydney chuckled and answered, "Funny story . . ."

Unst, Shetland Islands

SYDNEY SAT IN A BLUE PLASTIC CHAIR underneath a poster for *Where the Wild Things Are* and lied repeatedly to Detective Inspector Jennifer Glasheen of the Police Scotland's Organised Crime and Counter Terrorism Unit.

"I was scared and hiding under the bunk in my cabin."

"There were two explosions, but I couldn't see anything."

"I've never even heard of the stern thruster machine room. What's that?"

It wasn't that Sydney wanted to be unhelpful. It was just that, according to the United Kingdom Official Secrets Act, she was forbidden from disclosing her MI6 status to anyone. That included law enforcement, and there was simply no way she could say that she disassembled a limpet mine and performed two controlled explosions without getting a few impossible-to-answer follow-up questions. So the lies continued.

"I signed up for the trip because it's my dream to one day become a marine biologist."

The interview was taking place in a school library in the village of Baltasound on the island of Unst. Known for stunning sea cliffs, Shetland ponies, and the distinction of being the northernmost inhabited location in the United Kingdom, Unst was so quaint and remote that a police officer hadn't been stationed there in more than three decades. Yet, somehow it found itself at the center of one of the biggest crime stories of the year.

The bungled hijacking of the *Sylvia Earle* had occurred just offshore, and the island was now under virtual lockdown as a team of soldiers and police officers conducted a manhunt for Emil Blix and his henchmen. Meanwhile, the ship's passengers and crew had been brought to Baltasound Junior High, "The UK's Most Northerly

School," which could now be better described as "The UK's Most Northerly Temporary Emergency Response Center."

In addition to the detectives conducting interviews in the library, a trio of doctors was checking on everyone's physical and emotional well-beings in the gym, and the school's kitchen staff was serving a hot meal in the cafeteria. That's where Sydney came after she was done with Glasheen. And that's where she found Brooklyn devouring a late lunch.

"This bread is amazing," Brooklyn said, dipping a piece of it into a bowl of stew. "What's it called again?"

"Bannock," Sydney answered as she sat down next to her.

Brooklyn swallowed, smiled, and punctuated it with a satisfied "Well let me just say . . . *yum*!" She pointed at the remaining piece on a plate in the middle of the table. "You want that?"

"All yours," Sydney responded.

"You sure? Aren't you hungry?"

"No. I'm still too worked up about everything."

"Understandable," Brooklyn said as she scooped up the bread and slathered it with blackberry jam. "How was the interview?"

"Pretty straightforward," answered Sydney. "I was so terrified that I hid in our cabin for the duration of the hijacking and therefore have no useful information to pass along."

"Well, aren't you the scaredy-cat?" joked Brooklyn. "And the part about you saving lives and keeping the ship from sinking?"

"You know, I totally forgot to mention that," Sydney said as she gave her forehead a comical tap. "I've got such a shoddy memory."

"It's too bad, because what you did out there was amazing," Brooklyn said. Then her mood got a bit more serious and she added, "Of course, it would've been better if you'd told me about it beforehand."

"Told you about what?" asked Sydney. "That I was going to defuse a bomb underwater while holding my breath because my scuba tank had run out of air? That wasn't actually something I planned in advance."

"No, it wasn't," Brooklyn said pointedly. "The *plan* was for the two of us to meet in the cabin and work together. And when you didn't show up, I was worried. And then when one of the hijackers did show up, he almost got Alice and Judy."

Sydney shook her head in disbelief. "Are you actually

giving me a hard time about what happened? After what I just did? Do you know how difficult and dangerous that was?"

"More difficult and dangerous than I can imagine," Brooklyn said.

"I know you're Miss Superstar on the rise," replied Sydney, "but don't forget who was the alpha on this mission."

"I know exactly who was *supposed* to be the alpha," Brooklyn replied, matching Sydney's attitude. She let out a deep breath and added, "And I know who saved the day. I don't want to argue with you. I'm just saying that you should've told me that you were leaving the ship to go diving."

Sydney knew Brooklyn was right, but rather than admit that, she just said, "Well, I guess we can't all be perfect like you."

Just then a police officer came up behind them and asked, "Can you two come with me, please?"

Even though he was using a Scottish accent, both girls instantly recognized the voice. They turned to see Mother, in full undercover mode, dressed like a constable. He gave them a wink, but other than that, they kept to their roles.

"Yes, officer," answered Brooklyn.

Mother led them to a nearby classroom, and once they were alone, he slipped out of character into his own self—complete with his usual English accent. "It's so good to see you," he said with a deep sigh. "I was deathly worried. Are you okay? Are you hurt? Have the doctors checked you out yet?"

"Yes, no, yes," Brooklyn answered with a chuckle. "We're fine. So are Alice and Judy."

"And the explosions?" he asked. "I heard two bombs went off."

"Controlled detonations," Sydney said, the hint of a proud smile sneaking in.

"That was you?"

Sydney nodded.

"She was absolutely brilliant," Brooklyn said with no hint of the tension from the cafeteria. "She totally saved the day."

"Well, we got the right result," Sydney said modestly.

"And the SSAS alert?" asked Mother. "Was that one of the crew?"

Brooklyn raised a finger and said, "Actually . . ."

Mother beamed with pride. "Great job. Both of you."

Sydney felt uncomfortable with the praise and quickly

changed the subject. "Have they had any luck finding the hijackers?"

Mother shook his head. "No, and I doubt they'll find them on the island. Rescue got here right away, but it took a while for the search team. The hijackers had plenty of time to escape. My guess is that they rendezvoused with a fishing boat or a tanker and are halfway to Norway or Iceland by now."

Mother pulled out a folded sheet of paper from his pocket and opened it to reveal a police sketch of Emil Blix. "This is what they're working from," he said, handing it to them. "Does he look like the main guy?"

Brooklyn studied it for a second. "It's okay, except his hair was shorter and his beard was bushier. He also had a blue-and-red tattoo of a wolf right here." She pointed at a spot on his neck. "And a tattoo of three stars on the back of his left hand."

"Those are nice details," he said. He turned to Sydney and asked, "What about you? Do you have anything else to add?"

"No," she said. Then she added in a near whisper, "I never saw him."

This struck Mother as odd, but he didn't say anything about it. Instead, he turned back to Brooklyn and said,

"You should probably go to the gym and find the lead detective. Glasheen is her name. Tell her you have a few more details, and she'll put you together with the sketch artist so they can update the picture."

"Got it," Brooklyn said, heading for the door.

"And come back as soon you're done," he told her. "I want to get you both off the island and back home as soon as I can. So far the press hasn't been able to get here because the island's too remote. I want you gone before they arrive."

"Sounds good to me," Brooklyn said as she left the library. "I'll be right back."

Mother sat down at a table and signaled for Sydney to sit across from him.

There was a prolonged silence before he asked, "What's wrong, Syd?"

"Nothing," she said unconvincingly.

"Really?"

She nodded. "Everything's great. The mission's complete. It was a success."

Mother tried to read her eyes. "I've got to say that you don't seem like everything's great."

"I'm just tired," she said. "It's been a long and rather eventful day."

"How come you don't know what he looks like?" he asked. "Brooklyn sure got a lot of specifics."

"Of course she did," Sydney mumbled. "She's perfect."

"What's that supposed to mean?" he asked.

"It means exactly what it sounds like," she said, her voice rising slightly. "Brooklyn's perfect. She does everything right. She doesn't make any mistakes."

They sat silently for a moment until he asked again, "Why didn't you see him, Sydney?"

She couldn't look him in the eye when she finally answered, "Because I wasn't on the ship."

"What do you mean? How's that even possible?"

"I was goofing off," she said. "I went scuba diving."

"With whom?"

"By myself."

"That's incredibly dangerous, Sydney. What time was it?"

"A little before five o'clock this morning," she said. "It turns out Alice and Judy are world-class snorers. They woke me up, I couldn't go back to sleep, and besides, I really wanted to see the bioluminescent phytoplankton. Which you can only see in the dark."

"I don't know where to begin. You went on an exceptionally risky dive, and you left two protectees in the middle of a mission," he said, his temper growing. "What were you thinking?"

"It's not like I left them alone," she snapped. "They still had Queen B looking after them."

"Queen B? You mean Brooklyn?"

"Of course I mean Brooklyn," she replied, the jealousy in her voice completely unmasked. "What was that you called her on our last mission? A natural spy. The best you'd ever seen?"

"That was taken out of context," he replied.

"No, it wasn't," said Sydney. "And it wasn't wrong. You were absolutely right. She's utterly amazing. But how do you think that makes the rest of us feel? To know that even though she just got here, we're already second-rate?"

"That's rubbish," he said. "No one has ever said or even implied that you are second anything."

"Really?" she answered. "Then why are the two of you secretly working on a mission without us?"

"What are you talking about?" he asked. "There's no secret mission."

"Ever since we got back from Paris, the two of you have been working on something," she said. "We've all seen you have little meetings, and Brooklyn's been writing ridiculously complex algorithms. They aren't for school, so what are they for?"

Mother let out a sigh and rested his forehead against his clasped hands. He hadn't realized that he and Brooklyn had been so obvious. She had been helping him, but not with a mission. It was something personal about his family. Something he couldn't open up about in the middle of another crisis.

"You see," said Sydney. "You don't even deny it."

"It's complicated," he said.

"Of course it is," answered Sydney. "I get it. But you asked me what I was thinking and that's what I was thinking. I was sitting in my bunk in the middle of the night. I couldn't sleep, and I decided that I wanted to be away from those two loud, snoring girls who we were supposed to be protecting." And then she realized something and added, "And I decided I needed to be away from Brooklyn too. I was sick and tired of being cooped up in a room with Little Miss Perfect!"

They sat there for a long moment looking at each other. Neither said a word. In fact, the next voice came from over by the doorway. It was Brooklyn, and she'd come back into the room in the middle of the exchange.

"Well, it's a good thing," she said, trying to hide

the hurt feelings. "If you hadn't been in the water, you wouldn't have found the bomb. Good result. That's all that matters."

Sydney turned to the door and looked at her friend. "Brooklyn, I didn't mean—"

"I really don't want to hear it," Brooklyn said, devastation on her face. "The detective's left the building, but I'll go look for the sketch artist on my own."

Brooklyn disappeared through the doorway before either Sydney or Mother could say a thing.

The FARM

EARLIER THAT DAY, RIO HAD STOOD TRI-umphant, spread his arms out in victory, and started singing "We Are the Champions." Although, in his version, there was no "we." It was just about him.

"I am the champion, my friends. And I'll keep on winning till the end."

"Get over yourself, mate," Paris said with a laugh. "You just got lucky."

"Total fluke," added Kat.

"Luck had nothing to do with it," Rio replied proudly

as he dangled a stopwatch in front of them. "Read it and weep. One minute and forty-two seconds. That's not a fluke; that's an all-time record." He did a little victory dance and resumed singing.

They'd just been racing. But unlike other kids who raced to see who could run or ride their bikes the fastest, they were trying to see who was the fastest at cracking a safe while blindfolded. That's what life was like on the FARM, where being a kid and being a spy went hand in hand.

The FARM got its name from the Foundation for Atmospheric Research and Monitoring, the phony organization MI6 created as a cover story in 1953, when it converted a centuries-old Scottish manor house into a state-of-the-art spy center. To the outside world it was a weather station, but to the City Spies it was home.

It was also their training center.

This was where they learned martial arts like Krav Maga and Jeet Kune Do and where they studied code breaking, intelligence gathering, surveillance techniques, and all varieties of spycraft. Recently, they'd started Saturday Match Day, a weekly competition designed to make the training fun. Recent Match Day events determined who was fastest at completing an obstacle course in near-total darkness, who could build the most powerful explosive out of ordinary household objects, and who could memorize the longest string of numbers and letters.

In addition to bragging rights, the victor also received one-week ownership of an old football trophy Mother won in primary school, and with it the right to pick that week's dessert.

"I'm thinking carrot cake," Rio said.

"Blech," Paris said, sticking out his tongue. "I hate carrot cake."

"All the more for me," Rio said with a huge smile.

The trophy was bent and ugly and affectionately known as the Wretched Goalkeeper. Kat, who'd won the memorization challenge a week earlier, was presenting it to Rio when Monty entered the room.

Alexandra Montgomery, or Monty, was a world-class cryptologist, and the agent in charge of the FARM. She was also the other adult in their lives and shared the parenting responsibilities with Mother.

"There's been an incident on the *Sylvia Earle*," she said, trying to mask the panic in her voice. "We don't know what happened yet. We just know that the emergency signal was activated."

"Where's Mother?" asked Rio.

"On a plane to Shetland," she answered. "That's where it happened."

This was the part of spy work that wasn't fun: the moments of worry and concern about people who meant everything to you.

"We knew there might be trouble," said Paris, trying to sound reassuring. "That's the reason MI6 sent Brooklyn and Sydney. But they were well prepared. They're going to be fine."

The next few hours were excruciating as they waited for any information. BBC News had breaking reports, but all they knew for certain was that a distress signal had been sent and that British military scrambled to the scene. One journalist passed along the fact that the ship had been on an educational expedition "designed to encourage girls to pursue careers in the sciences," and another said there'd been reports of two explosions. While worrisome, this particular bit of news was oddly comforting.

"Explosions?" said Kat with the hint of a smile. "Sounds like Sydney."

Rio nodded and added, "Definitely."

Soon after, Mother called to say that both Sydney and Brooklyn were safe, as were all the passengers and crew on the ship. The team let out a cheer and Rio did his victory dance again, although this time the others joined in. After closing her eyes and saying a silent prayer, Monty started doing what she always did when she needed to burn off anxious energy.

She started baking.

In addition to being one of MI6's top cryptographers, Monty was an exceptional baker. Her mother owned an Edinburgh dessert shop, and growing up, she'd spent countless hours helping out in the kitchen. She was so skilled that the kids had come up with what they dubbed a Montyism: *Codes are for breaking; cakes are for baking.*

"We're starting with lamingtons," she said as she headed toward the kitchen. "Then we're going to make pineapple upside-down cake and millionaire's shortbread." She stopped and looked back at them. "Well, don't just stand there. Grab some aprons and get to work. They're not going to bake themselves."

They baked all afternoon, and by the time they were done, they'd also managed to make a double batch of snickerdoodles and a deep-dish apple pie in addition to the cakes. The air was filled with an intoxicating aroma of coconut, pineapple, and cinnamon, and the dining room looked like a bakeshop. But as sumptuous and tempting as it was, no one was allowed to take a single bite until Mother and Sydney and Brooklyn were home.

They went back into the living room, and by that time all the channels were covering the hijacking. Multiple reports confirmed that there'd been a failed attempt to seize the ship, as well as two unexplained explosions. There were also rumors that among the young passengers were a member of the royal family and the daughter of an MP, although both Buckingham Palace and Parliament refused to confirm anything. Additionally, there was a police sketch of Emil Blix, although at this point he had not been identified.

"He looks guilty," Kat said.

"No doubt," added Paris.

Just then the front door opened, and Mother called out, "We're here."

There was a mad dash to greet them, and the first to make it was Kat, who wrapped Brooklyn and Sydney in a three-way hug. "We were so worried," she said. "Are you okay?"

"Fine," Sydney assured her.

"Absolutely," said Brooklyn.

"All hail the conquering heroes!" Paris exclaimed as he traded fist bumps.

Everyone was so happy to see them safe and sound that nobody noticed their expressions were not at all celebratory. The tension between Sydney and Brooklyn had followed them home. They were exhausted from the ordeal and irritable toward each other, which became apparent when Rio made a grand gesture.

"I won this today, but I'm giving it to the two of you to share," he said as he presented them with the Wretched Goalkeeper. "You can decide how you split it up between you. You get to pick this week's dessert, although I think you'll find we're already off to a good start in there."

"Just give it to her," Sydney snapped. "She's the real hero. I only messed things up."

"No need to humblebrag to us," Paris said, trying to lighten the mood. "Let's have cake and you can tell us all about it. We made lamingtons, millionaire's shortbread . . ."

"Here it is in a nutshell," Sydney said tersely. "Total botch job by me. Brooklyn saved the day."

"No, no!" Brooklyn said. "That's not it at all—"

Sydney cut her off. "Listen, Brook. I don't need you to defend me. I can speak for myself." Sydney turned to the others. "I appreciate it, but it's been a day and I'm exhausted. I just want to go to sleep."

She moved past them toward the stairs as the others

watched, unsure of what to say or do. Monty traded a look with Mother, and he nodded that things would be all right.

"What about you?" Rio asked Brooklyn. "The news has been sketchy. Want to fill us in on what happened?"

"Villains tried to seize the boat, but Sydney saved the day with some well-timed explosives."

"I knew it," said Kat. "I knew that was Sydney's handiwork."

"Give us the details," said Paris. "We're on tenter-hooks."

Brooklyn gave a long sigh and said, "You know, I'm pretty tired too. I can tell it to you better in the morning. I haven't slept much this week. Our roommates were obnoxious snorers."

And with that, she headed toward the stairs and up to her room. "Good night, everyone."

Once she was gone, Paris turned to the others and said, "Well, among our many missions, I'd say that Operation Welcome Home was an epic fail."

"Is everything all right?" Kat asked Mother.

"It's been an emotional day for them," he answered. "A lot of drama. I think everyone will feel better in the morning."

After a week of living on a ship, both Sydney and Brooklyn were relieved to be back in their own rooms. Here, with no snoring roommates to keep them awake and no hijackers to fill them with fear, they each fell into deep, dreamless sleep. They slept for nearly twelve hours until Mother came and knocked on their doors.

"Ten o'clock, time to wake up," he called to them. "Meeting in the priest hole in twenty minutes."

The priest hole was a secret room deep beneath the house. It had been built hundreds of years earlier as a hiding place, but was now the command center for the team. MI6 had tricked it out with the latest gear and gadgets, including a virtual reality station, interactive touch-screen tables and monitors, and a massive Cray XC40 supercomputer that was the sixteenth fastest in the United Kingdom. This was where the team came for mission briefings and to do their most top-secret work.

Sydney was the last to arrive, having taken a quick shower. She sat at the end of the conference table next to Kat and assumed that Mother wanted to do a thorough breakdown of what happened on the *Sylvia Earle*.

"Good morning, everybody," he said, more business-like than usual. "Did you two sleep well last night?"

"Yes," said Sydney.

"Me too," answered Brooklyn.

"I didn't," said Mother. "In fact, I didn't sleep at all. Something happened yesterday that had me tossing and turning all night, and I think we need to address it. Right now. All of us."

"Are you talking about the hijacking?" Brooklyn asked.

"No, not that," he said. "We need to address that too. But first we need to clear the air about something that Sydney said."

Sydney couldn't believe he was going to make her apologize about hurting Brooklyn's feelings in front of everybody. She would've much preferred to keep that between her and Brooklyn. "Listen, I didn't mean to—"

Mother held up a hand, and she stopped. "Please. Let me say this."

Sydney was confused but nodded. "Okay."

Now all eyes were on Mother, and he was trying to figure out the best way to broach the subject. "I think the five of you are amazing. I think you are talented. Kind. Intelligent. Intuitive. Like I said, amazing."

"We think you're amazing too," Paris said, trying to add a little levity to the serious tone.

"If I have ever given any of you a reason to believe

that I favor one of you above the others, then that is a huge failing on my part."

Sydney sagged in her seat. This wasn't about her and Brooklyn. It was about her and Mother.

"I love and care for each one of you deeply, and equally," he continued. "And I value what you bring to this team equally. I hope you realize that."

Suddenly the mood in the room changed.

"I don't doubt that you care for us the same," said Paris. "And I don't know what Sydney said. But it's hard to argue with the idea that you do think of us differently when it comes to what we can do as spies."

"What makes you say that?" asked Mother.

"Well, for one, the secret project that you and Brooklyn have been working on for the past couple of months."

Sydney didn't say anything, but she felt vindicated. And now that the topic was out in the open, the others chimed in.

"Yeah," said Rio. "We're trained at surveillance. We do notice little things like the private meetings and hushed conversations you two have."

"We've all seen it," said Kat.

Brooklyn looked straight down at the table. For her this was an impossible situation. She didn't want to keep a secret from them, but she also didn't want to violate Mother's trust. She was still new to the group and was worried that something like this might make it harder for her to be fully accepted.

"Okay," Mother said, "it's true. Brooklyn and I have been working on a project that I've not told any of you about. Not even Monty."

He shot a look at Monty, and she forced a smile, realizing that he was wrestling with this.

"But the reason I haven't told any of you is because I want to protect you," he continued. "This is the type of information that is well beyond top-secret."

"But don't you see?" Sydney said, her frustration coming through. "That only proves our point. This is some super-secret project that you don't even tell Monty about, but you tell Brooklyn. How does that not make us feel second-rate?"

"But I didn't tell Brooklyn," he said.

"Really, then who did?"

Brooklyn looked up and directly at Sydney. "Clementine."

No name could have been more surprising.

"Clementine? As in Mother's wife?" asked Sydney.

"Yes."

"Clementine as in the agent who turned on her country and left MI6 to join Umbra?" said Rio.

"Maybe not," answered Brooklyn.

"So you're not sure it's her?" asked Sydney.

"I'm sure it was her," said Brooklyn. "We're just not sure she turned on her country."

"Really?" said Paris, jumping into the conversation. "Because I am. I was there. I saw it."

Five years earlier, Mother and his wife were both MI6 agents trying to infiltrate Umbra. But, in a shocking turn, she joined forces with Umbra and abandoned Mother, leaving him to die in a warehouse fire. He only survived because Paris saw what happened and braved the fire to save him.

"When did you meet Clementine?" asked Monty.

"In Paris," Brooklyn answered, referring to her first mission with the team. "At the hotel, she was the one who saved me. She was the one who helped me get to the embassy."

"What are you talking about?" asked Rio.

"I didn't tell anyone because at first I didn't know for sure that it was her," she answered. "I wanted to check with Mother."

"There's a chance she's a double agent still working

for MI6," said Mother. "That she has fully infiltrated Umbra. And if that's the case, the more people who know, the more endangered she is."

"Wait a second," said Paris, disbelieving. "Are you trying to protect us, or are you worried about her safety?"

"Both," Mother responded.

"Well, how do you even know for sure that it was her?" Sydney asked Brooklyn. "You've never seen her before."

"She gave me a thumb drive," said Brooklyn.

"And on that drive was this," said Mother.

He clicked a button on his computer, and a picture appeared on the big screen in front of them. It was a picture of a boy and a girl smiling at the camera.

"Is that?" asked Monty.

"Yes," Mother said. "It's Annie and Robert."

The team all stared at the image of Mother's children, and the room fell silent. Suddenly the secrecy made sense.

"You see," said Mother, "if Clementine is in danger, so are they. And I can't have that."

Caterpillar Logic

WHEN SHE'D FOUND THE LIMPET MINE
attached to the side of the *Sylvia Earle*, Sydney knew
exactly what to do. Her MI6 training had given her step-
by-step instructions for disarming an extremely sensitive explosive device. But here in the priest hole, as she
looked at the photo of Robert and Annie, she was at a
total loss. She didn't know what to think, what to feel,
and she certainly didn't know what to say. It turned out
spy training was fairly useless when it came to situations
in which the sensitive device was somebody's heart.

The people in the picture weren't suspects or spies. They were Mother's children. Children he hadn't seen in five years. Sydney had always known about them, but seeing them made it different. And seeing Mother look at them was completely gutting. Suddenly the situation was *real*, and Sydney didn't know how to disarm any of it.

She wasn't alone. There was an uncomfortable silence in the room while everyone waited for somebody else to talk first. Sensing that, Mother tried to make things easier.

"I know this is awkward," he said. "But while this picture is new to you, it's not for me. I've had a couple of months to wrap my head around it. Brooklyn and I have racked our brains, and all we've come to are dead ends. So please, share your observations. Give me your thoughts. Find something we've missed."

He pressed a button that projected the photo onto each of the wall monitors. That way all seven of them could study it without having to crowd around a single screen. In the picture, both kids flashed goofy vacation smiles that seemed to say, *We'll pose for you, but just this once*. Annie was tall, with braces and sun-bleached hair. She hugged her little brother around the shoulder and comically rested her head on top of his. Robert had pudgy cheeks, thick glasses, and wore a number eleven Liverpool jersey. Both seemed happy.

"He's got good taste in football," Paris said approvingly. "Unlike his father."

"He picked Liverpool for the same reason you did," Mother replied with a chuckle. "Because I love Everton, and they're our dreaded rivals."

Monty stepped up to one of the monitors and studied Robert's face. "Has he always worn glasses?"

"Since he was four," answered Mother. "Although Annie's braces are new."

"New braces," Sydney said eagerly, seizing on a potential clue. "That means there should be orthodontist appointments and medical bills." She thought for a moment and sagged. "Although we don't know what name she's using, where she lives, or when in the last five years she got them, so that only narrows it down to any girl with braces in the entire world. Sorry. It's a stupid idea."

"It's not stupid," Mother said. "That's exactly the type of thing we need to think about. That's what will lead us to them. We need to look at this like it's a jigsaw puzzle. No single piece gives us the picture, but if we can snap a few together, then suddenly the image might start to come into focus."

Rio pointed to where the edge of the photograph cut off some writing painted on the storefront window behind them. "That's Chinese, right?"

"I think so," said Mother. "Although with only part of the character visible and no others to go by, it could also be Japanese or Korean."

"Do you think that means they're in Asia?" Paris asked.

"It could," said Mother. "Although there's a Chinatown in virtually every major city in the world."

"We even set up a spreadsheet and tried to count them all," Brooklyn said. "We found more than fifty in the United States alone."

Everyone went back into thinking mode for a moment until Rio asked, "How old are they again?"

"Annie's fourteen and Robert's eleven," Mother answered. "Although when this picture was taken, he was still ten."

Sydney gave him a curious look. "How can you tell?"

"The metadata," he answered. "A digital photograph carries a wide range of technical information about the picture—everything from the type of camera and lens that were used to the date and time it was taken. This picture was taken last October on the fifteenth."

"Although we can't trust that completely," said Brooklyn. "It also said that the picture was taken thirteen minutes past midnight. Considering it's broad daylight, that's obviously wrong."

"Is there anything useful in the metadata?" Monty asked.

"A lot," said Brooklyn. "It lists the serial number of the camera, and we were able to track that to Clarendon Photo, a store in Oxford, where it was purchased by someone named R.F. Stroud."

"Or at least that's who they claimed to be," added Mother. "We've not found an R.F. Stroud living within fifty miles of Oxford."

"Do you think it's an alias that Clementine uses?" asked Paris.

"I would, except I can't imagine she'd go anywhere near there," Mother answered. "Do you know how many people from the Intelligence Service live and work nearby? Retired agents? Current ones? Not to mention the fact that Oxford University has long been one of MI6's main recruitment centers."

"That's where they recruited me," Monty interjected.

"Exactly," said Mother. "Clementine had to know that

the chance of being spotted was significant. I don't know why she'd risk it for something as mundane as a camera she could purchase in any of a thousand locations."

"So she used someone else's camera?" Paris replied. "Either someone who gave it to her or was traveling with her."

"And if Oxford is full of spies," Rio reasoned, "that means the camera could've belonged to another spy."

Mother nodded as he weighed this idea. "That makes a lot of sense."

"I'll tell you what doesn't make sense," Sydney said. "At least not to me." She turned to Brooklyn and asked, "What did she say again? When she gave you the thumb drive."

"She told me that Annie and Robert were happy and healthy and that Mother needed to stop looking for them," Brooklyn answered.

"That," Sydney said, trying to work it out in her brain, "that *doesn't* make sense at all."

"I may not have it word for word," Brooklyn replied somewhat defensively. "It was a crazy situation, and she just appeared out of nowhere."

"No, not that," said Sydney. "What *you* said makes sense. It's what *she* said that seems wrong."

"How do you mean?" asked Rio.

"You know Mother," Sydney said to him. "Is he ever going to stop looking for Annie and Robert?"

Rio shook his head. "Not until he finds them."

"Of course not," she said. "We all know that, and Clementine does too. Now add the fact that she gives him a massive clue. A photograph with both kids in it, knowing it will have the exact opposite effect. That it will make him look even harder." She turned to Mother. "She's super smart. So why would she give you the picture?"

"Because she feels guilty about everything?" Paris suggested.

"Maybe it's just what she told Brooklyn," Monty offered. "That she wants Mother to know that the kids are happy and healthy."

"No. That's not it."

The voice was forceful, and it took everyone a moment to realize that it belonged to Kat. She was away from the others, examining the photo on a monitor across the room.

"Why do you say that?" Paris asked.

"She may feel guilty, and she may want Mother to know that Annie and Robert are okay," Kat said. "But that's irrelevant to why she gave Brooklyn this picture. This particular picture was chosen for a specific reason." She stopped for a moment and analyzed it one more time before turning to them. "She picked it because she *wants* Mother to find them. Or at least to find where this picture was taken."

"And you think that because?" Mother asked.

Kat shrugged as if the answer were obvious. "Why else would she make it so easy to figure out?"

The others all shared an incredulous look.

"You think this is easy?" Paris asked. "Because it doesn't seem easy to any of us."

"That's because you're only seeing caterpillars," she said.

Paris tilted his head to the side and thought about that for a second. Then he smiled at Kat and said, "I love how when you explain things it actually makes them more confusing."

Kat tried to figure a way to put into words what was going on in her head. "If you look at a caterpillar, you're only going to see a caterpillar," she said. "And if you look at a cocoon, you'll only see a cocoon."

"And your point is?" Paris asked, totally baffled.

"You have to look at both of them," she tried to

explain. "You have to look at the caterpillar *and* the cocoon. And then you have to figure out how they fit together. . . ."

"If you ever want to find a butterfly," said Sydney, finishing the thought.

"Exactly right," Kat said.

"That's brilliant," Brooklyn said. "I'm not sure what it means, but I'm certain it's brilliant."

"You think if we stop looking for caterpillars, we can figure this out?" asked Sydney.

Kat nodded and tried to conceal her smile.

"Wait a second," said Sydney, suddenly excited. "You already figured it out. You already found the butterfly."

Kat could contain her smile no longer. She beamed as she said, "Yes."

Mother looked at Kat with total amazement. "How?"

"Start with the time," said Kat. "What time is it in the picture?"

"That depends," said Brooklyn. "It's 12:13 if you believe the metadata. But we know that's wrong."

"No it isn't," said Kat.

"You do see all the sunlight, don't you?" Rio asked skeptically. "You think it's midnight in that picture?"

"No," said Kat. "I think it's midnight in Oxford,

where the camera was purchased and the time and date were originally programmed." She pointed at the picture. "So how do we figure out what time it is in the picture?"

"Her watch!" Monty said, getting it. She used her fingers to zoom in on Annie's watch, which was visible where she had her arm around her brother. "Her watch says it's 4:13."

"Right," said Kat. "And if it's 12:13 a.m. in Oxford, where is it 4:13 p.m.?"

Mother started getting excited. "That's eight hours earlier," he said, doing the time zone math out loud. "It's five hours to New York and another three hours puts us in . . . *California*!"

Kat smiled. "Actually, it puts us on the West Coast of North America. It could be California, Oregon, Washington, British Columbia, or the northwest corner of Mexico."

"She's amazing," Sydney whispered to Monty.

Monty nodded. "Breathtakingly so."

"You said there were more than fifty Chinatowns in America," Kat said to Brooklyn. "How many are on the West Coast?"

"A bunch. Los Angeles, San Francisco, San Diego,

Portland, Seattle, a few others," Brooklyn answered. "And Vancouver in Canada."

"Which narrows it down," said Paris. "But it's still a lot of geography to cover. How do we figure out which of those it is?"

Kat smiled. "That's the best part."

She stepped up to the monitor and used her fingers to zoom in to a reflection in the store's window. In it the street was visible.

"What do you see?" Kat asked.

"The road," answered Sydney.

"And . . . ," replied Kat.

Sydney shrugged. "Nothing. Just the road. No cars even, just . . . asphalt."

"And train tracks," Rio said excitedly.

"Right," said Kat. "We've seen them in cities around the world. We've seen them so much we don't even notice them. Tracks for trolleys, trams, subways, trains. Except those tracks have *two* rails, and if you look closely, you'll see that this one has *three*."

They all looked closer and saw that a third rail ran down the middle of the tracks.

"What's that for?" asked Paris. "A third wheel?"

Mother gasped and covered his mouth with his hand.

He couldn't believe it. "It's a slot for a cable," he said. "Those are tracks for a cable car." He shook his head in disbelief. "How did I miss that?"

"And there's only one city in the world that still uses cable cars," Kat said triumphantly. "And it's in that time zone and it has a Chinatown."

"San Francisco," Mother said as tears welled up in his eyes. "They're in San Francisco."

There was stunned silence in the room until Paris exclaimed, "Well, I'll be a fuzzy caterpillar."

The others laughed, and Mother walked over to Kat and wrapped her in a hug.

"Thank you, sweetheart," he said. "Thank you so much."

"I know this is an emotional moment, and I hate to be critical at a time like this," she said. "But you really should've shown me the picture sooner."

"Lesson learned," he said, half laughing, half crying. "Lesson learned."

Operation Golden Gate

EVEN IN THE WORLD OF SECRETS, THERE were rules and records.

Officially, any MI6 spy mission had to be sanctioned by headquarters at Vauxhall Cross in London. Once approved, it was given a name, and a file was created to hold all the relevant information and documents. Eventually, that file was stored in a secure vault located just outside of Cheltenham in a building nicknamed the Doughnut. But there was nothing official about what Monty proposed. In the lingo of the spy trade, she was suggesting a "rogue op" that would be run "off the books."

"We're going to have to follow this lead wherever it goes," she said. "We'll call it Operation Golden Gate, but no one can know about it except for the seven of us."

She looked around at the others, and each nodded their agreement, with the exception of Mother, who was hesitant. "I don't think it's a good idea for any of you to—"

"We're doing it," Paris said, cutting him off. "And Monty's right. No one else can know. It's too risky."

The risk came from the fact that if Clementine was a double agent, there was no telling who at the Secret Intelligence Service might be threatened by that piece of information. More worrisome, if an Umbra mole secretly working inside the Service came across the file, Clementine's cover would be blown, and the consequences would be devastating.

"Let's begin with what we know," Monty suggested.

"All we can be certain of is that Annie and Robert were in San Francisco at 4:13 p.m. on October fourteenth," said Kat.

"I thought it was the fifteenth," said Sydney.

"It was back in Oxford," Kat explained. "But it was still the fourteenth in California."

Sydney sagged, embarrassed that she hadn't realized that on her own. "Of course. Eight hours earlier."

"What's our first step?" Rio asked. "Do we fly straight to San Francisco?"

"No," Monty answered as she studied the photo. "Not until we figure this out."

"I thought Kat already did that," Brooklyn replied.

"She figured out the when and the where," Monty said. "But we can't do anything until we know the why." She turned to Mother, who was silent as he tried to process everything that was going on. "Don't you agree?"

He stood there for a moment, still conflicted about all of it. "I don't know that I agree with any of this," he said. "If there's a mission, it should be mine alone. Running a rogue op can go pear-shaped in so many ways."

"No offense, Mother," she replied, "but you had the picture for two months and didn't figure out that it was in San Francisco."

He shook his head. "I know," he said. "I can't believe I missed that."

"I can," she replied. "This is too close to you. The fact that it's so personal makes it even more challenging. That's why we're going to help."

"Do you know what the fallout would be if MI6 finds

out?" he asked. "They'd quite likely disband this program. Break up the team."

"Except we're not a team," said Kat. "We're a *family*." She pointed at the picture of Annie and Robert and added, "And this is about family."

For this, Mother had no counterargument. For the second time in less than fifteen minutes, Kat's words had silenced the room.

Monty laughed and said, "For someone who never talks, you sure know what to say."

Kat smiled wryly and answered, "I pick my moments."

"Besides," Brooklyn added, "Clementine didn't give the picture to you. She gave it to me. *She* involved me, and when she did that, she involved all of us. So what's it going to be? Are you going to keep fighting us about this, or are you going to take charge and be the alpha?"

Mother took a few deep breaths as he scanned their faces and saw their determination. He was in. "Monty's right—we don't go anywhere until we figure out why Clemmie picked this picture. I guarantee that it wasn't to help me find the kids. The three of them were probably only in San Francisco for a few days. We have to find that reason, which means we have to find exactly where they're standing."

"How do we do that?" asked Sydney. "San Francisco's a large city."

"I've got an idea," Brooklyn said eagerly as she sat down at a computer keyboard and did a quick search. Within seconds, she found what she was looking for and put it up on the main wall monitor. "This map shows the different cable car routes in San Francisco. We know that they have to be alongside one of them."

"That's great," said Monty. "That focuses the search."

The map showed three separate lines. They were named after the streets they traveled along: California, Powell/Mason, and Powell/Hyde. Each was about a mile and a half to two miles long.

"We get on street view and take a virtual walk along each of these routes, building by building, until we find the storefront in the picture," Mother said. "We split up into three teams of two with each team taking one line, and each person taking one side of the street. That way we shouldn't overlook anything."

"Three teams of two is six," Brooklyn pointed out. "But there are seven of us."

"Right," said Mother with a grin. "That's because while we're going on street view, I want you and Beny to revisit all of those search profiles you've been using the last few months. Only now limit them to a fifty-mile radius around San Francisco."

Beny was the name they used for the massive supercomputer that was kept in a climate-controlled portion of the priest hole. For the past few months, Brooklyn had been using its power to search for Annie and Robert. She'd written a variety of algorithms, facial recognition programs, and search codes trying to locate them. But she had to use those to search the entire planet, which produced results that were unwieldy and hard to muddle through. Now she could concentrate that power to search every flight manifest, hotel registry, and database in San Francisco.

There was a buzz of excitement in the room, but also a hint of uncertainty. Sensing this, Kat turned to Mother to remind him of a good luck tradition they had at the start of every operation. "You know it's not really a mission until you say it."

This was as close to official as it would get, but it was an important step, a way for Mother to signal to the others that he was fully on board.

"This operation is hot," he said with a sly smile. "We are a go."

Fortune Cookies

SYDNEY LOVED HER TEAM, HER "FAMILY"
as Kat put it, and that only made her feel worse about
how things had been going lately. Before, she'd always
felt essential. Sometimes, she even thought of herself as
a star. After all, everyone said she was a natural, and she
was chosen to be the alpha more often than anyone else.
But she didn't feel like a star now.

In Paris, on the biggest mission they'd ever undertaken,
Brooklyn had been the hero, even though she'd had virtually no training. That continued on the *Sylvia Earle*.

Yes, Sydney defused the bomb and used the explosives to cause a distraction, but she'd also mishandled her role as alpha. Brooklyn was the reliable one who'd gotten Alice and Judy to safety. She was the resourceful one who twice defeated a hulking thug. She was the clever one who worked her way onto the bridge so that she could signal for help. Brooklyn proved time and again that *she* was the natural spy. And how did Sydney respond? She threw a hissy fit and hurt Brooklyn's feelings.

So far, Operation Golden Gate wasn't going any better. Kat solved a puzzle that Sydney knew she never could've cracked. And when it came time to convince Mother that they should take on the mission, it was the others who did the convincing. All Sydney did was make unhelpful suggestions and confuse time zones and dates. She felt useless. That's why she was determined to be the one to find the storefront as she took a virtual walk through San Francisco along Mason and Powell Streets. It was the kind of small but important contribution that could put her back on track. A way for her to help and maybe win back some of her confidence.

The work was tedious, made more difficult by the fact that the images weren't a picture of the streets now, but rather a collection of photographs taken over the course of the last few years. Businesses had changed hands, buildings had been repainted, facades remodeled, and there was little in the photograph to go on: just part of a window, half of a Chinese character, and the reflection of the street. Sydney clicked on the little arrow so she traveled down the sidewalk a few feet at a time until . . .

"Found it!"

A surge of excitement went through the room, just as Sydney had hoped. Only it wasn't directed at her. It was focused on Rio, who had made the discovery. He was across the room, tracing the cable car route down California Street along the edge of Chinatown. On his computer screen, he positioned the photo of Annie and Robert next to a storefront for a side-by-side comparison. "They've changed the paint," he said, "but you can tell that the window's the same, and there's a discoloration on the sidewalk in both."

Mother looked over his shoulder and studied it. "You're absolutely right," he said. "Great job!"

Rio beamed with pride, and the others hooted and hollered their congratulations. Loudest of all was Sydney, trying not to sound jealous as she said, "Way to go, Rio!"

"What's the name of the store?" Paris asked.

"Zee's Bakery and Confectionery," Rio answered as he clicked open the store's website. "According to this, Zee's has been a Chinatown fixture for more than a century. It was famous for helping popularize the fortune cookie, which was invented in San Francisco in 1907. The bakery now makes the cookies for restaurants throughout California."

"Unbelievable," Mother said.

"I know," Paris said. "I always assumed the fortune cookie was invented in China."

Mother chuckled. "That's surprising too. But I meant it's unbelievable that Clementine took the picture in front of a fortune cookie bakery. That is so like her."

"How do you mean?" asked Monty.

"Fortune cookies were a big deal with us," he said. "We used to joke that the fortune cookie was the ultimate symbol of spycraft, because it was a message hidden inside of something that had absolutely nothing to do with messages. We used it as a term to describe any coded communication." He paused for a moment. "It's even how I proposed."

"Wait, what?" asked Sydney.

Mother smiled at the memory. "There was a Chinese restaurant near Paddington that was our favorite spot for date night. The food was cheap but delicious. I had a special fortune cookie made, and I worked it out with the waiter to deliver it at the perfect moment. When Clemmie opened it, it read, 'Will you marry me?' And of course, Clemmie being Clemmie, she answered in Mandarin. I had to have the waiter translate to make sure she'd said yes."

"She speaks Mandarin?" said Sydney.

"Fluently," answered Mother. "Along with seven other languages."

The story was both sweet and heartbreaking. A reminder of when Mother and Clementine had been a happy couple.

"So now you think she's sending you a message?" Rio asked. "A fortune cookie."

Mother nodded. "I'm sure of it. I just hope this one's in a language I know."

Just then Brooklyn piped up. She'd been using Beny to perform big data searches and had found something interesting. "I think I know what it might be about."

"What's that?" asked Mother.

"R.F. Stroud," she said.

"He's the bloke who bought the camera in Oxford, right?" asked Paris.

"Yes," answered Brooklyn. "He's also the bloke who was found dead in Muir Woods on the morning of October fourteenth."

It was as if the air had been sucked out of the room as everyone rushed over to Brooklyn to look at her computer screen.

"What's Muir Woods?" asked Rio.

"It's a redwood forest just outside of San Francisco," said Brooklyn. "Listen to this incident report," she continued. "The body of a man was discovered by Ranger K. Gilson at 10:47 a.m. in the Cathedral Grove. The man was unresponsive, and the ranger administered CPR until paramedics arrived and took him to the UCSF Medical Center, where he was pronounced dead. The cause of death was determined to be a heart attack, and the man was later identified as R.F. Stroud of Watlington, United Kingdom."

"Watlington?" said Mother, his eyes wide with surprise.

"I used to visit a friend there when I was at uni," Monty said. "It's right outside of Oxford."

"I know exactly where it is," Mother said. "And now I know exactly who R.F. Stroud is."

"You do?" asked Brooklyn.

"He's a longtime spy named Parker Rutledge," Mother

said. "I worked on a team with him for the first couple of years I was in the Service. I learned a lot from Parker. He was brilliant. I heard he died of a heart attack while he was on holiday in California, but by the time it got around to me, there weren't any details."

"Then how can you be sure this is the same heart attack?" asked Rio.

"Watlington," he answered. "It's a small town, just a couple of thousand people. It's where Parker spent his whole life. His father was a professor at Oxford. He taught ornithology."

"That's the study of birds, right?" asked Brooklyn.

"Parker was heavy into it too," said Mother. "He was also a professor, and the president of the Oxford Ornithological Society. Ever since he retired from MI6, he's been traveling the world on bird-watching trips. That's what he was doing in California when he died."

"If you knew him early in your career," said Rio, "does that mean Clementine knew him too?"

"We were both on his team when we met," he said. "Parker was one of Clemmie's mentors."

"And the day he dies in San Francisco, she's in town using his camera?" said Paris. "That can't be a coincidence. There's got to be a connection that we're not seeing. Was there anything suspicious about his death?"

"Not that I know of," Mother answered with a shrug. "But like I said, by the time the story got to me, there weren't many details."

"There's something wrong about this," Brooklyn said as she continued searching for information with Beny. "According to the ranger's handwritten notes, Stroud—who's really Rutledge—was taken to the UCSF Medical Center, where he was pronounced dead of a heart attack. But there's no record of him arriving at the UCSF emergency room at that time."

"They list patients by name?" asked Monty, surprised. "I'd think those would be confidential."

"They don't list the names," said Brooklyn. "But they do list times and descriptions. There's no one within an hour of when he was picked up. And the closest ones are a woman with a severe laceration and a young man with a gunshot wound."

"What about the ambulance?" asked Paris.

"The same," said Brooklyn. "According to this dispatch log, the ambulance was sent out at 10:46, which matches the ranger's notes, but then there's no record of it returning. There's no mention of it until it goes out on another call at 12:41."

"MI6 must have erased it," Mother said. "You probably won't find a record of him staying at a hotel either."

"Then why didn't they erase the ranger's report?" asked Rio.

"They probably didn't know about it," said Mother. "You said it's handwritten, right?" he asked Brooklyn.

"Yes." She put it up on the wall monitor for them all to read.

"That means it might not have been scanned into the computer records right away," he explained. "You can't erase something if you don't know it exists."

"But why would they bother to erase any of it?" asked Sydney. "A retired agent has a heart attack. It's sad, but it's hardly a state secret."

"Unless he wasn't a retired agent on holiday," said Monty. "And he was actually an active agent on a mission."

11.

The Bird-Watcher

WATLINGTON, ENGLAND—TWO YEARS EARLIER

AFTER THREE DECADES WITH MI6, Parker Rutledge's retirement from the world of espionage lasted a grand total of sixteen days. On the seventeenth, he was tending to a flower bed in front of his quaint redbrick home when he looked up and saw something so surprising, he had to adjust his glasses to make sure his eyes weren't playing tricks on him.

Well, I'll be gobsmacked! he said to himself when he realized they weren't.

Walking directly toward him was none other than Sir

David Denton Douglas, a man who, despite the fact that all three of his names started with *D*, was universally known as C, the title historically given to the chief of the Secret Intelligence Service.

Douglas was Britain's top spymaster.

All the more curious was the fact that he seemed to have materialized out of thin air. There was no sign of the bulletproof SUV that dropped him off every day at Vauxhall Cross or the protection detail that escorted him on his frequent visits to Parliament and Buckingham Palace. There was just an aristocratic man in a finely tailored suit, carrying a briefcase as he walked along the very unaristocratic Watcombe Road.

"Good afternoon, C," Parker said, incredulous as he stood up and hurriedly brushed the dirt off his clothes. "What brings you here?"

"Just thought I'd stop by and have a cuppa with my favorite bird-watcher," the chief said with a smile and a wink.

Within MI6, "bird-watcher" was the most common slang for "spy," but for Parker it had double meaning. Like all agents, his role in the Service had been classified. As far as the rest of the world knew, he really was a bird-watcher. He taught ornithology at Oxford, just as his father had before him.

"Please come in," Parker said. "I'll put on a kettle."

A few minutes later they were sitting in the kitchen when C asked, "So, has the boredom of retirement driven you mad yet?"

Parker chuckled as he poured the tea and replied, "It hasn't had the chance. My farewell party was just three weeks ago."

"Right, right," C said as he took a sip. "As we were singing your praises, you mentioned something about working on . . . what was it again . . . your bird list?"

"My life list," said Parker. "It means everything to a birder. It's the record of every species you've seen in the field during your lifetime. My goal is to make it to a thousand. Like my father."

"I'm sorry I never got to meet him," said C. "He's the one who taught you the ways of birds?"

"Indeed," said Parker. "He's also the one who taught me the ways of spies, although he never knew it."

"How do you mean?"

"He was the director of the Edward Grey Institute of Field Ornithology here at Oxford," Parker explained. "From a very young age, I tagged along on his birding treks across Europe. And all the skills he taught me for spotting them—stealth, patience, attention to detail, and most importantly, the ability to observe without being observed—those are the same traits I used for thirty years to serve my country."

"And you served it quite well," said the chief, holding up his cup as if he was making a toast.

"Thank you, sir," Parker replied proudly as he returned the gesture.

The conversation stalled as Parker waited for the chief to say what had brought him out to see him and as C tried to figure out how to best broach the subject.

"How far have you gotten?" he asked. "On your list?"

"Eight hundred thirty-six," answered Parker.

"Impressive," said the chief. He leaned forward in his seat and added, "I have a suggestion for number eight hundred thirty-seven, but it'll be hard to track down."

"If it was easy, what fun would it be?"

"I was hoping you'd say that." The chief flashed a mischievous grin. "By showing what I'm about to show you, I'm in breach of at least three provisions of the Official Secrets Act. So let's keep this conversation between you and me."

"Of course, sir."

"For at least ten years, and probably longer, there has been a mole inside MI6 who's been funneling secrets to

Umbra. This double agent has cost us dearly. Security has been compromised, lives have been lost, and I'm quite sick of it. Yet, despite all our searching, we have very little to show for our efforts."

C placed a manila folder stamped TOP SECRET: EYES ONLY on the table between them. Parker opened it carefully. There was only one word written on the front page of the report: MAGPIE.

"If you're looking for a mole, why did you name it after a bird?"

"You tell me," said C. "You're the ornithologist."

Parker thought about it for a moment and began to see the reasoning. "A magpie blends in because it looks common, even though it's actually extraordinary. It's one of only a handful of animals in the entire world that can recognize itself in a mirror. Magpies are intelligent, calculating, and notorious thieves who steal from the nests of other birds to decorate their own. They are among the most deceptive creatures on the planet."

"Yes they are," C said coolly. "And one of them is loose inside MI6. I want you to find that magpie for me. There's your bird. There's your number eight thirty-seven."

Kinloch Abbey

SINCE THEY'D COME HOME FROM THE *Sylvia Earle*, Brooklyn had tried to avoid Sydney. And Sydney, sensing her friend's hurt feelings, had given her plenty of space. But as they returned to school on Monday, Sydney decided to test the waters during the train ride to Kinloch. She waited until they were almost there before she sat next to Brooklyn, who was flipping through her textbook working on an algebra problem.

"Hi," Sydney said, trying a little too hard to sound friendly.

"Hey," Brooklyn grunted, not bothering to look up.

There was an uncomfortable silence interrupted only by the sound of the train, until Sydney said, "So, what are you doing? Studying for a test?"

Brooklyn pointed at her textbook and then the papers spread out on the tabletop in front of her before saying, "That's amazing. Surveillance training is really paying off. How'd you figure it out?"

Sydney fought her instinct to snipe back and instead let out a deep sigh. "So, is that how it's going to be from now on?"

Brooklyn finally looked up from her work and asked, "What do you want, Sydney?"

"Nothing. I just wanted to sit here. With you."

"Is that so? Because the other day you made it abundantly clear that you did not want to be *with me*."

"I know that I said that," Sydney answered. "But I didn't mean it." She let out a confused groan. "Or if I did, not the way you took it."

"'*I was sick and tired of being cooped up in a room with Little Miss Perfect!*'" Brooklyn said, adding a hint of Sydney's accent as she did. "Am I quoting that accurately?"

Sydney sagged as she admitted, "Word for word."

"Well, how else was I supposed to take that?"

Sydney thought for a moment. "I don't know. I just know that my problem wasn't with you. It was with me. I wanted to be away from that. Away from how I was feeling. I wanted a little peace and quiet so I could try to figure out how I . . . fit in."

"How *you* fit in?" Brooklyn gave her an incredulous look. "That's rich. I'm the one who's trying to fit in. I'm the outsider joining a team that's thick as thieves. You guys have been together for years, and you were the second one, so that makes you an OG. I'm the noob. And after all you and I have been through these last few months, I thought we fit in together. I thought we were friends."

"We were. I mean we *are*. Of course we are. We're more than friends. We're best mates."

"Really? 'Cause talking like that about each other, that's not something best mates do."

"You're right. It's just some sort of twisted jealousy," Sydney said. "But I need you to be my friend. I need you to forgive me." She paused for a moment. "Because forgiving each other, that *is* something best mates do."

The train pulled into Kinloch, and Brooklyn quickly shoveled her papers into her backpack. "I am your mate and I do forgive you." She thought about that for a second while she zipped the bag shut. "Or, at least I will . . . but at the moment, I'm still mad."

When she stood up, Brooklyn saw that Paris, Kat, and Rio were avoiding eye contact as they collected their backpacks a row behind them. They'd undoubtedly heard every word, which explained why they were trying to sidestep her.

"Did you get all that?" Brooklyn asked them with a flash of New York attitude.

"We didn't get anything," Paris replied. "I had my earbuds in."

"Don't know what you're talking about," said Rio, feigning confusion and doing a lousy job of it. "Absolutely no idea."

"Wow, you two should really consider auditioning for junior drama club," Kat said, shaking her head at the two boys. "Come on, Brook, I'll quiz you for your algebra test while we walk to school."

Once they were on the platform, Brooklyn turned to Sydney. "I really do forgive you. I just need a little time and space to not be mad at you."

"I can do that," Sydney said, relieved. "I can give you all the time and space you need." To punctuate the point, she plopped down on a wooden bench so that Brooklyn and the others could get ahead of her. "See what I mean? This is me giving you space. You all go on."

Kinloch railway station consisted of a small blue-and-white building with a ticket window, four covered benches, and a dodgy vending machine that stole money far more often than it yielded candy bars or crisps. The platform was situated between the north- and south-bound tracks so passengers had to go up and over a wooden pedestrian bridge to get into town. While her friends crossed it, Sydney stayed on the bench and tried a quick meditation exercise she'd learned from Monty to help clear her mind. She hadn't felt like herself lately, and she was ready for that to end.

The footbridge offered a nice view of the town as well as a picturesque view of the school. This was where photographers would set up whenever it was time to take a photo for a new admissions brochure or to update the website. It was the can't-miss first impression that wowed prospective students and their parents.

Kinloch Abbey was one of the top prep schools in Scotland. It looked like a cross between a small college and a grand estate, with classic stone buildings and lush playing fields surrounding a stately manor house.

Despite her natural antiestablishment tendencies, even Sydney had to admit that it was beautiful.

"It's a wonderland," she'd said to Monty and Mother as they escorted her across the bridge for her first visit to campus. But looking at it now, she noticed something out of place. Unlike the panorama of the school, the view of the main gate was mostly obscured by the Kinloch Inn and the Bank of Scotland. Despite this, Sydney could see just enough to tell that there was some sort of activity going on there. She stood on her tiptoes and leaned over the railing far enough to see that a cluster of people was assembled just outside the entrance. That in itself was unusual. But when she leaned a bit farther, she saw something even more curious.

Why are there two TV trucks at Kinloch? she asked herself. She wondered if something newsworthy had happened while she was away on the *Sylvia Earle*.

And that's when it dawned on her.

What if she hadn't *missed* the story? What if she *was* the story? Her and Brooklyn.

Over the weekend they'd been so focused on Clementine, Parker Rutledge, and trying to figure out what happened in San Francisco that they'd lost sight of the fact that for the rest of Britain, the biggest news was the botched hijacking of the *Sylvia Earle.*

It had everything the tabloids and cable news craved: high-stakes drama, a rumored connection to Parliament and the royal family, and evil villains who were still on the loose. But most of all, it had mystery.

For three days, the media had been running reports with far more questions than answers. That was largely due to the fact that the crime had taken place in such a remote location. Unst didn't have a commercial airport—just a landing strip controlled by the government. By the time the press had managed to arrange for boats to take them there, most of the passengers and crew were gone. As a result, news outlets had virtually no firsthand information. There was no video of the aftermath. No interviews with traumatized victims. More importantly, because those passengers were minors, their identities had been kept secret.

Or at least, they were supposed to be secret. Was it possible that they somehow found out that the two of them were on board? If so, that would be very dangerous. Spies were supposed to blend into the background, not be on the news or have their pictures on the front page. Not to mention the fact that it wouldn't be a good thing for Emil Blix to know where they lived and went to school.

"Brooklyn!" Sydney shouted to no avail, her voice drowned out by distance and traffic. "Brooklyn!"

She raced after them but missed the light at the crosswalk, which put her farther behind. By the time she finally caught up, they were just around the corner from school.

"Brooklyn," she yelled, breathing a bit heavily. "Wait for me!"

Brooklyn finally stopped and turned to face her. "When I said I needed a little time, I meant more than three minutes." She said it as a joke, but there was more than a hint of seriousness in it.

"I know," Sydney replied. "And you can be mad at me again in a little bit. But right now, you've got to come with me. We need to get out of here."

"What are you talking about?"

"You can't see it yet," Sydney said. "But there's trouble right around the corner. I noticed it from the footbridge."

"What type of trouble?"

"Paps."

"Paps?" asked Brooklyn. "What are paps?"

"Paparazzi."

"Waiting for us?"

"Yes," said Sydney. Then she thought for a second. "At least, I think so."

"You think there are paparazzi waiting to take our pictures like we're celebrities?" Brooklyn said with a laugh. "You really have gone full mental, haven't you? Relax, Sydney. You and I are good. Apology's accepted. You don't have to worry about it anymore." She nodded toward the school. "And you don't have to make up insane situations in order to rescue me."

Sydney wondered if she'd done just that. If she'd caught a glimpse of one thing and manufactured it into some high drama that wasn't really there. That would be in keeping with her recent non-Sydney-like behavior. Her face flushed red with embarrassment.

"Sorry."

"Come on," Brooklyn said to her. "Walk with us."

Sydney remained embarrassed about overreacting up until the moment they turned the corner and realized she'd been absolutely right. Standing there just outside the school's property line were a dozen reporters and three television camera operators.

"There they are," one reporter said to her cameraman. "Start rolling."

Within seconds a chain reaction spread through them,

and they all moved toward Sydney and Brooklyn.

"You guys block for us," Sydney said to the others. "Try to buy us some time." She yanked on Brooklyn's arm and started sprinting down the street. "We've got to get out of here."

"They're running," another reporter called out, and soon the press started chasing after them. It was somewhat comical as camera operators lugged heavy gear, on-air reporters tried to run in uncomfortable shoes while not mussing their makeup or clothes, and newspaper and tabloid journalists sprinted into the lead.

"What's this about?" Brooklyn asked Sydney as they ran.

"The *Sylvia Earle*," explained Sydney. "It's a huge story and we're part of it."

"Yes, but how do they know that?"

"We can ask them if they catch us."

As they turned the corner, both girls looked back and saw that the first wave of reporters was gaining. The two of them started racing along High Street, sprinting past all the restaurants and shops.

"Shouldn't we go to the train station," Brooklyn said, "so we can get out of town?"

"There won't be another train for half an hour,"

Sydney said. "They'd have us cornered on the platform."

"Then where are we going?"

"Chip shop," said Sydney.

"Seriously?" replied Brooklyn, panting as they ran. "We just had breakfast. We're being chased by the paparazzi, and you want to stop for fish and chips?"

"Just trust me," said Sydney.

In the middle of the block stood Scrod Save the Queen, the best chip shop in town and a popular hangout for Kinloch students. But Sydney wasn't interested in their deep-fried deliciousness. She was headed there because of its basement.

"Morning, Calvin," Sydney said to the man behind the counter as she and Brooklyn scurried into the shop.

"Morning, Sydney," he replied. "Shouldn't you be in school?"

"On my way," she answered. "Mind if we lock up for a sec? We're trying to avoid some paparazzi."

"Fine by me," he answered as though this was an everyday request.

She turned the lock on the door and flipped the plastic sign so that it read CLOSED.

"Just give us a few, will ya?" she continued.

"Sure thing," Calvin replied.

Sydney led Brooklyn to the back of the store and down a flight of stairs.

"Okay, that was surreal," said Brooklyn. "You know him?"

"Calvin? For years. He's great and his chippy's to die for."

"Why are we coming down here?" Brooklyn asked. "Is this where we're going to hide?"

"It'll be easier to explain when you see it," Sydney replied.

They reached what appeared to be a dead end when they came to the rear wall of the basement. But Sydney moved with lightning efficiency as she quickly pushed some boxes out of the way and slid a cabinet to the side to reveal a metal panel with a bolt and latch. She opened it to reveal a set of stone stairs that descended into the darkness.

"Whoa," said Brooklyn.

"Come on," Sydney said as she flipped a light switch and illuminated a long brick tunnel. "Let's get you to that algebra test."

"What is this?" asked Brooklyn.

"Over the past five centuries, Kinloch Abbey has been a castle, a fort, a monastery, and a school," Sydney explained. "And no matter what it was, there have always been people desperate to sneak in or escape. There are various ways to do that, but this is my personal favorite. Legend has it that it was built in 1568 by Sir William Douglas as a way to smuggle Mary, Queen of Scots, whose cousin Queen Elizabeth wanted her dead. There's no way the paps will find their way down here."

Even though it was dark and damp, Brooklyn enjoyed the tunnel. Just the thought of it was exotic and exciting. It was narrow enough that she could touch both sides at once, and anyone taller would've had to duck to keep from bumping into the ceiling. It took them about ten minutes, just enough time to unwind from the unexpected adrenaline jolt of the morning.

They were about halfway when Sydney said, "I meant what I said on the train. I really am very sorry."

"I know," answered Brooklyn. She was quiet for a moment before she asked, "Did you also mean the part about being jealous of me?"

"Yes," Sydney said emphatically. "I know that's daft, but it's true."

"Why? How could I possibly make you jealous?"

Sydney stopped and turned back, half her face illuminated by a light bulb in a wire basket that hung from the ceiling.

"You're great at everything," she said. "Even without training."

"I wasn't great at figuring out that picture of Annie and Robert," Brooklyn replied. "In twenty minutes, Kat solved something that had baffled me for two months."

Even in the low light, Brooklyn could see a smile creep across Sydney's face.

"I quite liked that," Sydney admitted as she tried to stifle a laugh.

"Oh, you did?" Brooklyn replied, embarrassed and amused. "You enjoyed me failing miserably?"

"No," Sydney said. "You didn't fail at all. No one can think like Kat. But it was a good reminder to me that I'm not the only one who makes mistakes."

Minutes later, they reached an aged oak door and entered the school's boiler room. It was cramped and not unlike the school's version of the stern thruster machine room. There were old water tanks, hissing steam pipes, and an electric generator, among other machinery. Conspicuously out of place was the dapper man in a tweed houndstooth suit leaning against a wall, reading a book.

"Dr. Graham?"

Dr. Christopher Graham was the headmaster at Kinloch, and he closed the book and looked up at them. "Ah, Eleanor, Christina, so nice to see you," he said, calling them by the MI6 cover names they used at school. "Welcome back to Kinloch. I trust you had an . . . *eventful* . . . time on the *Sylvia Earle*."

"What are you doing here?" Sydney asked.

"Waiting for you, of course," he said. "First off, I'm terribly sorry about the horde that greeted you this morning. We did not see that coming, but trust me that we have lawyers in high places dealing with those media organizations as we speak. I was headed toward the train station to greet you personally when I saw the scrum and watched you run away. I knew I'd never catch up, so I decided to wait for you here instead."

Sydney looked around, trying to make sense of it all. "And you knew we'd be here because . . ."

"Because long before I was headmaster at Kinloch, I was a student at Kinloch," he said. "I too have snuck in and out through the secret passageway of Mary, Queen of Scots. I don't officially approve of doing so, but in this instance I'll look the other way."

Sydney and Brooklyn laughed. Dr. Graham was an unusual character but one students adored. Sydney had done some digging into his past and had an even greater appreciation for him than most. Before he was an educator, he was an army intelligence officer with the Royal Scots. She often wondered if his intelligence background had anything to do with why MI6 had placed them all at Kinloch.

"Now, on to more pressing matters," he said. "We have never talked about our"—he searched for the right word—"*peculiar* arrangement. You and your friends from FARM often disappear with little notice, and I know just enough to know that I shouldn't ask any questions. This time, however, I must force myself to violate that unspoken rule."

Sydney and Brooklyn braced themselves for whatever question he might ask.

"Are you okay? Is there anything I can do to help?"

The question was obviously heartfelt, and both girls were touched.

"I hold crown and country in the highest regard," he continued. "But I tell you with all sincerity that nothing matters more to me than the well-being of my students. I can't begin to imagine what you've been through."

"We're fine," said Sydney.

"Totally fine," added Brooklyn. "But thank you for asking."

He closed his eyes for a second of relief. "No more

questions," he said. "And perhaps this is just school spirit and personal pride talking, but until somebody disabuses me of the notion, I'd like to think that my two brilliant, resourceful, wonderful Kinloch students have a fair share of responsibility for the fact that the hijackers' plan failed so miserably. That perhaps you two are, in fact, the heroes of the day."

Sydney and Brooklyn both smiled as they shared a look. This was as close as they'd ever get to acknowledging their secret outside the circle.

"Well, I'm not going to *disabuse* you," Sydney said.

"Neither will I," added Brooklyn.

The headmaster slapped his hands together and beamed. "Deee-lightful." He gave each a firm, enthusiastic handshake, and then, once the moment of congratulations was over, he flashed a comically severe expression and said, "Well, off to class now. Heroes or not, I will not stomach tardiness."

They laughed and headed off to class, and as they did, they could hear him absently whistling the school song as he walked toward his office.

Feijoada

"WERE YOU TERRIFIED?"

"Is it true there was a royal on board?"

"What was it like when the bombs went off?"

"OMG, tell me everything!"

Sydney and Brooklyn were never as popular as they were that day at school. Everyone wanted to hear about the hijacking. Even their teachers. The algebra test Brooklyn had been so worried about had to be postponed because too much of the class time was eaten up by her recounting of the events.

Normally, they wouldn't say a word about one of their missions, but Mother worried that not talking about it would seem more suspicious and could possibly attract deeper curiosity and inspection. Besides, *Sydney* and *Brooklyn* were sworn to secrecy. But here at Kinloch, they were Ellie and Christina, two schoolmates who just happened to get swept up in the biggest news story in ages. It was no secret that they'd taken off from school to go on the trip. In fact, both were supposed to give presentations about it to their science classes. Only now, instead of talking about marine mammals and bioluminescent phytoplankton, they were discussing hijackers and rescues at sea. Throughout the day, both girls offered watered-down versions of the events, omitting any details that might hint at their actual roles. And even though neither would admit it, both liked being the center of attention at least a little bit.

"I've never been so scared in my life."

"Yes, she's a royal, but not one that you'd know."

"By the time the second explosion went off, I thought we were under attack."

After school, Dr. Graham drove them back to the FARM to ensure that there was no more trouble. Then he met with Monty, and they worked out a plan to make sure there wasn't a repeat.

"How did the press even know about them?" she asked.

"Our attorney thinks the media found out which schools sent students on the trip, and then they trolled through the social media accounts of any students at those schools," Graham explained. "Someone must have intercepted a message between two of our students who were talking about the girls being on the trip."

The team typically had chores around the house they had to take care of when they got home from school, but today those were postponed so they could all watch the news. With Emil Blix and his crew still at large, and so many unanswered questions about the hijacking, the *Sylvia Earle* still dominated coverage. The BBC had the best reporting, aided by the fact that one of their documentary filmmakers, Virginia Wescott, had been on board. She'd given an extensive interview while she was still on Unst, with the *Sylvia Earle* visible in the background, and she'd done a more formal one at the network's London studio.

"You know, I think she may have saved my life," Brooklyn offered.

"How so?" asked Kat.

"At the end, when everything fell apart, I think the head guy figured out that I might be to blame," she said. "He made a move toward me, and she stepped between us and warned him off."

"That's quite brave," said Monty.

"She's tough," said Brooklyn. "She told us some amazing stories about things that have happened while she was making documentaries."

During the interview Virginia explained that the government had seized all the footage she shot on the *Sylvia Earle* as potential evidence, although they allowed the network to show a few shots of the ship heading out to sea and of the crew with no students visible. It wasn't much, but compared to what the other networks had, it was a treasure trove.

They continued watching, and in the endless quest for "breaking news," the following stories led the way:

The hijackers were still at large, but the leader had been identified as Emil Blix, a shadowy figure from Bergen, Norway. He'd had past associations with several notorious crime syndicates, including Umbra and one whose symbol matched the wolf tattoo Brooklyn saw on his neck.

Much was being made of the fact that Frida Hovland, the ship's captain, was also from Norway. Although no one directly said that she was connected to the hijackers, that was the implication. This fit with a theory that someone in the crew might have helped the hijackers track the ship to such a remote location.

There was great interest in the explosions. According to the police statements, everyone on the ship heard both of them, but nobody saw either one nor could they explain why they didn't cause any damage. Each network had their own "expert" offer theories, the most ridiculous of which was that the Royal Navy had a top-secret program that trained dolphins and sea lions to detect and destroy underwater mines and explosives. This instantly led to the nickname Sydney the Sea Lion, to which Sydney responded by making a barking noise and moving her arms like flippers.

Interestingly, the person who was becoming most identified with the hijacking wasn't even someone who was on the ship. It was Judy's mother. Mary Somersby was using her position in Parliament to attack MI6, which she blamed for not preventing the assault. She made appearances on every network and, without naming her daughter, confided that someone close to her family had been on board. She cried during one clip that was frequently replayed and promised a thorough investigation into what went wrong.

"Isn't that just classic?" Rio complained. "She's attacking MI6, when it was a pair of MI6 agents who saved her daughter."

"Doesn't she know that?" asked Paris. "She's a high-ranking MP."

"Doesn't matter," replied Monty. "Everything this team does is behind the highest level of security. There'd be no way to explain that a pair of girls saved her daughter without her wanting to know more about that pair of girls."

"You'd think maybe her daughter would give her a little hint," Rio offered.

Sydney laughed. "You don't know this girl. She's concerned about her reputation and her reputation only."

"Do you think there could've been someone on the ship working with the hijackers?" asked Kat. "What about the captain? They seem to think she might be involved."

"I don't think so," said Sydney. "She's pretty awesome."

"I agree," said Brooklyn. "But there were two strange incidents that happened between her and Blix. Twice she yelled at him, and he just kind of took it. He didn't snap back at her."

"What did she say when she yelled at him?" asked Paris.

"I don't know," answered Brooklyn. "She yelled in Norwegian. I couldn't understand a word."

As they continued watching, they were relieved to see that the legal threats seemed to have worked. No channel had footage of Sydney and Brooklyn being chased through town. There was, however, an eleven-second clip shot on someone's phone that made it onto social media. But it wasn't of the two of them. Instead, it showed Paris standing firm like a brick wall as a camera operator slammed into him at full speed, only to comically crumble and crash to the ground. The user had added music and a bug splat sound effect, along with a banner that read STOP-ARAZZI!

That night, as everyone helped prepare dinner, Sydney the Sea Lion and Paris's budding online celebrity were the main topics of discussion.

"You just went over a thousand likes," Sydney said, checking her phone. "You're going viral!"

"You know," said Kat, "just like a disease."

The two girls traded fist bumps.

"What comes next?" asked Brooklyn. "Memes? A fan club? Stop-arazzi T-shirts?"

"Enough already," said Rio. "Can we just focus on dinner? I've already pushed this meal back a day. I will not have it ruined because of some stupid YouTube video."

"Stupid YouTube video?" Sydney said as she stirred a pan of rice. "Sounds like someone's got a case of the jellies."

"Jealous? Me?" protested Rio. "Of what? All he did was . . . stand there."

"Right," said Paris. "I guess no one thought to shoot any action footage of you hiding behind a car."

"I wasn't *hiding*," he said defensively. "I was . . . getting out of the way to avoid injury."

"How is that different from hiding?" asked Kat, bringing everyone to laughter.

Everyone, that is, except Rio.

"Just cook, okay?" he said.

Food on the FARM tended to have an international flavor, as both Monty and Mother felt it was important that the menu include dishes from everyone's homeland. As a result, the kitchen was a cultural melting pot, often filled with inviting aromas from around the world, like the smell of curry and saffron from a delicious Nepali dinner or the savory scent of piping hot Australian meat pies.

These so-called home table meals were prepared entirely by the kids and usually made on Sundays. But with all the craziness, this week's dinner had been pushed back a day, not unlike Brooklyn's algebra test. They were making Rio's favorite, a giant pot of feijoada, a beef, pork, and black bean stew that was served over rice with smoked sausage.

"This looks and smells amazing," Monty said as they sat down for dinner.

"Thank you," said Rio.

"The question is, how does it taste?" said Mother. He got a spoonful and was about to take a bite when the doorbell rang. "Hold that thought," he said, comically stopping the spoon inches in front of his mouth.

"I wonder who that is," said Monty.

"Probably a weather weirdo," Brooklyn answered as she got up and headed to the door.

Because the FARM was officially a weather research institute, people interested in meteorology would some-times show up at the door at odd hours. The kids usually referred to them as weather weirdos.

"Wait," Mother said. "Let me answer. I want to make

sure that no one from the media has tracked you down."

"If they have," said Sydney, "tell them we're not here."

"And if it's someone from my fan club, tell them I'm not here either," joked Paris.

Moments later, Mother returned and said, "It is neither a weather weirdo nor a reporter. Rather, it's a high-ranking official from MI6."

Into the room walked Gertrude Shepherd, known to everyone as Tru, a legendary spy who stood nearly six feet tall, walked with a limp, and was missing her left pinkie. After a long career as a field agent, Tru was now a command officer at Vauxhall Cross and was Mother's direct supervisor. She was also one of only a handful of people at MI6 who knew about the quintet of young operatives known as the City Spies. She was accompanied by her personal assistant, an agent in his late thirties wearing a coat and tie.

"Good evening, everyone," she said with a broad smile. "Smells delicious. Is there enough for two more?"

Tru

MI6 DIDN'T PLAN ON CREATING A TEAM
of underage spies. No right-thinking intelligence officer
would ever consider such a thing. But that unlikeliness
was part of why the squad had become so successful. It
had grown organically as the accidental byproduct of
a series of random events, beginning with the fire that
almost killed Mother.

As far as the rest of the world knew, Mother died
in that fire just as Umbra intended. But the unexpected
wild card was Paris. He was a homeless ten-year-old who

lived alone in the warehouse. He was used to hiding in the shadows and was able to free Mother and lead him to safety without anybody realizing. There was no way Mother was going to leave his rescuer behind, so he took him back to Britain and late one night they both showed up on Tru's doorstep.

Tru instantly realized that there was no more effective spy than a dead one. If the spy world thought Mother had perished, that would make it all the easier for him to continue pursuing Umbra. It was her idea to hide the two of them in a remote cryptography station in northern Scotland, which is how they came to Monty and the FARM. In addition to studying Umbra, Mother began searching the world for his children. Along the way, he came across other amazing children in need who he could not abandon. He brought them back to the FARM, and soon the City Spies were born: a team of young, skilled agents who could move unnoticed in situations where adults would stand out.

Keeping the team a secret was vitally important to both the team and the Secret Intelligence Service. As far as their effectiveness and safety were concerned, it was essential that as few people as possible knew about their existence. And as far as MI6's credibility was concerned, they simply could not let anyone know that they were using a team of kids aged twelve to fifteen.

Only four people at MI6 actually knew what was going on with Project City Spies, and only two of them were aware of Mother's true identity. Tru's assistant was not one of those people, which made the dinner conversation a little tricky.

"Everyone, I'd like you to meet my assistant, Jack Fissell," she said. "It's easy to remember: 'Fissell' rhymes with 'whistle.'"

"Nice to meet you," Jack said. "Tru's told me all about you."

"She has?" Sydney asked, surprised.

"Absolutely," Tru interjected. "I told him how you're all part of a special scholarship program run by the Foundation for Atmospheric Research and Monitoring."

"Oh," said Sydney, realizing that she hadn't *really* told him all about them. "Right, FARM."

"It's fascinating," Jack said. "You all hope to become climate scientists?"

"Or something in a related field," Paris said.

"FARM is dedicated to climate research," said Monty. "We have the FARM Fellows Program to give kids practical scientific experience no matter what career paths they choose to follow."

"Full confession," Tru said, directing the conversation again. "As my assistant, Jack is fully aware that Monty sometimes consults with MI6 with regard to issues of cryptography."

"You all know that too?" Jack asked the kids.

"It would be kind of hard to keep it a total secret," Sydney offered. "We live together."

"But we don't really know any specifics," added Brooklyn. "Just that her work involves Beny."

"Who's Beny?"

"That's what we call the Cray XC40 supercomputer that's the key to what we do here," answered Monty. "The reason that I sometimes consult for MI6 is because the exact model of computer used to make predictive weather patterns is ideal for cryptography."

As they ate, Tru explained that they were in the area for business and that she wanted to stop by and check in with Sydney and Brooklyn about the *Sylvia Earle*. "As you know, there's a lot of talk about MI6's role in responding to the hijacking, and I'm trying to piece together information from as many of the passengers and crew as I'm able."

Brooklyn started to tell her, but Tru waved her off.

"Not yet, sweetie," Tru said. "We can talk later. Now let's just enjoy the excellent company and this feijoada, which smells amazing. By the way, if you like, I can give you a little spy lesson."

"Really?" said Paris. "That'd be awesome."

"What is it?" asked Sydney.

"Feijoada is the national dish of Brazil, beloved across the country," Tru said. "But even if I didn't know where our friend here was from, I could tell you that this was a recipe specifically from Rio de Janeiro."

"How?" asked Brooklyn. "Because of the ingredients?"

"It's the meat," guessed Sydney.

"The rice?" said Paris.

"The beans?" suggested Kat with a shrug.

"No, no, and no," Tru responded.

"Then what is it?" asked Brooklyn.

Tru winked at Rio and he answered, "The orange slices."

Sydney had a confused look as she said, "But there aren't any orange slices."

"Exactly," said Tru. "In every other part of the country, they serve this with orange slices. But in Rio they steadfastly refuse to do so."

"Why?" asked Paris.

"I have no idea," said Tru. "That is one of life's great mysteries."

"I don't know either," said Rio. "I just know that it's true."

"How is that a spy lesson?" asked Brooklyn.

Tru smiled and said, "It's a reminder that sometimes when you're reading a situation, the answer lies not in what you see, but in what is missing."

The dinner was great. Tru told some amazing stories. And everyone had fun with the Stop-arazzi video of Paris and the cameraman.

"That's grand!" Tru said with a chuckle as she watched it on Sydney's phone. "Absolutely grand!"

She shot Paris a wink, and he smiled at the recognition.

After the meal, Tru suggested that they go down into the priest hole to discuss the hijacking. Jack Fissell started to follow, but she stopped him.

"Actually, I'll handle this on my own," she said.

"Don't you want me to take notes?" Jack asked.

She shook her head. "I want it to be a little less formal than that." She turned to the kids. "How about you three show Jack around this facility of yours. Give him the same tour you give to the weather weirdos who arrive unannounced."

"Gladly," answered Paris.

Jack looked wounded, but he didn't protest. He knew better than to contradict his boss. Tru went down into the priest hole with Sydney, Brooklyn, Mother, and Monty and made sure they secured the door once they were inside.

"First of all," Tru said as they sat around the conference table, "I want to tell you two how proud I am of you. You did amazing work on that ship, and you no doubt saved the lives of those girls."

Sydney and Brooklyn both thanked her.

"Now, I want you both to walk me through what happened," she instructed. "Go step-by-step and try not to leave anything out."

Each girl recounted her version of the events, careful to include as many details as she could remember. Sydney was honest about where she was and why. She was surprised that Tru didn't seem to mind that she'd broken some rules.

"The truth of the matter is this," Tru said. "If you hadn't gone scuba diving, the outcome might have been much less positive, so let's be happy this time that you're not so great when it comes to following rules." Sydney smiled and Tru added, "Although, in the future . . ."

"Yes, ma'am, I'll be better."

Tru had a briefcase and pulled a file from it.

"Can you confirm that this is the man who was in charge?" she asked as she handed a photograph to Brooklyn.

"Yes," Brooklyn said. "On the news they said his name was Blix, right?"

"Unfortunately," Tru responded.

"Why is that unfortunate?" asked Mother.

"Because he was once one of us."

"Blix was MI6?" asked Monty, surprised.

"Before he was turned by Umbra," said Tru. "Just like Clementine."

Sydney flinched almost imperceptibly at the mention of Clementine.

Tru turned her focus back to Brooklyn. "You say the captain yelled at him?"

Brooklyn nodded. "Twice."

"And all in Norwegian?"

"Yes," said Brooklyn. "I couldn't understand a word."

"What about her tone? Could you read that?"

"Angry. I'd probably call it defiant."

"Could she have been giving him orders?" asked Tru. "Working together with him?"

"She could've been," said Brooklyn. "But that's not what it sounded like."

"I don't think the captain was involved," said Sydney.

Tru gave her a raised eyebrow and asked, "And you're basing this on what?" Then she leaned in and added, "Considering you weren't there when this happened."

Sydney pulled back a bit and said, "Based on the fact that I spent time with her on the trip and . . ."

"You liked her?" Tru said sarcastically.

Sydney stopped talking and nodded.

"I'm willing to accept an agent who breaks the occasional rule," Tru said. "After all, rule breaking's kind of at the heart of what we do. But I cannot accept an agent who judges someone's potential guilt based on that person's likability. Despite what you've seen in movies, the villains don't all have scars and eye patches."

"Yes, ma'am," said Sydney.

"I have a question," said Brooklyn.

"What is it, dear?" asked Tru.

"What did the other agent say?" she asked. "Or better yet, who was the other agent?"

"Yeah," said Sydney. "When we planned the op, you said there'd be another agent on board the ship."

"And did I give you her name then?" asked Tru.

"No," said Brooklyn.

"So, I'm not going to give it to you now," she replied. "Just as she has no idea that you two were anything other than students on the trip. Anonymity is the key to everything we do. As to what she said, I haven't had the chance to debrief her."

"I think we know who it is anyway," said Sydney with a wry smile.

"Really?" said Tru. "Who?"

"The second mate," she replied. "Hannah Delapp."

"And what makes you say that?" Tru asked. "And please don't tell me it was a gut feeling."

"No," said Sydney. "The way she studied people. The fact that she had the night watch on the bridge yet still stayed up most of the day keeping an eye on things."

There was a long pause as everybody studied Tru's reaction, which gave away nothing. Finally she smiled and said, "Did you think I was going to tell you if you were right or wrong?"

They all laughed when they realized that she was not about to give them the slightest hint.

"What do you call those sayings of yours?" Tru asked Mother.

"Motherisms," he said.

"Here's the one that I live my life by," she said as she turned back to Sydney and Brooklyn. "*No matter what, my lips are sealed. My secrets will never be revealed.*" She let that sink in for a moment before saying, "Which brings me to the next topic. Mother thinks of you all first as children, and that's good. He should do that. But it's my job to think of you first as agents. And the two of you are very good agents."

They both smiled at this.

"But you're about to face something that will be very difficult."

For the first time that evening, Mother interrupted.

"What's that?" he asked.

"Not what, who," said Tru. "Bloody Mary."

"Who's Bloody Mary?" asked Brooklyn.

"Mary Somersby," answered Tru.

"Judy's mom?"

"Who also happens to be an MP who dreams of one day becoming prime minister," Tru said. "She plans on using this incident to make herself a star. In a day or two she's going to announce that she's leading a special Parliamentary inquest into the events that transpired. Everyone who was on the ship will be called to testify."

"Are you serious?" said Mother. "Will this be televised?"

"Thankfully, no," answered Tru. "It will all be held in secret to protect the identities of the students who were on the trip. That way, after every session, Bloody Mary can come out and address the press on her own."

"If it's going to be private, then why is it going to be difficult?" asked Sydney.

"Because I need you to lie," answered Tru. "Now, that's one thing for Brooklyn. She's only twelve. But you're fourteen, which means you're old enough to be sworn in."

"You want me to lie? In Parliament? Under oath?" Sydney couldn't believe it.

"It's not a matter of want," said Tru. "It's a matter of law. You have taken the United Kingdom Official Secrets oath. That supersedes any other oath. You cannot tell anyone that you are an agent of MI6."

"So no matter what I do, I'll be breaking at least one law?"

"I'm afraid so. Although I find it helps if you rely on your cover."

"What do you mean by that?" asked Sydney.

"Your cover identity is Eleanor King," she replied. "That was the name you used on the ship and the name you'll be sworn in under. Think of it as Ellie lying, not you."

"Can Mother and I be with them for the inquest?" asked Monty.

"You can, Monty, but not Mother."

"Why not?" asked Mother.

"Because Monty is their official guardian, so she has legal standing," Tru answered. "If you were there, it would only put you on the committee's radar, which is not something we want to happen."

She turned back to Sydney and Brooklyn. "Still, she won't be able to testify for either of you. You'll have to do all the talking. Do you understand?"

Reluctantly Sydney nodded. "Yes."

"You're a credit to the Service," Tru said. "Both of you."

Magpie

KIM PHILBY WAS THE BIGGEST VILLAIN in the history of British intelligence. While serving as a high-ranking MI6 official, he covertly led a group of double agents, known as the Cambridge Spy Ring, who passed secrets to the KGB for decades. His story was taught to incoming spies as a cautionary tale. Virtually all despised him because he betrayed his country and cost countless lives.

Magpie despised him because he got caught.

Like Philby, Magpie had spent years as a double agent

passing secrets to the enemies of the United Kingdom, primarily to the crime and terror syndicate known as Umbra. For nearly a decade, MI6 was aware that it had a mole but had been unable to figure out who it was.

Magpie eluded discovery by being careful and cunning, mixing bold actions with intricate planning. This had been a successful recipe up until the hijacking of the *Sylvia Earle*, where it failed miserably.

Magpie's search to figure out what went wrong led all the way to the Arctic Circle and the tiny Norwegian village of Reine. This was where Emil Blix had gone into hiding and where Magpie went looking for answers. They met alongside an old wooden *rorbu*, a fisherman's cottage built half on land and half on stilts over the water. It was red with a grassy sod roof, and the two of them sat outside, looking across the water as the sun set behind the craggy granite peaks of *Reinefjorden*.

"What happened?" asked Magpie.

"You tell me," said Blix, who had shaved his beard and dyed his hair blond to avoid recognition. "There were supposed to be two girls on that ship who you said would bring us millions."

"They were there," Magpie assured him. "You were just too inept to find them."

Blix didn't like being spoken to this way, but he knew he'd failed and was in no position to argue.

"They should've been in their cabin like you promised."

"What about the SSAS button?" asked Magpie. "Who pushed it?"

Blix considered mentioning that he thought Brooklyn might be the culprit. But that was just a fleeting hunch, and everything about the hijacking was already embarrassing. The idea that a twelve-year-old girl had derailed his plan would've been unforgivable and would've undoubtedly marked the end of his career with Umbra. He offered his companion a more reasonable theory instead.

"It must have been one of the crew," he said. "There was probably a second button hidden somewhere."

"Everything about this looks bad," said Magpie. "Which makes me look bad."

"You?" said Blix, trying to control his frustration. "I'm the one whose picture is all over the news."

"Exactly," said Magpie. "And I'm the one who picked you for this job. So when *Le Fantôme* looks to point fingers, they're aimed directly at me."

Le Fantôme was the leader of Umbra, and the mention of his name added to the seriousness of the conversation.

"Is he angry?" asked Blix.

"He doesn't get angry," answered Magpie. "He gets results. And if we cannot give them to him, he will move along to someone else, and we will instantly become expendable."

Blix nodded.

"Although," added Magpie, "he was irritated about the explosives. How could you have bungled that so?"

"I didn't bungle anything about the explosives," said Blix defensively. "I set that limpet mine myself."

"Then how do you explain the fact that there were two explosions instead of one? And if the explosives were attached with a limpet mine, why was there no damage to the ship?"

"The mine must have been tampered with."

Magpie laughed at the absurdity of this. "By whom?"

"Someone from MI6?"

"You're forgetting something," Magpie said. "I *am* MI6. I would know."

They were quiet for a moment and looked across the water toward the sky, now a brilliant swirl of reds, purples, and oranges.

"Maybe you don't know everything, because I set that bomb and it was perfect. Maybe MI6 put someone on board that you don't know about."

The Stamford Swizzle

IT HAD BEEN NEARLY TWO WEEKS SINCE Tru's visit to the FARM, and the entire team had come to London for Brooklyn's and Sydney's testimonies at Parliament. Since it was a secret hearing, only Monty would be allowed in the room during questioning, but the others wanted to be there for moral support. More importantly, they wanted to be there so they could make headway on Operation Golden Gate. London was just a short train ride from Oxford, where they could investigate all things Parker Rutledge.

This aspect of the trip had to be kept secret from everyone at MI6. Nobody could know what they were up to. Not even Tru. Mother told her they were coming down a couple of days early to do some sightseeing, and she arranged for them to stay at a safe house in Notting Hill, one of the nicest neighborhoods in the city. Normally, they wouldn't get such posh accommodations, but this was the only place available with enough rooms for them all. Besides, Tru wanted to reward the girls for their great work on the *Sylvia Earle*.

"We're staying here?" Sydney said in disbelief when they came upon the row of pastel-colored Victorian town houses lining Portobello Road. "It looks like an Instagram filter, only real."

"A gift from Tru," Mother said. "Her way of saying thanks."

"All hail Tru!" Paris replied as he and Rio traded a high five.

"Much nicer than the concrete bunker I was expecting," Kat added in her typically understated manner.

MI6 safe houses tended to be small flats in nondescript neighborhoods, but this one was an exception. It was designed for high-level representatives from foreign governments and was well appointed with nice furniture, a deluxe kitchen, and a state-of-the-art home theater. It was also well equipped with listening devices, hidden cameras, and a wide array of cutting-edge surveillance equipment.

MI6 spied on everyone, including its friends, a point Mother reiterated as they navigated the maze of vendors, artisans, and merchants whose stalls filled the street for the Saturday Portobello Road Market.

"You have to assume that someone is always listening and that your every action is being monitored and recorded," he said. "When you're in the house, you cannot say a word about Golden Gate."

They spent the day sightseeing, just as they'd told Tru they would. It was Brooklyn's first visit to the city, and they wanted to show it off. They watched the changing of the guard at Buckingham Palace, posed for pictures on Tower Bridge, and checked out the Rosetta Stone at the British Museum. After a delicious dinner at an Indian café in Covent Garden, they capped off the whirlwind by seeing a West End musical.

As Mother suspected, their movements were tracked, albeit loosely. An MI6 agent posing as a produce seller noted their arrival at 9:47 a.m. and their subsequent departure at 10:21. The artificial intelligence software that monitored all conversations in the safe house detected none of the key words that might initiate deeper surveillance. And Tru was notified by her assistant, Jack Fissell, when the group arrived at the Lyceum Theatre. She'd arranged for the tickets in part as a reward, but also so she could keep an eye on them.

"Interesting," Mother said to Monty as they entered the theater.

"What's that?" she asked.

"Don't look now, but Jack Fissell, who rhymes with whistle, is sitting at one of the outside tables at the Wellington pub," he answered. "No doubt he just told Tru that we are where we're supposed to be."

"We assumed she'd keep an eye on us," Monty replied. "Why's that *interesting*?"

"She's using her personal assistant," he said. "Someone we could recognize. That means she's not overly concerned. It also probably means she has limited manpower and resources."

"So tomorrow?"

"We shake them early and we should be fine."

"Excellent."

Operation Golden Gate began in earnest the next morning with a maneuver Monty dubbed the Stamford

Swizzle. The goal was to make it virtually impossible for someone to follow them, but in a way that wouldn't arouse suspicion. For this they needed a massive distraction, and Mother chose the football match being played between Chelsea and Liverpool at Stamford Bridge, one of the UK's most legendary stadiums.

They took the tube to Fulham Broadway station, where they waded into a sea of supporters in bright blue jerseys who sometimes broke full-volume into songs like "Keep the Blue Flag Flying High," which was sung to the tune of "O Christmas Tree." Up at street level, Mother bought everybody shirts at a souvenir stand and quickly handed them out.

"Here you go," he said. "Put these on over what you're wearing."

Paris was incredulous. "You want me to wear Chelsea blue to a Liverpool match?"

"No," Mother answered. "I want you to blend in and disappear." Then he smiled and added, "And it's my good fortune that it will be much easier to do that with you wearing Chelsea gear."

"But there are plenty of Liverpool supporters here," he countered. "Let me wear red."

"Sorry," Mother replied, clearly enjoying Paris's

predicament. "It stands out too much. You're the needle and the haystack's blue."

Paris shook his head in disbelief as he grudgingly pulled it on. "You're only doing this because we've won four straight against Everton. You're jealous."

Mother laughed and said, "I don't know, Paris. Blue's a good color on you. Maybe you should switch teams."

And then, to add to Paris's grief, Sydney snapped a quick picture on her phone.

"What's that for?" he asked.

"You never know when you might need an instant blackmail photo."

Paris wagged a finger at her. "Had I known you were a traitor, I wouldn't have used my body to block that cameraman chasing after you."

Despite Paris's complaining, the plan worked perfectly. It soon became impossible to pick them out from the mass of people slowly herding their way down Fulham Road. Once their tickets had been scanned at the turnstile, they entered the grounds and looped halfway around the stadium before exiting back onto the street.

For Paris, this was even worse than wearing the wrong team's jersey. "I can't believe we have tickets to see Liverpool play at the Bridge and we're not going to use them," he said, shaking his head. "It's one cruel trick after another today."

Mother threw a consoling arm around his shoulders and repeated one of his sayings: *"Most can go where fortune falls, but a spy must go where duty calls."*

Paris gave him a look and replied with an impromptu Motherism of his own: *"I know that is what you think, but as for me, I think it stinks!"*

Mother roared with laughter. "Very clever, Paris. I think it's the Chelsea shirt. It makes you smarter."

Once they were out of the stadium, they took the tube to Paddington to catch a train for Oxford. Along the way, they made sure to use cash so there'd be no digital trail left by swiping their Oyster cards, the specially made debit cards used to pay for fares on the London Underground. They had to assume MI6 could track them whenever they were used.

The train to Oxford took about an hour, and they were able to find an empty car where no one could overhear them as they discussed their plans. Monty was the Oxford expert. She loved her time there as a student, and because of her extensive local knowledge, she briefed the team during the train ride.

"I'm so excited that you're finally going to see the

dreaming spires," she said, referring to the steeples and towers that made up Oxford's skyline. "The first thing you have to know is that it's not laid out like most universities. Instead of a main campus with dormitories and lecture halls, the university is made up of thirty-nine different colleges set in clusters around the city. The best one, of course, is Exeter, which is where I went. But the others are good too. Think of the colleges as planets and the university as a solar system that holds them in orbit."

"If they're the planets," asked Kat, "then what's the sun?"

"The Bodleian," answered Monty. "The massive library right in the middle of everything. It's gorgeous. They used it as the library in the Harry Potter movies. And it will be our rendezvous point."

"If we have a rendezvous point," said Paris, "does that mean we're separating?"

"Yes," answered Mother. "We've got to get a lot done quickly so we're splitting up into four groups. Brooklyn and Kat are heading to the store where Parker bought his camera, Sydney's going with me to visit his aged mother, Monty's going to use her alumni connections to check out the college where he taught, and you and Rio will attend the monthly meeting of the Dodos."

"The what?" asked Paris.

"The Dodos," Mother replied. "It's what the members of the Oxford Ornithological Society call themselves. They meet the third Sunday of every month at the Museum of Natural History."

"Bird-watchers?" said Paris. "I'm missing a football match at Stamford Bridge so I can listen to a bunch of bird-watchers?"

"You're not just going to listen," Mother said. "I'm sure they'll have pictures."

Strange Birds

THE OXFORD UNION WAS ONE OF THE oldest and most respected debating societies in the world. For nearly two hundred years, leading figures, including presidents and prime ministers, had participated in lively and often heated discussions about topics ranging from the arts and sciences to global politics.

The Union was located on Frewin Court off Cornmarket Street, and as the City Spies passed by, they too were locked in a passionate debate.

"Gelato," Kat said firmly.

"Cupcakes," countered Paris.

"I'm with Kat," added Brooklyn. "The gelato place looked amazing."

"Well, I'm with Paris," said Rio. "And all that matters is what I think."

"Really?" asked Sydney. "Why's that?"

"Because I set a lock-picking record and won Saturday Match Day," he said proudly. "And the winner gets to pick what we have for dessert."

"Not *forever*," said Sydney. "That was two weeks ago, and it shouldn't count anyway because Brooklyn and I were getting hijacked at the time."

"I didn't hijack you, and it's not my fault we've been too busy to have another match," said Rio. "So until we do, I'm the reigning champion. Rules are rules."

"Except didn't you hand the trophy over to Sydney and Brooklyn when they got home that night?" said Monty. "You were so happy to see them safe and sound. It was very sweet and lovely."

"It was, wasn't it?" added Mother. "I was touched."

"But . . . but . . ." Rio sagged in defeat.

"So gelato it is!" Brooklyn said triumphantly. "I think I'm going with one scoop of coconut and one scoop of chocolate."

"Um, not so fast," said Sydney. "He gave the trophy to both of us, and my vote is for that pie shop we saw in Piccadilly. It smelled amazing."

Monty and Mother smiled at the back-and-forth, and when they reached the corner where they were supposed to split up into their groups, Mother made a suggestion. "How about we hold a Match Day right now, here in the field?"

"Ooh," said Monty, "that's brilliant. Whoever comes back with the best bit of information wins the match and picks dessert."

"Real world Match Day?" said Sydney. "I like it."

"So do I," added Brooklyn. "I can already taste the coconut."

"No way," protested Paris. "That's not even close to being fair. We got the worst assignment. We're going to a bloody bird-watching society."

Sydney laughed and said, "Well, at least you'll fit right in."

"Why's that?" asked Paris.

She got up in his face and said, "Because you're a giant chicken." She started flapping her arms like wings. "Bawk, bawk. I can't uncover information as well as Sydney and Kat and Brooklyn. Bawk, bawk."

Now everyone was laughing. "That's war," Paris said. "You are on and I'm calling it now: Tonight it will be cupcakes for everyone."

"Well, great," said Monty. "Now that we've got that settled, do you all know when and where we rendezvous?"

"Three thirty at the library," they replied in unison.

"Then I've just got one more thing to say," she replied. "This operation is hot, and we are a go."

RUTLEDGE HOME, WATLINGTON

Mother and Sydney took a taxi to Watlington and the house on Watcombe Road that Parker Rutledge called home for most of his life. Mother had visited on multiple occasions, including once for Christmas dinner. At the time, he was a member of the so-called Zoo Crew, a spy team led by Rutledge that worked for the London Zoo as their cover. During this period, Mother went by the alias Gordon Swift, which was how he introduced himself when Parker's mother answered the door.

"Hello, Mrs. Rutledge," Mother said with a bright smile. "My name's Gordon Swift. I was a colleague of Parker's back at the London Zoo."

The elderly widow had only cracked the door as wide as the security chain would allow, and she eyed him suspiciously through the gap. "I don't remember you."

"I was over one Christmas dinner and accidentally dropped the pudding on the kitchen floor," he said.

She brightened and replied, "You made a right mess, didn't you?"

"Dreadfully so, I'm afraid."

"I remember *that*." She flashed a smile and undid the chain to open the door. "Gordon, was it?"

"Yes, although your son always called me Gordo." He motioned to Sydney. "This is my daughter, Eleanor."

"Ellie," Sydney said pleasantly with a wave.

"We came by because we were in town and I wanted to offer my condolences about Parker," he added as he held up a bouquet of flowers he'd picked up at a florist next to the railway station. "I was heartbroken to hear he'd passed."

"Thank you, dear," said Mrs. Rutledge. "Please come in. Sorry to seem so unwelcoming, but I've had a couple of break-ins and you can't be too careful."

"No you can't," said Mother. "You can't be too careful at all."

CLARENDON PHOTO SHOP, OXFORD CITY CENTRE

Clarendon Photo was a quaint camera shop with a bright yellow storefront and helpful employees in matching blue polos. The cameras were arranged by manufacturer in display cases, and Kat and Brooklyn looked around until they found the same model Rutledge purchased.

"Three thousand, five hundred pounds?" Kat gasped when she saw the price tag. "Are they serious?"

"That can't be right," said Brooklyn.

"Look for yourself."

Brooklyn checked and was equally stunned. "That's unbelievable." She checked the nearby cameras, which were far less expensive. "Why wouldn't he buy one of these? They're so much cheaper."

"That's a great question," said Kat.

A saleswoman came over and asked, "Can I help you two?"

"Yes, please," Kat said. "We're curious about this camera. Why's it so expensive?"

"It's top of the line, the latest DSLR," she answered, as if any of that made sense to normal people.

"DSLR?" asked Brooklyn.

"Digital single-lens reflex," said the woman. "It's a cross between a camera like the one you have on your phone and a more traditional one designed to let you swap lenses. But you two wouldn't need anything this advanced. We have plenty of inexpensive models that take beautiful photos."

"Then why would someone pay this much?" asked Brooklyn. "Who would even use a camera like this?"

"Mostly professional photographers," she answered. "It shoots still images and video, so you can use it to shoot anything from portraits to weddings."

Kat picked up the camera and studied it. "Can you think of any reason why someone who's really into bird-watching might want it?"

The woman thought for a moment and said, "You know, about a year ago a bird-watcher came into the store, and I helped him pick out a camera. Come to think of it, I think this is the model he settled on."

"Do you remember anything about him?" asked Brooklyn.

"It's been a year and I sell a lot of cameras," she said, trying to recall the memory. "What was his name? Dowd? Proud?"

"Stroud?" suggested Kat.

The woman smiled. "That's it, *Stroud*." Then she gave them a quizzical look. "Do you know him?"

There were more than seven million objects in the collection of the Oxford University Museum of Natural History, but the most famous was the Oxford dodo. It was a soft-tissue specimen of a bird species that'd been extinct since 1680, and there was nothing like it in the world. As a symbol of pride, the dodo served as the logo of the museum and was the namesake of the bird-watching society that met there once a month.

The birders gathered in a small lecture hall with heavy oak chairs and dark wood paneling. Every meeting featured a presentation by one of its members, followed by an informal discussion and snacks, usually tea sandwiches. Paris and Rio had trouble finding the room, and they walked in just as the presentation was about to begin. Despite the interruption, the eleven members in attendance seemed delighted by their arrival.

"Are you here for the meeting?" asked the club's leader, an older man with wispy white hair and a long thin nose.

"That depends," said Paris. "We got a little turned around, and I'm not sure we're in the right place. Are you the . . . *Dodos*?"

"Are we the Dodos?" the man said excitedly as he

turned to the rest of the group and they all started making loud squawking noises.

Paris shot Rio a side-eye that asked *What have we gotten ourselves into?* before saying, "I'm guessing that means yes."

"It sure does," the man answered happily. "Are you budding ornithologists?"

"Yes, sir," said Rio, trying to sound convincing. "We're very interested in all things birds."

"Well, you have excellent timing. Marni's just about to show the pictures from her trip."

Paris and Rio both forced smiles and tried to sound convincing when they answered.

"Great."

"Can't wait to see them."

At the front of the room stood Marni Stern, mid-thirties, sporting a khaki shirt and khaki pants, her long black hair pulled back in a ponytail. She was a researcher with the Edward Grey Institute of Field Ornithology and had just returned from a three-month expedition studying, as she said in her very detailed introduction, "the causes and consequences of inter-specific competition between species in the Nyungwe Forest National Park."

"See what I mean?" the leader said to Paris. "Impeccable timing."

"Yes," Paris answered. "Sounds fascinating."

Marni showed pictures from her trip on a monitor hooked up to a laptop. The other Dodos oohed and aahed like they were watching a fireworks display while she offered narration, using words such as "avifauna," "endemic," and "taxonomic."

Within five minutes, Rio was already struggling to keep his eyes open, and Paris could only think about the Liverpool–Chelsea match that he could've been watching instead.

THE KING'S ARMS PUB

Monty was not at all surprised to learn that Parker Rutledge had been on the faculty at Lincoln College. MI6 recruited heavily throughout Oxford but nowhere more than Lincoln. The connection to the Secret Intelligence Service was so strong that the four racing shells used by the college's rowing club were named *Tinker, Tailor, Soldier,* and *Spy* in honor of the bestselling espionage novel written by former MI6 agent and Lincoln alumnus John le Carré.

She also knew that if she really wanted to find out what Rutledge had been up to during the last year of his life, her best plan of action was to bypass the students and faculty and go straight to a porter.

The porters were the backbone of Oxford life. Their lodges were at the entrances of each college, which literally made them the gatekeepers of the school. They had a front-row seat to all the comings and goings, and their services were a mix of security, support, and sometimes even counseling.

Monty had been so close to some of the porters when she was a student at Exeter College that she still exchanged Christmas cards with them. Luckily, Lincoln and Exeter were literally next door to each other, and the staffs knew one another well. One of Monty's friends vouched for her with Nigel Tompkins, the senior porter in the Lincoln lodge, who agreed to meet with her during his lunch at a nearby pub called the King's Arms.

They took a table in the back along the windows and away from the televisions, where most of the patrons were watching the Chelsea–Liverpool football match that the group was supposedly attending. Nigel had a steak pie along with a pint of Guinness, while Monty had a basket of triple cheesy chips and a ginger ale.

"I got hooked on these my first year at uni and I have to have them whenever I come back," she said. "This was the comfort food that got me through exams."

"They must've worked," he replied. "Thomas said you were an exceptional student, even by Oxford standards. He also said you had questions about one of our professors."

"Yes," she said. "A late professor, sadly. His name was Parker Rutledge."

The porter paused for a moment as he dipped a forkful of steak in its sauce. Then he looked up at her and asked, "What would you like to know about him?"

"Anything you could tell me, really," she said, leaving the door open for him to share as much as possible.

He answered just before he took a bite, "Well, I know he was a spy."

Monty was so surprised by this that she choked a little bit on a chip. "What makes you say that?"

"Twenty-plus years of collecting his mail, watching him come and go, observing some rather peculiar habits," he replied. "It's not much of a leap, really."

He took another bite and added, "Besides, you're not the first one to come asking about him. There've been two others, and they couldn't have been more obvious if they played the double-oh-seven theme when they walked in the room."

Monty wasn't sure if this meant he assumed she was a spy too, but she just skipped over that and asked, "Two others? Can you tell me about them?"

"The first one came a week after Parker passed," he said. "I didn't care for him at all. He was big and burly with black hair and dark sunglasses. Walked like a boxer. He said he was a nephew and had come to collect some of Parker's books."

"What did you tell him?"

"I told him that Parker Rutledge had two nephews and that I knew both personally because they'd been students at Lincoln. That kind of put an end to that conversation."

"Lucky break that you knew them," said Monty.

"I didn't know them." He smiled slyly. "I made that part up. But Mr. Sunglasses didn't know that."

Monty chuckled. "What about the other one?"

"A woman," he said. "At least she was clever. You could tell. She told me that she was an ornithologist and had worked with Parker in the field."

"Did she mention anything about a book?"

He nodded. "She said she wanted to look at his journal so that she could check some of the notes he took when they were on an expedition together. I told her that all his personal belongings had been returned to his family."

"And you feel certain both of them were with the Secret Intelligence Service?"

He shrugged. "I feel certain both of them were spies. Whether they were MI6 or not, I guess I don't know. The man had a hint of a Scandinavian accent, so that doesn't fit so well."

"Could you describe the woman for me?"

"Average height, physically fit, blond, but it could've been a wig."

"Did she ask for anything else?"

"No. Just the journal."

RUTLEDGE HOME

Unlike the porter at Lincoln College, Parker Rutledge's mother gave no indication that she knew her son was anything other than a college professor and avid birder. As they sat around the kitchen table, she told Mother and Sydney long, rambling stories about him and his travels. Mother didn't interrupt at all. He knew she missed him, and he wanted her to be able to bring him back, even if only in conversation. When one story came to an end, he said, "You mentioned something about break-ins. What happened?"

"There were two of them," she answered. "One climbed in through the window in Parker's bedroom and the other broke in through the back door."

"Were you home when they happened?"

"Thankfully no. I was shopping the first time and visiting my sister the second."

"What did they take?" asked Mother.

"Well, that's the strange part," she answered. "They didn't take anything. Not even my rings, and they're quite nice."

"Are you certain? Maybe they took something of Parker's."

"They couldn't have," she said. "I'd donated everything."

"What do you mean?" asked Mother.

"Parker was a man of few possessions," she explained. "Once he passed, I took his clothes to the homeless shelter. They were nice and well kept."

"Of course," said Mother.

"And I took all his papers and books to the Bodleian."

"The library?"

"Yes," she said. "My late husband's work was already there, so I donated Parker's as well. They're for future ornithologists."

Mother smiled. "How very generous of you."

CLARENDON PHOTO

Kat and Brooklyn told the saleswoman that they didn't really know Stroud, but that he'd given a lecture at their school.

"We were doing a unit on birds in our science class," Brooklyn said. "And he came in and showed us a bunch of pictures."

"If he took them with a camera like this, I bet they were beautiful," said the saleswoman.

"Amazing," said Kat.

"He told me that he'd done his research and called this model the bird-watcher deluxe," the woman continued. "For example, he liked the fact that it was mirrorless, because that meant it didn't make any shutter noise, which tended to scare birds away. He also liked that it shot HD video, even in low light. He said he often shot video of birds in flight early in the morning and at dusk when it was dark."

Kat and Brooklyn both quickly recognized that in addition to bird-watching, a silent camera that shot high-quality video in poor lighting would be ideal for a spy.

"And then there was the Bluetooth," the saleswoman said. "That was an essential feature for him."

"I know what Bluetooth is," said Kat. "But you think of it for earbuds or your phone. How is it useful for a camera?"

"This camera can load pictures directly to the cloud," she answered. "Normally, you have to wait until you download the images onto your laptop, but these go straight up. He wanted that. Said it was vital."

OXFORD UNIVERSITY MUSEUM OF NATURAL HISTORY

Paris checked his watch. They were forty-five minutes into the presentation, and Marni Stern had given no indication that she was nearing the end. She pressed a button on her clicker, and the image changed to one of a small red-and-brown bird sitting on a branch.

"This is a red-collared mountain babbler," she said. "Very sociable and noisy. Notice the rufous neck, breast, and rump. Now, an interesting tidbit about this species is that it was moved from genus *Kupeornis* to genus *Turdoides* in 2018."

"And why was that?" asked one of the Dodos.

"That was the determination of a molecular phylo-genetic study," explained Stern.

"Yes, yes," said the man. "Very interesting."

Rio swallowed a snore halfway and leaned over to Paris. "Are they still speaking English? Because I have no idea what they're talking about."

"Shh," said Paris, trying to decipher it. Despite the fact that much of the terminology was alien to him, he found himself surprisingly interested in the presentation. "Ms. Stern," he said, raising his hand.

"Please, call me Marni," she replied. "The Dodos are all on a first-name basis."

"Why is the number three hundred seventy-four marked in the upper right corner of the picture? Does it have something to do with its location?"

"No," she said. "It's part of my life list. The red-collared mountain babbler is the three hundred and seventy-fourth species I've seen in the field."

"And how do you get the number on the picture?" he asked.

"It helps to have a professor of quantum information

science in the club," she said, motioning to the man with the wispy mustache who'd welcomed them earlier. "Simon designed a wonderful program that tracks numbers for all of us."

"It's actually much simpler than it sounds," Simon said modestly. "It's a basic computation logarithm. We upload images directly into our cloud account and mark which ones are new, and the program automatically adds the number."

KING'S ARMS PUB

The meal was wrapping up, and Monty felt she had gleaned a good surface knowledge of Parker Rutledge. Nothing helpful in the particular situation, but all useful in a general way of understanding him.

Nigel Tompkins studied her for a moment, sizing her up in a way. He considered something before asking, "Do you know who Kim Philby was?"

"Of course," said Monty. "He was the treacherous double agent who sold out MI6."

"And do you know where he went to university?"

This made Monty smile. "Cambridge."

"That's right," Tompkins said disdainfully. "His whole

gang were Cambridge men. Although, you know, he tried to recruit here at Oxford. In fact, he tried to recruit John le Carré at that table right over there."

"Seriously?" said Monty. "Here in the King's Arms? I've never heard that before."

"Of course our boy said no," Nigel said proudly.

Monty was completely charmed by the porter and wondered if he knew so much about MI6 because he too had some connection to it.

"Now, I'm not saying those two other agents who came poking around were Cambridge types," he continued. "But I'm positive they didn't go to Oxford."

"Why's that?"

"Because if they'd gone to Oxford and understood how everything around here works, they would've known the right question to ask the porter of a college. But they didn't." He leaned forward and asked, "I wonder if you know it."

He was obviously trying to lead her somewhere, but she didn't know where. She racked her brain thinking about all the things a porter does, and then it came to her. There was one key thing that porters handled for everyone at the college.

"The mail," she said.

"What about the mail?" he asked coyly.

"Did you receive any mail for Parker Rutledge that you never got the chance to deliver to him?"

He smiled and she knew she was right.

And then he said, "No."

She sagged in her chair, totally confused.

"Although," he added, "I did receive an envelope for R.F. Stroud."

Monty's eyes opened wide with anticipation.

"Have a nice day," Tompkins said as he stood from the table. "It was lovely to have lunch with you."

He walked away, and she looked down to see that he'd placed a thick yellow envelope on the table. It was addressed to R.F. Stroud in care of the Lincoln College porter's lodge. There was no return address, but it was postmarked San Francisco, California.

It was unopened.

Bernhard Berliner, MD

MONTY DIDN'T OPEN THE ENVELOPE
until after everyone had ordered their food. They were at
a hamburger joint down the street from Oxford station,
and the anticipation was killing her.

"It may be nothing," she reminded them all as she
used a knife from the table to neatly slice it open.

"And it may be the key to everything," Paris added
hopefully.

The thickness of the envelope came from its pad-
ding. Inside, there was only a thin pocket calendar with

a simple black cover that had the year imprinted on it in silver lettering, as well as the words ALL WEATHER— WATER-RESISTANT. Each two-page spread represented a single week. Throughout the book, Parker Rutledge had written down his appointments in very precise hand-writing, always using pencil. Some weeks were empty and some were crowded, but there didn't seem to be any pattern to the appointments.

Monty flipped through the pages until she got to the last one with writing. "The final entry is for October fifteenth."

"That's the day *after* he died," added Paris.

"Meeting. Four p.m. Bernhard Berliner, MD," Monty read.

"So that's who he was supposed to meet with," said Mother. "Maybe this Dr. Berliner has the key to what this is all about."

Brooklyn did a quick search on her phone and read aloud to the others. "Dr. Bernhard Berliner. Born in Hanover, Germany. Educated at the University of Leipzig. Settled in San Francisco, where he became a noted psycho-analyst."

Mother gave her a curious look. "I wonder why Parker was meeting with a psychoanalyst?" he asked. "Though he wouldn't be the first spy who needed some therapy."

"Died: November twenty-fifth, 1976," Brooklyn continued.

"Wait, what?"

"Bernhard Berliner, MD, has been dead for more than forty years," said Brooklyn. "I don't think he's going to be of much help to us."

"Then how was Rutledge planning to meet him?" asked Rio, confused.

"Excellent question," said Monty. She flipped back through some pages, looking, and asked, "And how did he meet with him twice the week before?"

They were all quiet for a moment. It was frustrating because it felt like an important clue, but it also felt like a dead end. Literally.

"We'll study this book carefully, and maybe those answers will come to us," said Mother. "But let's put Dr. Berliner on hold for a moment and talk about what we learned today. Figure out who's going to pick dessert."

"We learned that cameras can be really expensive," said Kat. "Rutledge's cost thirty-five hundred pounds."

"Wow!" said Sydney.

"Apparently, it was important for him to load his

pictures directly to the cloud," said Brooklyn. "Why, we have no idea."

Rio looked over at her and smiled. "We know," Rio said, pointing toward Paris. "It was for his life list."

"What's a life list?" asked Monty.

"It's a record of all the bird species a bird-watcher sees in the field during their lifetime," Rio answered. "It's a very big deal for the Dodos. They were talking all about it. There's even an ongoing competition between them. Rutledge had the most."

"Why does that involve the cloud?" asked Sydney.

"Because that's where they keep their lists," Paris answered. "When you see a bird for the first time, you take its photo to document it. They keep them up on the cloud so they can look at each other's pictures."

"And by loading directly," Rio said, "it lets you prove who saw the species first."

"Sounds like you guys enjoyed your afternoon with the Dodos," said Mother.

"Paris liked it more than I did," answered Rio. "But the tea sandwiches were delicious."

"What else do we know?" asked Monty.

"We know that there were two break-ins at Parker's house soon after he died," said Mother.

"How soon?" asked Monty.

"One a week after he passed away and the other a few weeks later."

"Interesting," said Monty. "That syncs up pretty well with the timeline of a pair of visits to Lincoln College. The porter said two people, one man, one woman, both of whom he was quite certain were spies, came looking for a book or books belonging to Rutledge."

"Did they find them?" asked Brooklyn.

"No," Monty answered. "They left empty-handed."

"Following that logic," Mother said, "if those same two people were the ones who broke into Parker's house, maybe they were looking for the books there. Although if they were, they struck out again. Nothing was stolen."

"I wonder what the books are?" asked Kat.

"His bird books," Rio interjected. "They may have been looking for his bird books."

"I think you're right," said Paris.

Rio loved the rare moments when he knew more than the others. "Looks like we're the only ones who got useful intel today, Paris."

They traded a fist bump.

"What are bird books?" asked Monty.

"The Dodos raved about them at the meeting," said Rio. "Once we got started talking about Rutledge, they couldn't stop. They loved him. He was like their rock star."

"And he had these intricate journals he kept," said Paris. "Drawings, details, facts about different birds. He called them his bird books. They all started making them too."

"Marni showed us some of hers," said Rio.

"Marni?" asked Mother.

"She's a field ornithologist with the Edward Grey Institute," Paris answered. "She just had a fascinating trip to Africa."

"Did the journals look like this?" Monty asked, holding up Rutledge's datebook.

"No," said Paris. "They're hardbacks. Like those blank book diaries you can buy at the stationer's."

"Of course," said Mother. "Why didn't I think of that? I remember those. He was always doodling in them." He thought about it for a moment and the memory took on more significance. "But they weren't just about birds. That's what everyone thought. But they were really about our missions. He had these little codes to track our operations."

"Well, that would definitely be something MI6 would want to get their hands on," said Monty. "Do you think they found them?"

Sydney shook his head and smiled. "No. They didn't."

"How do you know that?" asked Kat.

"Because Mrs. Rutledge donated them to the Bodleian."

"So that means we're having cupcakes tonight," said Rio.

"Wait a second," said Sydney. "I was part of the team that found out about the Bodleian."

"Ahem," said Monty. "Are we forgetting this?" She held up the pocket calendar.

"Match Day is for young people only," protested Rio.

"Says who?" asked Monty.

"I don't remember that rule," said Mother. "All we said was best information gets to pick dessert."

"Which will be macarons," said Monty, "from the French bakery by Paddington station." She paused for a moment and added, "But it's going to have to wait."

"For what?" asked Rio.

"For Paris, Sydney, and me to get back to London," she said. "You guys are going to go now, and we're going to come back on a later train."

"We are?" asked Paris.

"Yes," she said. "I'm going to take you over and show you around my old college. And then, when it gets dark, maybe the three of us will break into the Bodleian and steal those bird books."

19.

The Bodleian Job

PASSING THROUGH THE PORTER'S LODGE into Exeter College was like stepping into another time. For Paris and Sydney, it was as if they'd wandered back into the Middle Ages as they looked up at the medieval architecture of the centuries-old buildings. But for Monty, the time travel was a much shorter trip. She felt like she'd gone back fifteen years to when she was a student and this was home.

"It's perfect," she said gleefully as they walked across the grassy quad. "It hasn't changed a lick."

"Yeah," added Paris, "not since Charlemagne."

Monty shot him a look and smiled. "Exeter's old, but not quite *Charlemagne* old. It was founded in 1314," she said, assuming the role of tour guide. "Famous alumni include J. R. R. Tolkien, who first began writing about Middle-earth while he was an undergraduate living right over there."

She pointed toward a building across the quad, and Paris, whose favorite book was *The Hobbit*, looked over in amazement.

"Other notable Exonians include author Philip Pullman, actor Richard Burton, and Sir Roger Bannister."

"Who's Sir Roger Bannister?" asked Sydney.

"A prominent neurologist who also happened to be the first person to run a mile in less than four minutes," Monty answered. "He set the mark just down the street at Iffley Road Track after spending the morning doing his rounds as a med student at St. Mary's Hospital."

"You certainly know your school history," said Paris.

"Of course I do. The Junior Common Room is the society of undergraduate students, and in my last year I was the president." She gave Paris a sly wink and added, "Just like Tolkien was during his final year."

They reached Palmer's Tower, which Monty informed

them was the oldest building at the college. "It's the residence for some of the school's most distinguished professors, including the person I want you to meet."

On the second floor, they reached an apartment and could hear someone playing violin inside. Monty smiled and paused, as if reconnecting to a fond memory, before knocking on the door.

There was no reply, just the continued playing of music, so she rapped three more times, only louder than before.

The music stopped and a perturbed voice called out from within. "Can't you tell that I'm practicing?"

"Is that what you call it?" Monty called back. "You've been *practicing* since I was president of the JCR. You think you might've gotten at least a little better by now."

They heard movement from within, and then the door opened wide to reveal esteemed mathematician and mediocre violinist Duncan Fletcher, late fifties, tall and lanky with a thick head of silver-gray hair. Paris's first thought upon seeing him was that he'd make an excellent Doctor on *Doctor Who.*

"Alexandra Montgomery!" Fletcher beamed, a huge grin on his face. "Tell me you've come to repay the money you owe."

She laughed. "You mean the five quid that I've paid back at least a dozen times?"

"Compound interest is a complex and confusing concept. You might know that if you paid more attention during my tutorials."

"So good to see you, Fletch," she said as she gave him a warm hug.

"Lovely to see you too, Monty. It's been much too long."

"I'd like to introduce you to my friends, Eleanor and Lucas," she said, using their cover names.

"Nice to meet you both," he said, shaking their hands. "Let me warn you now, do not loan money to this woman. She may look trustworthy, but I assure you she's a charlatan."

"Good to know," replied Paris, delighted to be included in their inside joke.

"Come on in," Fletcher said, motioning to his room. "The lodgings are meager, but I should be able to rustle up a tin of biscuits."

"Actually, we just ate," Monty said.

Fletcher turned back and gave her an arched eyebrow.

"Although a couple of biscuits might be nice," she conceded.

"I thought so," replied Fletcher.

The apartment was teeming with cramped book-shelves and antique furniture, but every inch was meticu-lously organized and spotlessly clean. They sat around a coffee table in the main room and had Earl Grey tea with custard cream cookies.

After some pleasantries and brief catching up, Fletcher asked, "So what brings you back to Exeter? I mean, other than exquisite music and engaging conversation."

"I need your help."

"Of course, my dear, anything. What is it?"

She stood up and pulled open the curtains to reveal a spectacular view of the Bodleian library. "We need to break into that," she said. "Preferably tonight."

"Break into the *Bod*?" he replied, laughing. "And what after that? The Tower of London?"

Sydney and Paris were shocked to realize that Monty had meant what she said earlier. They really thought they were just paying a friendly visit.

"Oh, and Eleanor is scheduled to appear before a secret inquiry at Parliament tomorrow," Monty added. "So it would be best if we didn't get caught and arrested."

"Wait a second," Fletcher replied. "You're serious?"

"Quite."

"I will do no such thing," he said. "I'm a don at this

university, and the Bodleian is a sanctified repository of priceless books and manuscripts. There's a Gutenberg Bible in there. Not to mention four original copies of the Magna Carta."

"We're not interested in any of those," she said. "But we would very much like to get our hands on some recently donated bird-watching journals. Trust me when I say that no one will notice when they're gone."

"Oh, so you're not just breaking in?" he said. "You're also planning to steal what you find? The crimes keep multiplying."

"We're not criminals, we're spies," she said. "This is an MI6 directive."

He gave her a disbelieving look and gestured toward Paris and Sydney. "Does security mean nothing to you?"

"Don't worry, they know I'm a spy." Then she turned to the kids and said, "And don't you worry. He not only knows I'm a spy, but he's the one who recruited me for MI6." She smiled as she realized something. "Come to think of it, that means you're to blame for all of this in the first place. So you *have* to help me."

"You're a spy?" Paris asked Fletcher.

"Less spy, more consultant," he said. "And part-time talent scout." He turned his attention back to Monty.

"And even if I were inclined to help, I wouldn't have the first clue as to how. The Bodleian's a highly secure building."

"That was built when the cutting edge of security was a moat and a man with a pointy stick," Monty said with a laugh. "I'm guessing there must be a few vulnerabilities in that old medieval armor. Besides, I don't believe for one moment that you've spent years looking out this window at that gorgeous building and not figured out how to break into it." She gave him a look. "Or more to the point, how Newton Isaacs would do it."

"Newton Isaacs?" said Sydney. "Don't you mean Isaac Newton?"

"Isaac Newton is the great scientist and mathematician," said Monty. "Newton Isaacs is the main character in the Principia Murders, a series of mystery novels written by none other than Duncan Fletcher."

"You're an author?" asked Sydney.

"Yes," he said with a slight bow. "Although my books are only printed by a small press and sell about as well as you'd suspect novels written by an applied maths professor would sell."

"They're wonderful," claimed Monty. "And so is Newton. He's a brilliant Oxford mathematician and a cunning detective. And I guarantee that you've worked out a way for him to get into that building."

Fletcher paused for a moment before coyly admitting, "I may have sketched out a few ideas. Or, to be more precise, six feasible scenarios."

"I knew it!" said Monty.

Sydney and Paris exchanged happy looks, delighted at the unfolding developments.

"Just give me a second." Fletcher went over to a wooden file cabinet and pulled out an aged manila folder, which he placed on the table.

"What's the Bodleian Job?" asked Paris, reading from the tab.

"It's an idea for a novel in which someone is murdered the same night that the Gutenberg Bible is stolen," he explained. "They're seemingly unrelated events, but Isaacs realizes they are, in fact, part of the same crime."

"I'd read that," Paris replied.

"So would I," added Sydney.

Fletcher sighed comically and said, "I wish you'd been there to tell my editor that. She was unimpressed." He opened the folder and pulled out a small stack of type-written pages, the corners of which were yellow with age, and started leafing through them.

"Let's see, here's a good one," he said, running his finger down the page as he read. "Oh wait, no. For this to work, there needs to be a large New Year's Eve celebration on the lawn outside the library." He looked up from the paper. "I don't suppose you can wait until late December?"

"No," said Monty, "we can't."

This process continued through the other scenarios. For each, he'd study the paper, point out a disqualifying element, and turn the page over as he moved to the next one.

"We'd need a Russian spy."

"Doesn't work without a full moon."

"The temperature has to be below freezing."

"We'd never be able to arrange for a flock of sheep this late in the day."

Paris turned to Sydney and mouthed, "Sheep?" All she could do was shrug.

Six ideas quickly winnowed down to one as he reached the last scenario. He looked hopeful as he scanned it, until he reached the bottom and said, "Oh dear, I'm afraid this one won't work either."

"Why's that?" asked Monty, deflated.

"The break-in's fine," he answered, "but the escape

requires rappelling on ropes from the roof of the library."

Monty looked to Sydney and Paris, and all three of them smiled.

She turned back to Fletcher and said, "Go on."

20.

Great Tom

FOR MONTY, IT WAS AS IF SHE WAS A student back in one of Fletcher's tutorials again. She sat on the couch next to Sydney and Paris and took notes while her favorite professor explained the intricacies of a complicated process. Only instead of discussing probability and outcome, this time the subject was breaking and entering.

"This is going to be a four-step enterprise," he said, counting steps off with his fingers as he listed them:

STEP ONE—Enter the library
through the Rad Cam and the
Gladstone Link
STEP TWO—Access the upper reading
room via the north staircase
STEP THREE—Extract the bird books
STEP FOUR—Exit by way of rappelling
from the roof

"For this to succeed, it will take a total of five of us," he continued.

"Five?" asked Sydney, confused.

"Yes," Fletcher answered. "You three are the burglars. I will be the diversion. And then there's Great Tom. He's our ringer." He smiled and said, "Quite literally."

Monty laughed. "I love it."

"Love what?" asked Sydney. "Who's Great Tom?"

"London has Big Ben; Oxford has Great Tom," he answered. "He's the massive bell atop the clock tower in Christ Church. Every night he rings one hundred one times to signal what was once the university's curfew. It's during this period that the Bodleian has a 'vulnerability in its medieval armor,' as Monty put it."

He walked them through the steps of the break-in

until they had it all memorized. Then they had to run two errands to, as Fletcher put it, "acquire the proper tools necessary for the burgling."

The first stop was at the Oxford University Mountaineering Club. Fortunately, Fletcher was a long-time member and was able to borrow the equipment they'd need to rappel off the building. It was used and somewhat smelly, but more than good enough to do the trick.

Next they headed over to the library.

"What are we getting here?" asked Sydney. "A book about how to *burgle*?"

"She's a cheeky one," Fletcher said to Monty.

"Tell me about it."

"Actually, my dear, we're getting library cards," Fletcher said to Sydney.

Paris gave him a curious look. "We're getting library cards so that we can steal something from the library? Isn't that the one thing we don't need?"

"It seems counterintuitive, but it's quite necessary," said Fletcher. "What was step one?"

"Enter the library through the Rad Cam and the Gladstone Link," Paris and Sydney repeated in well-practiced unison.

"Exactly," said Fletcher. "And you cannot enter the

Rad Cam without a reader card. So that's what we're going to get."

Once they were inside the library, Paris and Sydney did what they'd been trained to do. They began creating a mental map of the building, studying the flow of people, memorizing exit points, looking for any potential trouble spots in the plan. Monty, however, didn't need to do any of this. She'd spent so much time here that she could draw it with her eyes closed.

Fletcher led them into an office and up to a desk marked BODLEIAN LIBRARIES ADMISSIONS.

"Good afternoon," Fletcher said to the young library aide who was working at the desk. "I am Dr. Duncan Fletcher, Fitzhugh Senior Fellow of applied mathematics, director for the Oxford Centre for Nonlinear Partial Differential Equations, and executive liaison between the university and the Alan Turing Institute. And you are . . . ?"

The aide looked up at him, more than a little intimidated, and meekly answered, "Shawna."

"Ah, yes, Shawna, pleased to meet you," Fletcher replied. "We're here today because my three associates need to get reader cards so they can access the Bodleian for research."

Shawna went from *intimidated* to *confused* as she eyed Paris and Sydney suspiciously. "But they're . . . kids."

"Very astute, Shawna," Fletcher replied. "Good eye on you. They are indeed young. But they're quite accomplished, I assure you. They are assisting me on a project for the Turing Institute, and have extraordinary intellect." He turned to Sydney and said, "Go ahead, dear, demonstrate your intellect."

"What?" Sydney asked, totally confused.

"Say something smart."

Sydney was on the spot and had no time to prepare, so she just blurted out the smartest-sounding thing she could think of. "To manufacture trinitrotoluene, you must first produce mononitrotoluene by nitrating toluene with a mixture of sulfuric and nitric acids. This must be renitrated to dinitrotoluene and then nitrated to trinitrotoluene by using an anhydrous mixture of nitric acid and oleum."

The library aide looked up, stunned.

"See what I mean," said Fletcher. "Brilliant." He gave a side look to Monty and added, "And a wee bit scary."

"Okay," Shawna said as she nodded. "Let me get the paperwork."

She walked over to a filing cabinet to get some forms, and when she was out of earshot, Paris leaned over and whispered to Sydney, "Was that an explanation of how to make a bomb?"

Sydney gave him a sly smile and answered, "Maybe."

The three of them filled out forms and had their pictures taken, but before they could be given their library cards, they had to recite the Bodleian oath.

"Is this for real?" Sydney asked Fletcher as she looked at the paper she was handed.

"Oh yes," he replied. "This oath dates back centuries to Thomas Bodley himself. It's been translated into more than one hundred languages, and you can take it in whichever one you please."

"I think I'll just go with English," she said.

She looked down at the paper and recited, "I hereby undertake not to remove from the Library, or to mark, deface, or injure in any way, any volume, document, or other object belonging to it or in its custody; not to bring into the Library or kindle therein any fire or flame, and not to smoke in the Library; and I promise to obey all rules of the Library."

"And you're good," Shawna said as she handed Sydney a reader card.

Paris was next, and when he stepped up, he asked, "The oath has been translated into a hundred languages?"

"More than," said Shawna.

"Is one of them Swahili?"

"Of course," said Shawna.

"I would like to take the oath in Swahili," Paris replied with a delighted smile. He turned to the others and explained. "It was my grandfather's language, and he was a great lover of books. I think this would make him proud."

"I'm certain it would," Monty said sweetly.

After Paris took the oath in Swahili, Monty decided to make a similar gesture to her grandfather and took it in Scottish Gaelic. Once they were done and had their cards, they made the short walk back to Exeter and Fletcher's apartment for some final preparations. There they packed the rappelling gear into three backpacks, ate a few more custard cream cookies, and Monty called Mother and gave him a rundown of the plan and told him not to expect them back until late.

They waited in the apartment until it was one hour and fifteen minutes before closing time at the library.

"All right, everyone," Fletcher said. "From this point

on, we are on the clock. Every minute matters. Right place, right time, or we're dashed."

"Don't worry, Fletch," Monty said. "Newton Isaacs's plans always work. They're foolproof."

STEP ONE—*ENTER THE LIBRARY THROUGH THE RAD CAM AND THE GLADSTONE LINK*

The Radcliffe Camera had nothing to do with photography. The domed circular building was a stunning example of neoclassical architecture and was the iconic image of Oxford. Its name referred to the Latin word "*camera*," which means "room," and among students it was fondly called the Rad Cam, Radders, or simply the Camera.

Although it was a separate building, it was technically a reading room of the Bodleian and was closed to the general public. Ironically, this is why Fletcher wanted the team to use it as the point of entry. Once they'd scanned their reader cards and made it past the first wave of librarians, they'd already breached the library's security. They were inside. Had they entered through the Old Bodleian building, which was open for public tours, they would've needed to navigate additional layers of librarians and security officers.

"Remember we are on the clock," Monty reminded them as she led them past the computer bay toward the right rear stairwell. Paris and Sydney both had to resist the urge to stop and gawk at the library's beautiful interior.

They took the stairs down to the Gladstone Link, an underground library that connected the Rad Cam to the Bod. It was modern looking with bright fluorescent lights and orange architectural accents that stretched along the ceiling.

Monty checked her watch and stopped. "Three minutes and twenty-seven seconds until our diversion kicks into gear. Let's wait here."

"Got it," said Paris.

The Gladstone Link closed forty-five minutes before the rest of the library to allow security a chance to make a thorough sweep. It was almost that time, so the students in the area were packing up to go.

"You know, this part of the library is named after Prime Minister William Gladstone," Monty said, reverting to her tour guide mode.

"Why's that?" said Paris. "Was he the one that approved the money to build it?"

"No," she said with a chuckle. "Believe it or not,

he's the one who came up with the idea for shelves with wheels so that libraries could store more books."

Sydney laughed. "The things you know, Monty."

"All right, everyone," said a security guard standing at the help desk. "It's closing time. Up and at 'em."

Monty, Paris, and Sydney were on the move again, trying their best to blend in among the students leaving the Gladstone, although they left the opposite way from where they came and exited through a black-and-white tunnel that looked more like it belonged in a *Star Wars* movie than a four-hundred-year-old library. It led them to the base of the north stairway in the Old Bodleian building, where they waited until they heard a commotion.

"There's my boy," Monty said. "And I guarantee he's loving every second of it."

On the ground floor, Fletcher was playing the perfect model of the dotty, absentminded professor when something in his briefcase "accidentally" set off the alarm system at the reading room's entrance. This drew the attention of the librarians who staffed the reader services desk right next to the stairwell, and as a result none of them noticed the three people who quickly came up the stairs and entered the nearby toilets.

This was not the first time the members of the City Spies had used a bathroom as a hiding place. Paris was in the men's room, sitting atop the toilet tank in the rear stall with his feet pulled up on the commode so no one could see them under the door, which he'd securely locked. The ladies' room had a supply closet that was big enough for both Monty and Sydney to hide inside. They had to wait silently for nearly an hour until it was time for step two.

STEP TWO—*ACCESS THE UPPER READING ROOM VIA THE NORTH STAIRCASE*

This was how Duncan Fletcher explained the flaw in the library's state-of-the-art security system:

"Security is extremely important at the Bodleian, but so is history," he'd said during their tutorial. "Put another way, you have to protect the treasures inside the library, but you also have to protect the actual library, because it too is a treasure. And, as Monty pointed out, it's a treasure that was constructed hundreds of years ago when security was a much more simplistic endeavor."

"So how did they solve it?" asked Sydney. "How did they upgrade the library without hurting it?"

"The university hired a preeminent museum and library security company to design a system tailor-made for the Bod. It's a company out of Tokyo, and they did an amazing job. They wanted to preserve the architecture in the main reading rooms, so they focused their attention on entry points and stairwells, each of which now has a state-of-the-art motion-activated alarm system. There are lights, cameras, lasers—the whole deal. To illustrate how sensitive it is, one time a small rat got into the south stairwell and triggered every single alarm within twenty seconds."

"Okay," Paris said skeptically. "Considering we're much bigger than a rat, how are we going to make it up the stairs?"

"That's where Great Tom comes in," said Fletcher. "Every night Great Tom tolls one hundred one times to signal what was once the university's nine o'clock curfew. Because Tom is very loud and because the bell tower is very close to the Bod, the security firm knew that the bell would set off the alarm. So they built that into the system. Every night at nine o'clock, an algorithm inside the programming cancels the sound of the tolling."

"Which helps us how?" asked Sydney. "If it only cancels the sound of the bell, wouldn't it still detect us?"

Monty started to laugh as she realized the problem.

"Why don't you explain it to them, Alexandra?"

"Because Great Tom is at Christ Church and the college has long been run by some very stubborn men." She laughed heartily. "That's bloody brilliant, Fletch."

Paris and Sydney were utterly confused.

"You see, what the security company did not know— and to be honest, I can't blame them because it's ridiculous," Fletcher said, "is that in 1880, when all time in the United Kingdom was standardized, the lone holdout was the swath of one hundred seventy-five acres that make up Christ Church, Oxford. The college steadfastly refused to adapt and was determined to remain on what was known as Oxford Time, five minutes and two seconds behind the rest of the country."

"So their bell tolls five minutes later than the security system was programmed for," Paris said, getting it.

"Exactly," said Fletcher. "When the system was booted up, the bell set off the alarm every single night. It was maddening for the staff, and they had to make a decision. They could either pay a fortune to have the software completely rewritten and reinstalled, or . . ."

"They could turn it off," said Monty.

"Which is exactly what the cost-conscious decision-makers opted for," he said. "It turns off every night for the duration of Great Tom's big number. And during that time, the stairwells are completely blind and vulnerable. All you've got to do is take the stairs to the third floor and make it to the main reading room before it's done." Then with dramatic flair he recited a famous line of poetry: "'Ask not for whom the bell tolls, it tolls for thee.'"

"How do you know all this?" asked Sydney.

"Well, they try to keep it a secret," he said. "But luckily, one of the people in this room is also on the faculty oversight committee."

Paris smiled as he ran through the conversation in his mind. He'd been hiding in the rear stall for nearly an hour, and it was almost time to make the mad dash to the third floor. He checked his watch and saw that it was three past nine. He put his feet down on the floor and was about to unlock the latch when he heard the door open and someone walk into the bathroom.

Paris quickly pulled his feet back up and leaned over to peek through the space that separated the stall door and its frame. In one of the mirrors he saw a reflection of a custodian heading over to the urinals. Paris checked his watch. It was time.

Bong. Bong. Bong.

Great Tom started tolling, and all Paris could do was keep hiding in the stall.

Bong. Bong. Bong.

He counted each ring as the custodian finished at the urinal and headed over to the sink.

Bong. Bong. Bong.

After washing his hands, the man primped in the mirror, trying to fix the part in his hair, and it took everything Paris had not to let out a scream.

Bong. Bong. Bong.

By the time the custodian left the restroom, Great Tom had already rung sixty-eight times by Paris's count. That left thirty-three more for him to make it up to the top level and into the upper reading room. Originally, he'd planned to go up the stairs slowly and carefully, but there would be no time for that now.

He peeked out the door into the hall to make sure the custodian was gone, and then he hit the stairs at a full sprint.

Bong. Bong. Bong.

He tried to keep track of the number in his head, but it was hard in all the rush and he was no longer sure.

Bong. Bong. Bong.

When he made it to the top level, he saw Monty and

Sydney holding open the door to the reading room, signaling him to hurry.

He sprinted full speed across the entryway and actually slid the last few feet across the marble floor into the room.

Bong. Bong.

He'd made it with only two left to go.

"Where were you?" asked Sydney.

Paris shrugged nonchalantly and answered, "In the loo."

STEP THREE—*EXTRACT THE BIRD BOOKS*

Once they'd made it into the upper reading room, the team only had to rely on old-fashioned skulking and sneaking. They'd evaded the high-tech portion of the security system. Now they just had to stay quiet, make sure they didn't attract attention, and listen for any security guards who might be on their rounds.

"We're looking for room two zero two five," said Monty, who'd searched the library's online directory to learn the location of the library's ornithology special collections. They found the door quickly enough, but it took them a while to pick the lock.

"What's the problem?" Sydney asked as Paris fiddled with it. "I thought you were good at lock-picking?"

"You're thinking of Rio," he said. "I'm pretty good when it comes to modern locks, but I've never picked one this old. None of my tricks work."

They heard a guard approaching, so they ducked behind a bookcase until the coast was clear. Once it was, Sydney took a crack at the door and had the lock picked in forty-five seconds.

"You can use a flashlight," Monty said once the door was closed. "No one should be able to see us in here."

Sydney turned on the flashlight app on her phone and almost let out a scream. Just inches in front of her face was a stuffed hawk made to look as if it was in full flight and ready to swoop in for a kill. The light reflected in the fake eyes that looked like black-and-yellow marbles.

"I think it's safe to say we've found the ornithology special collections," she said, her heart still racing.

They scoured the room for about fifteen minutes until they found three boxes stacked in a corner and marked PARKER RUTLEDGE. The boxes were still taped shut and obviously hadn't been opened in the six months since

Mrs. Rutledge had dropped them off. Monty wondered if the library staff considered them as educationally vital as Parker's mother did.

STEP FOUR—*EXIT BY WAY OF RAPPELLING FROM THE ROOF*

Duncan Fletcher stood on the lawn that separated the library from the nearby Sheldonian Theatre. His eyes were focused on the roof of the Bodleian, and when he saw a quick double flash of light, he knew they'd made it that far.

He checked to make sure there was no one nearby, and when he was certain it was safe, he gave the "go" signal of three quick flashes.

The first one down was Sydney, followed just thirty seconds later by Paris. Monty trailed the group, and the instant her feet hit the ground, Sydney and Paris started pulling down the rope and coiling it up.

Less than two minutes after Fletcher had signaled them, they were walking back toward Exeter College and looked like any group of students and faculty out for a stroll.

"How was the burgling?" asked Fletcher.

"We got all the books," answered Sydney.

"How many is that?"

"Twenty-seven," said Monty. "It was quite a haul." She looked at her old friend and said, "Sorry to turn you into a criminal."

"Not a criminal," he said. "A spy. Besides, I haven't had this much fun in years."

It was late by the time Monty and the kids made it back to the safe house, but the others were still awake, waiting to see what happened. They had to be careful what they said because they knew there were listening devices in the house.

"Everything good?" Mother asked.

"Everything's great," Monty replied.

They went into the home theater because it didn't have any windows and seemed like the most secure room in the house. There, the three of them unzipped their backpacks and started pulling out bird books. They lined all twenty-seven of them up across a table, and the others were stunned.

"Wow!" said Brooklyn.

"You got that right," said Sydney. "Wow."

Exhausted by the day, Monty, Paris, and Sydney plopped into a row of leather recliners. It had been a long day with twists and turns, but they'd managed to navigate it expertly. They'd eluded whoever may have been following them, beat the Bodleian's state-of-the-art security system, and managed to bring back the bird books. They were tired but felt great.

"So what do you think?" asked Mother.

"It's a lot of information," answered Monty.

"We'll start sifting through it tomorrow when you guys are at Parliament," he said.

"I flipped through some of them on the train," said Sydney. "And I think the key has to do with someone named Magpie."

Mother held his finger up to his mouth to signal quiet. He had long known about MI6's attempt to locate Magpie. But his warning was too late. With the mention of that one word, the artificial intelligence program monitoring conversations in the safe house was triggered. "Magpie" was a golden word, and the system instantly began recording all conversations in the house and an alert was sent to a computer in Vauxhall Cross.

Parliament

EVEN THOUGH SHE DIDN'T GET MUCH sleep, Sydney felt great when she woke up the next morning. Some of that may have been due to the fact that the town house was furnished with top-of-the-line luxury mattresses. But mostly it was because the break-in at the Bodleian had been just what she needed. It was fun, exciting, illicit, and a great boost to her confidence.

It also helped that Monty had selected her for the job. It was a reminder that she believed in her.

"Ready for today?" Mother asked when Sydney came into the kitchen for some breakfast.

"Absolutely," she answered. "Tru gave us instructions on how we should testify. And she very specifically reminded us about the Secrets oath. I know what to say and what not to say."

"Great," replied Mother. "And the truth is, the questioning should go easy on you and Brooklyn. After all, you're the victims. Bloody Mary isn't going after you. She's going after MI6."

"Is Tru going to testify?" asked Sydney.

"That'll happen afterward in a separate closed session," answered Mother. "That way they can take everything you all say and throw it right at her."

"I feel sorry for her," Sydney said. "She's a patriot. She's dedicated her life to protecting this country. And they're going to attack her when she did nothing wrong."

Mother chuckled. "She's tough. She's handled far worse than an overly ambitious member of Parliament. Besides, remember what she said was her rule to live by."

"*No matter what, my lips are sealed. My secrets will never be revealed,*" said Sydney.

"That's right," he said smiling. "She lives up to that."

There had been some debate about how they would

dress for their testimony. At one point, Monty suggested they might wear their school uniforms, which Sydney shot down instantly. She had a strong sense of style, and after a week of having to blend in on the *Sylvia Earle*, she was looking to show her true self. So while Brooklyn went the conservative route with a simple navy dress, Sydney wore black pants and a white blouse with a fitted houndstooth blazer and a bold red belt. This was her power outfit, and it made her feel strong, which is what she needed at the moment.

They took a taxi from Notting Hill but got out a couple of blocks early. Monty wanted to walk up so that she could get a read on the situation. Even though the hearing was private, the press knew something was going on. Monty wanted to make sure there wasn't media crowding around the entrance, looking for any school-age girls coming to testify.

"Now remember, Sydney," Monty said as they walked along Victoria Street next to Westminster Abbey. "Brooklyn's too young, but you're going to be sworn in. Are you going to be okay lying under oath?"

"It won't be my first time," replied Sydney.

"It won't?"

"Don't you remember last night? *I hereby undertake*

not to remove from the Library . . . Once you've broken one oath, you've broken them all."

She tried to make light of it, but Monty knew it wouldn't be easy. Sydney's moral compass was strong, and lying, even for the right reasons, was hard for her. It also didn't help that she was going to have to do it in one of the most famous—and most intimidating—buildings in the world.

Although people often referred to the building as Parliament, it was officially the Palace of Westminster. Just as most tourists thought its giant clock tower was named Big Ben when that was actually the name of the bell inside it.

To avoid the media, the passengers and crew of the *Sylvia Earle* bypassed the visitors' entrance on Cromwell Green and entered through a much less conspicuous door normally reserved for staff. Although it had been only a few weeks since the ordeal, it felt like a reunion of old friends when they all gathered in an ornate reception area with a name that was not particularly friend-like— the Strangers' Dining Room.

The room was large enough that they were able to break up into smaller groups. The three scientists were in the middle of the room, making a point of checking in on everyone. The captain of the ship, Frida Hovland, stood in one corner with a few members of her crew, including Hannah Delapp, the second mate.

"The one talking to the captain is the one we think is MI6," Sydney whispered to Monty.

"Although if she is, I didn't see her do anything useful during the assault," added Brooklyn.

"What we do is not always noticeable," Monty reminded her.

Much to Sydney and Brooklyn's surprise, Judy Somersby approached them, but she seemed different than she had on the ship. Rather than having the confidence she exuded on the *Sylvia Earle*, she now seemed tentative in her manner, with her shoulders dipped and her eyes downcast.

"Hi," Judy said pleasantly. "It's nice to see you two."

Sydney didn't know what to make of the friendly gesture; after all, she'd hardly spoken to them when they shared a room. Still, Judy was playing nice, so she replied in kind. "Nice to see you too."

"How are you doing?" asked Brooklyn.

"Okay, I guess," she said. "Still kind of rattled. How about you?"

"Same," said Brooklyn.

"I never got a chance to properly thank the two of you," she said. "It was crazy on that island, and when I looked for you, I couldn't find you."

"No thanks necessary," Sydney said flatly, not fully trusting this new and improved Judy.

They stood there awkwardly for a moment, and Judy added, "I also wanted to say I'm sorry about my mother. I've kept it a secret like you told me to, but I'd really like to tell her. I still don't understand who you are, but I know that Alice and I are extremely lucky that you were there on the boat. So thank you."

"We appreciate it," said Brooklyn. "But it really is best if you keep it between us."

"Just so you know, though," Sydney added pointedly, "*luck* had nothing to do with it."

"Right," Judy said. "Thanks again." She started to walk away, but as she did, she turned back to Sydney and said, "By the way, I really love your belt."

"Well?" Monty said once Judy was out of earshot. "What do you think?"

"I wish she hadn't complimented my belt," Sydney said.

"Why?" asked Brooklyn.

"Because just when I decided she was insincere and full of garbage, she made me like her a little," she answered.

"What makes you think she's insincere?" asked Monty.

"The way she treated us all week on the ship," answered Sydney. "She acted like we weren't even there. That we were beneath her."

"I don't know," said Brooklyn. "She sounded sincere to me. Maybe the hijacking changed her."

"I'm not convinced," said Sydney. "It's easy to come over here and thank us when nobody can hear. I still think it's an act."

"And the comment about the belt?" asked Monty.

"Oh, she totally meant that," joked Sydney. "Say what you want about her people skills, but she's got a great sense of style."

Monty and Brooklyn laughed, and then a hush came over the room as Mary Somersby entered with a small entourage of aides and addressed the group. "First of all, thank you for being here today." She looked out solemnly at the faces of those assembled. "What happened to you is inexcusable. Your government—more specifically MI6—let you down. As a representative of that government, I offer my most sincere apology, along with a promise that my committee will get to the bottom of this. The proper punishments will be doled out, and the perpetrators will be captured and brought to justice."

There was polite applause around the room.

Sydney turned toward Judy, who had a look of disdain on her face.

"Doesn't seem like Judy's much of a fan of dear old mum," Sydney whispered to the others, who noted the expression.

"Now, I want to talk to you about how the day is going to work," Somersby continued. "We're just trying to get as much information as possible from each of you about what happened on the ship. To do that, we're going to bring in groups of four, which keeps us from having to repeat too much and lets each of you have plenty of time to talk. Moreover, for the passengers, we're going to bring you in by cabin, so you'll be with the roommates you had for the trip. We think this will help you remember details better."

"That's good for us," Sydney whispered to Brooklyn.

"Why's that?"

"Because Judy and Alice will be the focus and they'll do all the talking," explained Sydney. "All we have to do is nod along quietly."

"Now, one thing that's really important," Somersby continued. "You have to remain in this room until you testify. That's to protect you from the press as much as anything. If you need to use a restroom, one of our wonderful visitor's assistants will escort you to a nearby room typically reserved for members. Also, once you've testified, you will not be able to come back into this room, so make sure to bring everything you have with you. And finally, we're going to need to collect your phones until the session is complete. Trust me, they'll be completely safe, but it's a necessity. There are a few security guards coming around the room to collect them."

"What's with all that?" Brooklyn asked Monty.

"For one thing, they want to make sure no one records anything and that no one posts on social media," Monty answered. "But more importantly, I'm guessing they don't want the crew to be able to coordinate with one another or give warnings about what questions are being asked."

"Why not?" asked Brooklyn.

"Because they may think that somebody in the crew is involved," she said, "that they helped the hijackers. And they're going to want to catch them off guard in that hearing room."

"Again, I am sorry for all the inconvenience of the day," Somersby said. "We'll try to move along speedily in the hearing room, and as soon as I'm done here, we have some delicious food that's been catered and will be brought in. Thank you all. And once again, I promise that this government will bring you justice."

As far as her promises went, Somersby was fifty-fifty. About as well as could be expected from a politician. The catering was delicious as advertised. It was mostly finger foods, but there were plenty of them and they included the best scones Brooklyn had ever tasted. As for the speediness of the proceedings, however, that was a less accurate description.

Each group seemed to take forever, and the hearing lasted hours. Unfortunately, the Strangers' Dining Room didn't exactly offer hours worth of entertainment potential. In addition to the food, there were nine paintings on the walls, mostly portraits of past speakers of the house. With nothing better to do, Brooklyn and Sydney spent a great deal of time studying the minutiae of the artworks, and among their insightful observations was the fact that eighteenth-century Prime Minister William Pitt and twenty-first-century Hollywood star Brad Pitt had nothing in common other than their last name.

Monty tried to read the room as the different people were called out. She especially studied the captain, who seemed troubled by the whole situation. Monty tried to strike up a conversation with her, but after a few curt replies, she gave up the attempt. She had more luck with Virginia Wescott, the documentary filmmaker.

"What are some of the documentaries you've made?" Monty asked. "Any I might've seen?"

"Let's see," Wescott said. "I did one a few years back about the coal miners strike back in the mid-eighties and another about the women code breakers who worked at Bletchley Park during World War II."

"I saw both of those," Monty said. "I quite liked them. Especially the Bletchley Park one. The story's fascinating."

"Amazing," said Wescott. "You know, some of those women had never let on about the work they'd done. Lived for decades with their spouses and never once uttered a word about Bletchley Park. They said they'd sworn to secrecy and that they'd take it to their graves."

Monty had actually enjoyed the Bletchley Park documentary so much that she'd watched it several times. Virginia Wescott moved up in her esteem several places.

"I spent the last few years making a multipart docuseries about the history of the Olympics."

"I saw that," Sydney added, beaming as she joined the conversation. "It was excellent."

"Thank you," said Wescott.

Sydney and Brooklyn were among the second-to-last group to be called in to testify. The only ones still left were Virginia Wescott, Captain Hovland, and two of the marine scientists who were on the trip.

The first person Sydney saw when she entered the committee room was Tru, who sat in the corner and shot her a quick wink. Sitting next to her was her personal assistant, Jack Fissell. There were nine members of Parliament sitting at a U-shaped table with Mary Somersby in the middle spot reserved for the chairperson. They all faced a long wooden table where Judy, Alice, Brooklyn, and Sydney sat side by side.

"Welcome, girls," Somersby said. "In the United Kingdom, people of any age are permitted to provide testimony, but those fourteen and older must be sworn in. So before we ask any questions, Alice and Eleanor," she said, referring to Sydney by her cover name, "I'd like each of you to raise your right hand and repeat this oath. 'I promise before Almighty God that the evidence which I shall give shall be the truth, the whole truth, and nothing but the truth.'"

For the second time in less than twenty-four hours, Sydney took an oath that she knew she was going to break instantly. The MPs questioned the girls in order from left to right, starting with Judy and then Alice. The questions were general at first, asking them how they happened to go on the trip and what the experience had been like. They got more specific when it reached the events of the day of the hijacking.

That's when the questions got tricky. Mary Somersby knew it would be inappropriate for her to ask questions of her own daughter, so she yielded to another MP from her party.

"How did you know the ship was under attack?" the woman asked.

"Alice and I were awoken when Emil Blix started speaking over the intercom to inform us that they'd taken control of the ship," said Judy in a well-practiced answer.

"And how did it come to pass that you hid in the . . ." The MP went to read the name of the room in her notes, but Judy filled in the answer for her.

"Stern thruster machine room," she answered as though she were now a nautical expert. "It was instinct, really. Considering that I had a mother in Parliament and that Alice is a member of the royal family, it only made sense that we'd be targets of the hijackers."

"That's very quick thinking," said the MP.

"Thank you, ma'am," answered Judy. "In preparation for the trip, I had studied the *Sylvia Earle* extensively, and I knew our best chance was to look for a place to hide down on the engine deck."

"Very brave," said the MP. "Brilliant and brave."

Even though it was exactly what they needed Judy to say, the testimony drove Sydney crazy. Here Judy was, getting all the credit that Brooklyn deserved. Brooklyn was the one who had been brilliant and brave.

There was a similar line of questioning for Alice and then for Brooklyn. Although after a basic introduction, Mary Somersby asked Brooklyn something surprising, more accusatory than inquisitive.

"Why weren't you on the marine mammal observation platform?" she asked.

"I'm sorry, ma'am, I don't understand."

"It's not that difficult a question," Somersby said. "According to the testimony we've heard today, all of the other girls were on the marine mammal observation platform, but you weren't. Why not?"

Monty, Tru, and Sydney all paid close attention to how Brooklyn handled this question. They were about to find out how quickly she could talk on her feet.

"That testimony's not accurate," Brooklyn said.

"Are you calling the other girls liars?"

"No, ma'am."

"Then are you calling me a liar?"

"No, ma'am," Brooklyn answered. "It's that all of the girls weren't on the platform. Alice and Judy were both hiding in the machine room. And Eleanor was hiding in our cabin."

And with that, the others relaxed. As she had been with many other aspects of spying, Brooklyn seemed well-suited to handle this one.

"Of course," Somersby said, scrambling. "But, unlike them, you were actually up on the main deck. You were close to the platform. But instead of putting you with the others, Emil Blix took you, and you alone, to the bridge. Why was that?"

At this point, Brooklyn had to make a quick judgment. She had to assume that one of the girls on the platform had overheard her conversation with Blix and had testified about it. That meant she had to tell the truth about what happened. At least, most of the truth.

"He took me there because I promised to tell him where Alice and Judy were hiding."

Suddenly the tone of the room changed.

"And did you know where they were hiding?" asked the MP.

"No, ma'am," Brooklyn said.

"Then why did you tell him you did?"

"Because he was threatening me and I wanted to make him stop."

Bloody Mary eyed her suspiciously. "And what happened on the bridge?"

"There are detailed maps of the ship on the bridge, and on one of them I pointed to the forecastle anchor room," said Brooklyn.

"And why did you tell him that?"

"Because I wanted to send him on a wild goose chase."

Monty realized that the answer was a mistake and could tell by Bloody Mary's reaction that she did too.

"Then I'm confused," Somersby said. "Moments ago you said you *didn't* know where they were hiding."

"That's right, I didn't."

"Then how did you know that you were sending him on a wild goose chase?" Somersby asked, pouncing on the slip-up. "How did you know that the girls weren't actually in the anchor room?"

Brooklyn didn't even miss a beat. "I saw them heading toward the rear of the ship."

"Wait a second," Somersby said. "I thought you just said you didn't see them."

Brooklyn was unflappable. "No. I said I didn't know where they were. But I did know that they'd headed to the stern of the boat, which is precisely why I selected the place farthest from the stern." She paused for a beat and added, "I was trying to help your daughter."

Bloody Mary deflated a bit, disappointed that she hadn't been able to trap Brooklyn. But her big prize was yet to come.

She didn't even bother with cursory questions to establish the baseline of Sydney's story. She just went straight for the strike. "Why was your hair wet?"

"I beg your pardon," answered Sydney.

"According to testimony, nobody saw you during the assault, but afterward, when everyone was together, your hair was wet," she explained, as focused as a laser. "But in your statements to the police you said only that you were hiding in your cabin. Although neither Judy nor Alice saw you there. So I ask again, why was your hair wet?"

"I . . . um . . . don't . . . ," Sydney started to say as she looked for an answer.

"And I remind you that unlike your friend, *you* are under oath," Somersby stated.

Sydney hadn't even given an answer, but Mary Somersby had knocked her off guard and she was already scrambling. She gave a somewhat desperate look toward Tru, but there was nothing she could do to help her.

"I lied to the police."

This stunned the room, and every MP was now fully engaged in the testimony.

"You did what?" asked Somersby.

"I lied to the police. I didn't tell them because I was doing something I shouldn't have been," Sydney said haltingly, her eyes shooting another sideways glance at Tru.

"What were you doing?" asked the MP.

"Taking a shower," said Sydney. "There's only one shower on the *Sylvia Earle*, and it was reserved for the officers and scientists. After nearly a week at sea I couldn't take it anymore. My hair was greasy and disgusting so I snuck into the shower for a quick rinse. When I came out, I heard what was going on, and I hid, right there in the captain's stateroom. That's why my hair was wet. That's why the others didn't see me."

"And you felt this was worthy of lying to the authorities?"

"Looking back, I think that was pretty stupid of me,"

Sydney said. "But hijacking or no hijacking, I was breaking a rule, and I was worried that might lead to me getting in trouble at my school. I've already maxed out on demerits for the term."

Somersby looked unconvinced, but she moved on. "I notice your parents aren't here today."

This question was really harsh, and it triggered all of Sydney's antiestablishment tendencies. "And that's relevant how?"

"It's just that the Duke of Covington made time to be here with Alice," she said. "And my ex-husband was able to break free from his legal duties to be here with Judy. But your parents aren't here."

"I'm here as her guardian," Monty said.

"Excuse me," Somersby said, glaring at Monty. "You've not been sworn in, and you will not speak unless directly spoken to."

"I am here as her guardian and advocate to protect her from treatment like this," Monty said, not backing down. "She's a child and you're making insinuations that are wholly inappropriate."

"It's okay, Monty," Sydney said, looking at her over her shoulder. "I can explain." Sydney turned back to Bloody Mary and smiled. "I appreciate that both the duke and your ex-husband were able to make time to be here with their daughters," she said. "I'm sure one of my parents would too if they weren't both dead. That makes it kind of hard, unless you've got a crystal ball or a Ouija board back there. So Ms. Montgomery is going to have to do."

This brought chuckles from some of the other MPs and members of the gallery.

"It's interesting you say that," she responded. "Because there is no mention of your parents anywhere. The record trail for Eleanor King starts fresh three years ago with your enrollment at Kinloch Abbey. It's as if you just materialized out of thin air. Or perhaps there's a different identity tucked away in there somewhere."

Sydney looked first at Monty and then at Tru, completely unsure what to say next, so she just sat quietly, trying to come up with an answer.

"What?" Somersby said sarcastically. "No clever reply. Well, we'll get back to that, because I feel like this next question is going to open up the floodgates."

Sydney's eyes opened wide as she braced for whatever might come.

"Two months ago, did you or did you not order the ingredients necessary to manufacture an explosive device from a chemical company in Southampton?" the MP held up a receipt. "And once again I remind you that you're under oath."

This is when Sydney realized the depths of where the MP was willing to go. She was trying to implicate her in the hijacking. First the sketchy alibi. Then the undocumented past. And now explosives. Sydney had bought them for a Saturday Match Day training exercise on the FARM, but Bloody Mary was going to say that she was part of the terror team. She was accusing her of being a criminal. Yet, if Sydney told the truth, she would actually become a criminal.

Never before in her life had she felt more vulnerable. She had no idea what she could say in her defense.

"This is absurd!" Monty said, leaping to her feet.

"Bailiff, silence that woman," Somersby thundered as she pointed at Monty. She focused on Sydney and continued, "Tell us the truth. You're connected to all this, aren't you? You're a mole that was placed by foreign agents determined to—"

"APPLE JACK!"

The interruption was startling and caught everyone by surprise.

"APPLE JACK!"

Sydney turned to look down the table and saw that it was Judy.

"Judy, what are you doing?" Somersby asked her daughter.

"Before I went on the trip, you told me about apple jack," said Judy. "Just like the duke and duchess told Alice."

Alice nodded her confirmation.

"You told us that if anyone said 'apple jack,' we had to stop what we were doing and follow their instructions," she continued. "Well, I'm saying 'apple jack' to you for the same reason. To tell you to stop what you're doing."

"Apple jack has nothing to do with this," the MP said crossly.

"Apple jack has *everything* to do with this," her daughter replied firmly. "Apple jack is the reason that Alice and I weren't locked up in some tiny closet on a ship sailing to Iceland. It's the reason the two of us are still alive. And it's the reason you should stop accusing these two girls and start thanking them. Because they're not suspects. They're heroes."

"And how's that?" roared the mother.

"I can't tell you how," Judy replied.

"Because?"

"Because you don't have a high enough security clearance."

Tru tried to stifle a laugh with a cough.

"I don't know what's gotten into you," Somersby said. "But I am here not as a mother to be spoken to petulantly by her spoiled rotten daughter. I am here as the representative of the government and the people of Southgate, and I will question as I see fit."

"Well, I'm going to lay it out for you, Mum," Judy said. "You've got two options, and I'm going to let you pick which one to pursue."

"How generous of you."

"Option one, stop your ridiculous questions, thank these two girls for saving your daughter's life, and go out to the members of the media who you've been feeding information to and announce that after a thorough investigation it is evident that MI6 made no lapses with regard to the hijacking of the *Sylvia Earle*."

"And option two?"

"You continue your ridiculous questions, and I go out and address those same members of the media," Judy said coolly. "And I tell them all about our family. I tell them about the late-night phone calls you make when you think I'm asleep and can't hear who you're doing business with. And of course, I explain to them why it is I live with my father and not with my mother." The color drained from Bloody Mary's face. "I don't know how the fine people of Southgate will like what they hear, but I'm sure the press will be fully entertained by the pathetic soap opera that is our family."

The room fell into stunned silence until Alice stood up and pointed directly at Judy. "What she said!"

22

The Doughnut

MAGPIE HAD ALWAYS BEEN OVERLOOKED.
First, it was growing up in a family that focused its praise
and attention on the oldest son. Then it was boarding
school, where the children of the rich and powerful were
given the best opportunities. Now, it was MI6, where
spies with the right connections got all the flashy assign-
ments and hero treatment.

At each of these stages, Magpie had been successful,
but never too successful. A likable child, a good student,

a well-regarded agent. Solid but not special. Certainly not spectacular.

This pleased Magpie intensely.

Stars got all the attention, which meant their every move was scrutinized. Understudies could scurry around in the shadows, which is exactly where Magpie wanted to be. The shadow world was rife with opportunity for anyone who had talent but lacked morals.

One person who did not underestimate Magpie was Le Fantôme. Their collaboration had been very profitable, and he found the agent to be incredibly skilled, which is why he wanted them to work together on a special project. A few months earlier, an Umbra plan had failed miserably in Paris. The organization intended to release a deadly virus during a youth summit on the environment, but the man responsible for executing the plan suddenly disappeared. Le Fantôme suspected MI6 had something to do with it and tasked Magpie with finding out.

Rather than dig into files about the summit or Umbra, which could attract attention, Magpie devised a more devious scheme and orchestrated the hijacking of the *Sylvia Earle*.

"How will this help uncover what happened in Paris?" Le Fantôme asked.

"It might not," answered Magpie. "But MI6 lacks creativity and is prone to repeat itself. Like the youth summit, this scenario features students in a scientific setting. They may try to repeat whatever worked for them in Paris; perhaps placing an agent on board as a scientist or crew member." The double agent paused for a moment and added, "And even if they don't, you'll still make millions from the ransom."

Le Fantôme laughed and said, "I think you may be the only person I've ever met who's more deplorable than me."

"I'll take that as a compliment."

"I meant it as one."

At the time, the plan seemed brilliant. Magpie made sure MI6 intercepted a communication about the hijacking and then got out of the way. At least one agent was placed on board, but there was no indication that she disrupted the hijacking at all. She didn't need to. Emil Blix had bungled everything on his own.

Or had he?

When they met in Norway, Blix was adamant that someone had tampered with his bomb. Magpie thought this was a desperate attempt to salvage his reputation, but the investigation in Parliament had changed things.

Despite the hearing's "secret" status, Magpie had managed to get access to all the testimony. Originally, this was to make sure none of it led to Blix or helped connect him with Umbra. But now it had Magpie questioning whether perhaps MI6 had been clever enough to place more than one agent on board. Multiple agents working independently could explain Blix's failure. Had the mole underestimated the Secret Intelligence Service?

"Who's there?" asked the security guard making his hourly rounds.

"It's just me," Magpie answered innocently with a friendly wave. "The boss had some emergency late-night files that needed to be pulled for a meeting tomorrow morning."

The guard shook his head and replied, "Isn't it always that way? It's the boss's emergency, but you're the one working late at night while he's sound asleep."

"Always," Magpie replied, not bothering to point out that the boss was, in fact, a she and not a he.

"Take care and turn the lights out when you leave," said the guard as he resumed his rounds.

"I will. Have a good night."

That's how easy deception was when people continually overlooked you. The guard was so used to seeing

Magpie coming and going to perform menial tasks such as dropping off or picking up files that he didn't think twice about the situation. Even in the middle of the night at GCHQ, the government communications headquarters. This was the building, universally known as the Doughnut, where MI6 stored its most sensitive records. Magpie had come looking for one in particular. A name had cropped up out of nowhere and suddenly seemed worth looking into.

The label on the file read ALEXANDRA MONTGOMERY.

23.

Kat

KATHMANDU, NEPAL—THREE YEARS EARLIER

MOTHER AND MONTY WERE LOOKING for a coffee shop hidden somewhere in the maze of crowded alleyways that made up the Thamel neighborhood of Kathmandu, Nepal. Here there were no sidewalks—just narrow strips of pavement teeming with beat-up cars, sputtering motorbikes, and wayward pedestrians.

"I've never seen so many signs in all my life," Mother said, shaking his head in amazement.

Signs were everywhere. They covered the walls of each

254

building, adorned every light and electrical pole, and hung from balconies and banners that stretched across the street. They advertised everything from souvenir shops and Internet cafés to budget boarding houses and Himalayan mountain treks.

"Well, one of them says Lhasa Café," Monty said as she gave him an encouraging pat on the back. "All we have to do is find it."

He chuckled and replied, "I love your optimism."

It took them about twenty minutes of looking, but they finally found the narrow storefront tucked between a money exchange and a small shop selling local crafts. The coffee shop was barely wider than the front door. Inside there was a bar with stools and three wooden tables. A young woman in her twenties was sitting at one of the tables. She looked up and smiled at them.

"Alexandra?" asked the woman.

"Yes," replied Monty. "You must be Elaine."

"I hope it wasn't too hard to find, but my mum said you wanted to meet off the beaten path," Elaine answered. "Besides, this place has the best coffee in KTM," she said, calling the city by its nickname.

Monty introduced Mother, and they all sat around the

table. Following Elaine's recommendation, they ordered a breakfast of aloo chana, a curry dish of potato and chickpeas.

"You know, your mother's my all-time favorite doctor," Monty said.

"I think it's something of a mutual admiration society," replied Elaine. "She raves about you. She says you're a mathematical genius and told me I should do whatever I can to help you, no questions asked."

"Did she give you any indication where I work?"

"That was the one question I was specifically told not to ask," she replied. "But judging from all the cloak and dagger, I have a pretty good guess."

Monty smiled. "Let's just leave it at that."

"All right, then, what brings you to Nepal?"

"I know from your mum's annual Christmas letter that you work for UNICEF helping children here in Kathmandu," she said. "And as crazy as it sounds, I was hoping you could help me find a particular one."

Monty pulled a piece of paper from her purse and handed it to Elaine. It was a photo printed from the Internet that showed a Nepali girl holding a piece of fabric with geometric designs painted on it. The girl was about ten years old, and rather than looking directly at the camera, she was focused slightly down and away from it.

"You want to find this girl?" asked Elaine.

"Very much," answered Monty.

"You know there are over a million people in Kathmandu, not counting the tens of thousands who are here because they've been displaced by earthquakes and floods," said Elaine. "It's going to be really hard to find her."

"Actually, finding this café was really hard," said Mother. "It's going to be practically impossible to find her." Then he flashed a grin. "But practically impossible is our specialty."

While they ate their breakfast, Elaine studied the picture, looking for clues that could help. "This is called a *yantra thangka*," she said, pointing at the artwork. "It's used in meditation."

"I found the picture on a UNICEF website," said Monty. "There were a couple of other girls, and the article said they were part of a program that teaches orphaned girls how to make handicrafts. But it didn't list the name of the specific program."

"There are a number of them," said Elaine. "But I know one of the guys who writes the posts for the website. He should be able to help us."

They spent the rest of the morning and all afternoon following one dead-end lead after another until they arrived at a small school just outside of the city.

"You have to be careful when dealing with the local agencies," Elaine said. "Not all of them are legitimate, but with so many children in need, the social services are just overwhelmed."

"How does this one rate?" Mother asked.

"Good," she said. "The woman who runs it really cares about the girls. It's what's known as a transitional learning center."

The three of them met with the director, and as they'd instructed her, Elaine introduced Monty and Mother as representatives from a British aid society.

"What brings you to us?" she asked.

"We would very much like to meet this girl," Monty said, showing her the picture. "Is she here?"

The director had a slightly pained look on her face. A look that they would soon realize was one of pity. "Yes," she said. "Her name is Amita."

"And her family?" asked Monty.

The woman shook her head. "She lost her family in an earthquake two years ago."

"Can we talk to her?"

"You can try," she replied. "But Amita barely speaks at all."

"Is she not able to talk?" asked Mother.

"Oh no," said the woman. "It's not that. She just chooses not to."

"Not even to her friends?" he asked.

The woman thought about this as they walked out of the room and she led them toward Amita. "I don't know that she really has any friends. At least, not like the other girls."

The school managed to be both modest and impressive. There were dorm rooms along one hall and classrooms along the other.

"The girls live here and go to school here," she explained. "We also try to teach them handicrafts so that they might have a trade when they're grown."

"Let me guess," said Monty. "Amita is one of your best students."

"By far the best," said the director. "How did you know?"

Monty nodded knowingly. "Just a guess."

They passed through a studio with several looms, where teenaged girls were learning how to weave decorative carpets, and finally found Amita in a room by herself. She was stringing turquoise and coral beads onto a necklace she was making.

Speaking in Nepali, the director told Amita she had visitors, but the girl didn't look up. She just kept stringing the beads.

"Can you translate for me?" Monty asked the woman.

"Of course," she replied.

"Hello, Amita, my name is Alexandra."

She sat down on the opposite side of the table as the director translated for her.

"I want to ask you about your artwork," she said. "Your *yantra thangka*."

Monty slid the paper across the table to her.

"Where did you get your design?"

She waited anxiously during the translation. Amita didn't respond at first, but then, still without looking up, she answered softly.

"She just made it up," the woman told her.

"She didn't have a pattern she copied?" asked Monty. "There wasn't any kind of computer program that helped her?"

"No," answered the director. "We have nothing like that."

"Is it possible that she was ever exposed to calculus or advanced geometry?"

The woman laughed. "I'm afraid you think too highly of our school. We are not equipped to teach those types of subjects. Why do you ask?"

"Because the design on that *thangka* is the visual representation of a rather complex mathematical principle," Monty said. "It's made up of perfectly formed fractals, something I might expect to see produced by a doctoral candidate with a computer, not hand-painted by a ten-year-old girl with a limited mathematical education."

The woman looked at the picture for a moment as she considered this. "I don't know what to say."

Monty let out a sigh as she tried to think of what to do next. She looked at Amita, whose eyes were still focused on the necklace she was making.

"Can I speak to her alone for a moment?" asked Monty.

Mother laughed. "Did you suddenly learn Nepali when I wasn't paying attention?"

"No," Monty said. "We'll talk in math."

Elaine, the director, and Mother all left the room, and Monty quietly watched Amita continue working.

Monty was shy by nature, but nothing like Amita.

During college, she'd worked part-time as a nanny for a family whose daughter was extremely shy. She recognized the same far-off look and the aversion to eye contact. She knew the key to communication was not to force anything but just leave the door open for Amita to connect with her.

"I've come a long way to meet you, Amita," she said sweetly, even though she knew the girl couldn't understand her. "Do you mind if I make a necklace too?"

She pulled a foot of thick thread off of a spool and tied a knot at one end.

"I learned how to make necklaces from my grandmother," Monty continued. "But I always had trouble deciding which color beads to use."

As she talked, she started sliding beads onto the thread. First, she put on a single coral bead followed by a turquoise one. She followed this with two coral, three turquoise, and five coral.

"Let's see, what should I do next?" she said. "How about eight turquoise?"

She strung the beads onto the thread and laid it on the table directly where Amita was looking.

"How many coral beads should there be?"

She just waited, and after nearly a minute, Amita picked up the necklace and starting stringing coral beads. Monty counted while she did, and when Amita was done, she laid the necklace back on the table.

"I'll call your thirteen and raise you twenty-one."

Monty slid twenty-one turquoise beads onto the necklace and placed it back on the table.

Amita let out a faint giggle and picked up the necklace. She put thirty-four coral beads onto the string, and instead of laying it on the table, she handed it to Monty. For the first time, she looked up at her.

The two of them locked eyes for a moment, and Monty smiled.

"It's nice to meet you, Amita. So very nice."

Soon the others returned to the room.

"What a beautiful necklace you two are making," said the director.

"It's more than that," Monty said. "It's a Fibonacci series. Each number progresses by adding the last two numbers. It first appeared in ancient India and was introduced to the West in the 1300s by an Italian mathematician known as Fibonacci. I'm guessing you haven't studied that here in school."

"No," the director said with a laugh. "We have not."

"So you didn't learn it," Monty said to Amita. "You just know it."

The woman started to translate, but Monty waved her off.

"No, tell her this instead." Monty took a deep breath. "Amita, my friend and I live in a place that's far from here, but is very nice. We'd like to know if you'd like to move there and live with us. You'll have your own room, and you'll get to learn everything there is to know about math."

The woman paused for a moment, surprised at this development, but then she translated for Amita.

The girl looked up again and maintained eye contact with Monty. The corner of her lips slowly formed a smile, and she nodded.

24.

Rosetta Stone

AISLING, SCOTLAND—PRESENT DAY

KAT WAS STILL QUIET AND SHY, BUT NOT like she had been back in the orphanage. She'd come out of her shell in the three years since she'd left Nepal, especially here on the FARM, surrounded by the people who were now her family. Still, it was quite rare for her to call a meeting with the intention of purposefully getting in front of the group to speak. So when she did, Paris's first thought was that she was joking. Especially considering the timing.

"Seriously?" he said. "You want everyone in the priest hole, *now*?"

"Yes," she answered. "What's wrong with now?"

"Actually . . ."

He'd been all set to sit down and watch Liverpool play Arsenal. It was a week after they'd had tickets to see the Liverpool–Chelsea game only to leave the stadium before kickoff. His chores were completed, his homework was done, and the snacks were ready and delicious. He'd looked forward to this for days. But in that nanosecond, it dawned on him how unusual it was for Kat to call a meeting. If she wanted them all together so she could tell them something, it had to be important. Even if for no other reason than it was important to her.

"Actually . . . *now's* perfect," he said. "I'll help round everyone up."

The group gathered around the conference table with Kat at the head and Brooklyn right next to her with a laptop. The others were beyond curious about why they were there.

"I don't know about you guys," Mother said as he settled into his seat, "but I'm guessing this is going to be amazing."

Kat smiled shyly and simply said, "Yes."

Kat saw the world as a series of interconnected math problems. To her, everything was some sort of equation or pattern, which is why she was such an incredible code breaker. The hard part was translating that. It was often much easier for her to decipher a code than it was to explain how she'd done so. That's why she'd enlisted Brooklyn to help with the presentation.

First, though, she wanted to check one thing to make sure she was right.

"Mother, when you were on the spy team with Parker Rutledge, was Clementine on the team with you?"

"Yes," Mother answered. "At MI6 we were known as the Zoo Crew because our cover was that we worked at the London Zoo."

"And during this time, did she go by the name Robin?"

Mother gave her an astonished look. "Yes. How did you know that? Her alias was Robin Lynch."

"That is very good news," Kat replied, pleased. Then she turned to Brooklyn and said, "First slide, please."

Brooklyn pressed a key, and a picture appeared on the wall monitor. It was one of the group taken a week earlier at the British Museum.

"What's this?" asked Kat.

Rio looked around, not sure if this was some sort of trick question. "It's us around the Rosetta Stone."

"That's right," she said. "And why is the Rosetta Stone important?"

"It's important because . . ." Rio started to answer, but then it dawned on him that he really had no idea why it was important. He just knew that it was a big deal and that everyone who came through the museum made sure to check it out. "Because it's a . . . really old rock with writing on it."

"That is *less* right," Kat said with a raised eyebrow.

"It's important because it broke the code," said Monty.

"Yes," said Kat. "Up until the Rosetta Stone was discovered, no one in modern times could understand hieroglyphics. But the stone was inscribed with a decree that was written in three languages: ancient Egyptian hieroglyphs, which was the language appropriate for the priests who made the decree; demotic, which was the language used by the people at the time; and ancient Greek, which was the official language of the government. Because ancient Greek had been recorded and translated into modern languages, linguists were able to compare the three versions of the decree and translate the ancient Egyptian. Then, once they understood those hieroglyphs and how they were used, they were able to decipher the entire language wherever they found it."

"That's great," said Paris. "But why is that important to us?"

"To help explain this," she said as she held up the pocket calendar that Parker Rutledge had mailed to himself. "This is the Rosetta Stone of Parker Rutledge. It is the key to understanding everything."

Mother leaned forward, excited by what she was saying.

"We have twenty-seven of his bird books dating back sixteen years," she said. "Each covers a period of about six to nine months, and they are filled with notations that can be as confusing to decipher as the hieroglyphs." She nodded to Brooklyn, who clicked her mouse.

Four images appeared on the screen. They were pages from different bird books, and they featured an amalgam of drawings, diagrams, symbols, maps, and numbers alongside short entries about birds. All of it was written in the same precise penciling they'd seen in his calendar.

"It's a bloody mess," said Sydney.

"Yes," said Kat. "But it's also a beautiful mess. I don't believe they were meant to be read by anyone else. They were personal notes to himself. They detail his travels and the birds he saw in the field. They include information and scientific notations. But they also track his work for MI6 and the missions he undertook. And what makes it so confounding and beautiful at the same time is that he wrote about everything as if he were writing only about birds."

Monty loved the fact that in what most people saw as confusion, Kat saw beauty.

"Remember you're talking to a remedial group here," Paris joked. "Can you explain what you mean by that?"

"When he was part of the Zoo Crew, Mother's alias was Gordon Swift. Swift is a type of bird." She walked over to the monitor and pointed to a page that featured a drawing of a bird. "This page is from that time, and this drawing is of a swift. When he writes about this bird, he's really writing about Mother."

She pointed at the next page. "Now, this one talks about a swift and a robin."

"Also a bird," said Sydney. "But it's actually about Mother and Clementine."

"Exactly," said Kat.

"And how can you tell when he's writing about

birds or when he's writing about other things?" asked Monty.

Kat held up one of the bird books and the pocket calendar. "These overlap by three months. So for those three months, I can compare the two."

"Like with the ancient Greek and hieroglyphics," Paris said. "That's brilliant."

"But there's more," said Kat. "Brooklyn, why don't you show them?"

With a click of a mouse, Brooklyn opened a massive photo gallery on the monitor. The images were almost all of birds taken around the world at locations ranging from tranquil mountain lakes to busy urban landscapes.

"Remember that Parker wanted a camera that had Bluetooth built into it?" she asked.

"Right," said Rio. "So he could upload his pictures to the cloud for the rest of the Dodos to see."

"These are those pictures," Brooklyn said. "I hacked into his cloud account. There are thousands of photos, and they date back at least ten years."

"How hard was it to hack?" asked Monty.

"For me with a supercomputer at my disposal?" Brooklyn said with a smile. "Not hard at all. But to be fair, they were barely encrypted. He intended to share them with the other Dodos."

"The good news is that they're all dated," said Kat. "So when you compare them against the bird books, it fills in even more information. We've only begun to scratch the surface, but we already know that he traveled a ton over the last few years."

"Berlin, Beijing, Moscow, Paris, Tokyo, Mexico City," said Brooklyn. "He was crisscrossing the world and there doesn't seem to be any pattern to it."

"And you know how I hate it when there's not a pattern," joked Kat.

"Well, I know one pattern," said Mother. "I'm not sure about which birds are there, but I do know those cities would make for an all-time greats spy tour. They represent some of the most important espionage centers over the last fifty years."

"And he went to all of them, multiple times, even though he retired from MI6," said Brooklyn.

"Now here's where it gets most curious," said Kat. "During that time, the bird he's most interested in is the magpie, which is odd, because magpies are common. You can find them across Europe, Asia, and western North America."

"Right, magpie," said Sydney. "That's the name I read in the bird books and blurted out at the safe house when I shouldn't have." She turned to Mother and said, "You shushed me and told me we're not to talk about it, but you never said why."

"Magpie is the code name given to a double agent working inside MI6," said Mother. "I only know about it because I helped out on a sting attempt once. For at least ten years there's been someone inside MI6 passing secrets along to Umbra. Since I was trying to infiltrate Umbra, they asked me to help plant some bad information to see if it would help, but it didn't."

"So Rutledge was going all over the world trying to figure out who Magpie was?" Rio asked.

"That would make a lot of sense," said Mother. "Especially because of his retirement."

"What do you mean?" asked Brooklyn.

"Magpie's literally inside MI6 and therefore could potentially interfere with any investigations MI6 is running," he said. "But a retiree outside the Service can move around more easily without attracting attention."

"Until he did," said Kat. "You tell them, Brooklyn. You're the one who figured it out."

"Okay," Brooklyn answered.

She flipped through the photo gallery until she reached the last page of images.

"We're missing one bird book," she said. "The one Rutledge was using when he died."

"And he took them everywhere, so it would still be in San Francisco," said Mother.

"But we do have the pictures he took right up until the end." She clicked on the final image, and it expanded and filled the screen. It was a picture of three large birds with black feathers. "This is the last one."

"Are those magpies?" asked Sydney.

"That's what we thought at first," said Kat. "But they're actually ravens. They're similar looking and belong to the same family, but they're a different species."

"And here's the strange part," said Brooklyn. "They were taken two days after Rutledge died. And we checked the metadata on the picture and know that it was taken with the same camera."

Mother had a totally confused look on his face. "You mean the camera Clementine used to take the picture of the kids?"

"Yes," said Brooklyn.

"So Clementine took this picture?"

Brooklyn nodded. "This is the fortune cookie," she said. "This is the secret message she's sending you."

"I don't understand," said Mother. "Why would she send me a picture of three ravens?"

"Do you know what a group of ravens is called?" Brooklyn asked.

"No," he said. "What?"

"There are two terms, actually. I came across them while we were trying to identify the pictures. A group of ravens is called a conspiracy or a murder."

The Underground

THE CHIEF OF THE SECRET INTELLIGENCE
Service arrived at work every day in an armored SUV
driven by a specially trained agent and accompanied
by a personal protection officer, known as a PPO. This
was necessary for security reasons and appropriate for
someone in charge of such an important and sensitive
agency. As for the rest of the senior staff, most of them
also arrived in impressive vehicles driven by imposing
agents. The business of who had which make and model
of car, and which specially trained driver, had become

something of a status symbol among the group, which was made up primarily of men, all of whom were highly competitive.

Tru took the tube.

"If the London Underground was good enough for my father to take to work every day, then it's certainly good enough for me," she once said to one of her status-conscious colleagues who'd asked her about it. "Besides, I like to look at my people."

"My people" was the term Tru used to describe regular British citizens. Not the ones who were on the telly or sitting around a conference table at MI6. But real people with briefcases and backpacks, runny noses and slobbering babies. These were the ones she'd sworn to protect, and seeing their faces to and from work was a twice daily reminder of how important her job was.

She was walking among them in the King's Cross St. Pancras tube station on a Monday morning when a man began to carefully follow her. During his years with MI6 he'd had high-level surveillance training, but he hardly needed those skills for this. Because of her height and limp, Tru was easy to pick out, even among the crush of commuters.

He never had to get closer than fifteen meters to keep

her in his sights. To make sure she didn't see him, he wore a blue cap and sunglasses, and when they reached the platform for the Victoria line, he turned the other way and kept his eye on her by watching in the security mirror hanging from the ceiling. When the train heading toward Vauxhall Cross arrived, he waited until after she boarded before getting on one car behind her.

They'd only just pulled out of the station when his phone buzzed, signaling the arrival of a series of texts:

I saw you the moment I stepped foot in King's Cross.

Meet me at the Wilton Road exit of Victoria station.

The hat and glasses are fooling no one.

Mother shook his head and laughed. He should've known better than to think he could outfox the fox. He'd come to London for just one reason: to talk to Tru. It had reached a point where he needed to tell her about Magpie, and he had to do that face-to-face and away from the prying eyes and ears of Vauxhall Cross.

Now that he suspected Rutledge may have been murdered, he wanted the team to go to San Francisco, and he couldn't do that without looping in Tru. A day trip to Oxford was one thing. But the seven of them flying off to California would be impossible to hide. Besides, if they uncovered Magpie's identity, he'd need to tell her.

His problem was that he didn't want to mention anything about Clementine or the photograph of the kids. If his wife was, in fact, a double agent, then the odds were that Tru already knew and was somehow involved. He wanted to get the green light to go to San Francisco without letting on that he was getting closer to finding Clemmie.

Mother got off the train at Victoria station and exited onto Wilton Road. There he saw Tru waiting impatiently, her collar flipped up to fight the morning chill, her face frozen in a disapproving scowl.

"What took you so bloody long?" she asked, irritated.

"I came straight up from the train," he said. "You couldn't have been waiting more than fifteen seconds."

"Not what took you so long to meet me on the street," she replied. "But what took you so long to come down to London to have this conversation. I've been waiting for days."

He looked at her totally confused.

"I assume you've come to discuss Magpie."

So much for his carefully made plans. Just as she'd been throughout his career, Tru was five steps ahead of him.

"You know?"

"I know you've been digging around."

"I knew you bugged the safe house."

"Of course I did," she said. "I'm a very tall woman who stands out in a crowd, yet has still managed to have quite a successful career in espionage. I didn't last for thirty-nine years at MI6 by trusting people and leaving them to their own devices. Now, let's talk about Magpie and let's do it quickly. I have an eight-fifteen with C, and I am never late."

Mother explained that he felt certain Rutledge had been murdered and explained the photo gallery of bird pictures and the ominous meaning behind the image of the three ravens.

"The picture was taken with his camera two days *after* he died," he said. "Someone is trying to send a message," he added, making no guess as to who that someone might be.

He didn't mention the bird books, because that would've required him to admit to the break-in at the Bodleian. But he did tell her about the pocket calendar, offering only "It came in the mail after his passing and was given to Monty by a porter she knew at Oxford."

Tru had many questions, but she neither had the time

nor the inclination to ask them. How this information came to light was not nearly as important as the fact that it had. Besides, despite what she said about not trusting people, she trusted Mother implicitly. If she sometimes snooped or eavesdropped, it was only out of her wish to protect him.

"What's your plan?" she asked.

"All seven of us will go to San Francisco. We'll come up with a cover story to explain why, but when we get there, we'll use his calendar to retrace his final days and see if we can make headway into who may have killed him."

"If you can answer that, you may well discover Magpie's true identity."

"Exactly," he said.

"Okay, the mission is approved. But it will be a verbal approval only. Just this conversation. No record. No communication. No one in Vauxhall Cross will know. There's no telling what Magpie hears in that building, so we'll have to maintain radio silence."

"Of course," he said.

"If there comes a moment of dire need to communicate while you're in the field, you are to contact me directly on my private mobile, not the work one I just texted you on."

He gave her a look. "I don't have the number for your private mobile."

"Yes you do," she assured. "I put it into the contacts on your phone while I was standing here waiting for you."

"You can do that?" he asked, surprised.

"I'm Tru. I can do whatever I please. It's under the name Harrison Marcus."

He smiled. "You don't much look like a 'Harrison Marcus.'"

"Says the man named 'Mother.'"

He smirked and asked, "Anything else?"

"Yes," she said. "You desperately need to work on surveillance skills. Today's demonstration was pathetic. You've really gotten rusty."

"Yes, ma'am," he said, duly chastened. "But to be fair, I was intending for you to see me. I just didn't want to approach you close to home or close to work."

"Tell yourself that if it makes you feel better," she said with a wink. She started to walk away, but stopped and turned back to say, "And make sure to tell Sydney and Brooklyn that they were outstanding during their testimonies in Parliament. I was quite proud of them both." There was a pause, and then she added, "You and Monty have done a right good job with them. All five of them."

"Thank you, ma'am."

That evening, Mother returned to the FARM and informed everyone that they were heading to California for Operation Golden Gate. He was at the dining room table working out the cover story with Monty and Sydney when Brooklyn entered the room with a stunned look on her face.

"Are you okay, sweetie?" asked Monty.

"Yeah, Brook," said Sydney. "You look like you've seen a ghost."

"I found them," Brooklyn said slowly, almost as if she didn't believe what she was saying.

"Who?" asked Sydney, confused.

Brooklyn looked directly at Mother and said, "I found Robert and Annie."

Chloe and Griffin

"WHAT DO YOU MEAN YOU FOUND ROBERT and Annie?" a thunderstruck Mother asked, his voice loud enough to attract the others from the neighboring rooms.

"I mean I've identified the names they're using and the school they attend," Brooklyn said. "It's possible that Clementine's withdrawn them, but they were there as recently as a few months ago."

Mother sat in a daze as he wrapped his head around this development.

"Did I hear that right?" Paris asked as he hurried into the room with Rio and Kat right behind him.

"You found them?" asked Rio. "How?"

"Ever since Kat figured out that the picture was taken in San Francisco, I've been running different search protocols through Beny," Brooklyn said. "First, I checked hotel registers within fifty miles of the city on the dates around when the picture was taken. But that didn't work because there were just too many rooms and no way to know if Clementine had put all of them on the register. Or even if she was using a hotel. Then I searched flight manifests for arrivals at nearby airports for the three weeks leading up to that date and departures for three weeks after," said Brooklyn. "That's six weeks of flights to and from three large international airports."

"Wow," said Sydney. "That had to be a bigger number than the hotel rooms."

"Much bigger," said Brooklyn. "But it was also a precise number. I knew that if they flew to San Francisco, each of them had to have a ticket. I also knew that Clementine is an expert at lying low so I thought about the way we fly: usually on separate reservations, but always on the same plane. So I had Beny search for every combination of three people who arrived and left on the same flights during those time frames. Then I narrowed that to only include groups in which at least one of those passengers was a child."

"And what did that leave you?" asked Rio.

"A massive number," she answered. "But we've got a supercomputer that can perform five hundred trillion floating-point operations per second." She flashed a proud smile. "My boy Beny was engineered for massive numbers. So I had him start searching for each of those people on social media."

"There's no way that Clemmie would let the kids be on social media," said Mother.

"Right," said Brooklyn. "That's when Tru came to the rescue."

"You told Tru about this?" Mother asked, panicked.

"No," she said. "Of course not. But I thought about what she said that night we ate feijoada. She said that she could tell the recipe was from Rio de Janeiro not because of the ingredients it had, but because it was missing the orange slices."

"*Sometimes the answer lies not in what you see, but in what is missing,*" Sydney said, repeating what Tru had told them.

"Exactly," said Brooklyn.

Kat smiled. "You had Beny identify which names *didn't* have social media accounts."

"Yes," answered Brooklyn. "I told him to eliminate the names of anyone whose picture he found more than five times. I figured there might be a couple of slip-ups or photos that were tagged wrong."

"So he's looking for people who aren't there?" said Sydney. "That's . . ."

"Brilliant," said Monty, finishing the sentiment.

"Thanks," Brooklyn said. "That still left a lot of people, especially because we're dealing with a bunch of kids who are too young to be on social. But now it was a much more manageable number. So I took things that we know about Robert and Annie and included them as search variables, like Robert's glasses and asthma, and the fact that Annie is an excellent swimmer and wears braces. That led me to Chloe and Griffin Mass. His eye doctor is right across the street from her orthodontist. And even though her water polo team is championship caliber, she's always missing from the photos celebrating their victories."

"Chloe and Griffin?" Mother said, his voice full of emotion. "Chloe was the name of Clemmie's best friend when she was growing up, and Griffin is her mother's maiden name." For him, this was confirmation. "You really have found them. That's amazing. Where are they?"

This was the part that made Brooklyn hesitate. The one gray cloud in the happy news.

"Rose Hill," she said. "It's a boarding school in Australia. Just outside of Sydney."

The news hung in the air for a moment before Paris turned to Mother. "I thought you checked out all the boarding schools in Sydney a few years ago."

"Not all of them," Sydney said softly, her voice cracking.

This was the reaction Brooklyn had worried about. Three and a half years earlier, Mother had rushed to Australia after Clementine was spotted at the Sydney airport. He had a list of all the boarding schools in the area and visited them one by one, posing as a police officer looking for a pair of missing children.

"He still had three schools left to check when he met me," she continued. "Or rather, when he got stuck with me." She looked up at him, tears in her eyes. "I'm the reason you missed them. It's my fault. I'm so sorry."

"Sydney, that's not how it is at all," he said. But it was too late.

She tried to stop the tears, but she couldn't. Instead, she darted out of the room and up the stairs.

Mother chased after her, but paused quickly to say to Brooklyn, "Thank you so much, Brooklyn, but I have to . . ."

"Of course," Brooklyn said.

Mother chased after Sydney and caught up with her in her room. She was sitting on the edge of her bed sobbing, her face buried in her palms.

Mother sat down, put his arm around her, and pulled her in tight, his body rocking ever so slightly. "You are not to blame for anything. You must understand that."

She went to reply, but she couldn't make words come out. So she just closed her eyes and nestled against him, and continued to cry.

27.

Bletchley Park

THE WORK DONE AT BLETCHLEY PARK was arguably the greatest achievement in the history of the Secret Intelligence Service. During World War II, the mansion and its surrounding estate were converted into a clandestine code-breaking facility. MI6 staffed it with mathematicians, linguists, and even chess champions. At one point, the Service surreptitiously ran a crossword competition in the *Daily Telegraph* and then secretly contacted the winners to recruit them as well. That was how desperate the British government was to find people who were good at solving puzzles.

It paid off. It was thought by many that the work accomplished at Bletchley Park shortened the war by two to four years and swung the outcome in favor of the Allies.

Interestingly, although the heroes of war are often imagined as strong young men, seventy-five percent of the people who worked at Bletchley were women. There were nearly eight thousand in all, and after the war they were forced to keep their service a secret for more than thirty years.

That always bothered Magpie, whose grandmother had been one of them. She was a Wren, the name given to female members of the Royal Navy, and she worked in Hut Eight, which played a crucial role in Bletchley's history. This is where the team led by Alan Turing first deciphered the unbelievably complex codes created by the German Enigma machine, which was the key to Bletchley's success. Magpie had no problem idolizing a woman who'd help save Britain, while at the same time working with its present-day enemies to undermine it.

Now that it was finally declassified, Bletchley was a historic park open to the public. Tourists would come to learn about the vital work that took place here. Couples and families would come to picnic and enjoy a pleasant day walking around a grand estate. And Magpie would come for inspiration when a problem, or enigma, seemed too hard to solve. There was no better location for finding solutions than sitting on a bench and looking across the lake toward Hut Eight.

What's the code, Nan? How do the pieces fit together?

The puzzle currently bedeviling Magpie had to do with Alexandra Montgomery.

After studying her MI6 employment record, Magpie knew that she was a supremely talented cryptologist stationed at a research center known as the FARM. Interestingly, the FARM wasn't just an MI6 cover. It was also an actual working climate research station. And it had a peculiar outreach for young people from difficult backgrounds who aspired to be scientists.

That was the part that was vexing Magpie.

How do the children fit into all this?

They were officially known as the FARM Fellows, and Magpie tried to learn more about them by performing a quick phone search. There was some information on the FARM website, but it was vague and offered no indication of how children were selected for the program. Additionally, none of the current fellows appeared to have social media accounts, which seemed unusual for children of this age.

Magpie knew that two girls on the *Sylvia Earle* attended the elite Kinloch Abbey, which was close to the FARM. And it was the web search of Kinloch that yielded the breakthrough.

It was a viral video. An eleven-second clip titled "Stop-arazzi." In the clip, a television cameraman slams into a student and comically collapses to the ground outside the front gate of the school. Magpie recognized the boy, having seen him with the others in London.

Magpie watched it over and over at least twenty times, laughing at each viewing. Laughing first because of the humor of the pratfall, but later because of the recognition of what the boy had done.

It was easy to miss.

At first glance, it appeared only that Paris had stood tall and the cameraman had slammed into him and fallen. But after repeated viewings, Magpie realized Paris had actually adjusted his feet and made a subtle turn. If he hadn't, he would've been bulldozed, or they both would have crashed.

It was so reflexive that Paris probably didn't even realize he'd done it. That's what happens when you've been trained well. You do things automatically when a situation arises. This wasn't an instinctive maneuver; it was something that had been taught and learned.

Magpie had learned the same maneuver at the MI6 training academy.

"Well, look at you," Magpie said to the screen. "You're not a boy. You're a spy." And if he was a spy, then perhaps the two girls on the ship were spies too.

This Operation Is Hot

OF ALL THE THINGS SHE DID WELL, AND there were many, one of the most important skills Monty had was the ability to inject humor and lightness into moments that otherwise felt overwhelming. The way she did this wasn't by sidestepping problems, but rather by taking them head-on. That's the approach she took as they drove from Aisling to the Edinburgh Airport in an oversize passenger van, well past its prime, painted ocean blue with the FARM logo on each side.

She was behind the wheel, as usual, and noticed that

things were particularly quiet behind her. In the rearview mirror, she saw that everybody had their earbuds in and was lost in their own world, their faces deep in thought.

"Headphones out," she called back. "You'll have plenty of time to vegetate on the flight to America. Besides, if you want to listen to music, we have a perfectly good sound system on the Blue Whale," she said, calling the van by its nickname.

"You call that a sound system?" asked Sydney. "It's a cassette player. It's from the 1900s."

"Yeah, well, so am I," Monty replied.

"I don't even think they make cassettes anymore," said Kat.

"They don't have to," Monty said. "Because I make my own."

There was a groan throughout the van. Monty's homemade mixtapes were filled with what they collectively called "old people music."

"Here's the deal: We can either talk or I can play one of my mixtapes," offered Monty.

"Talk," Sydney said quickly. "We can talk."

"That hurts, Syd, but it's good for us to talk," she replied. "So tell me, why the glum faces? What's bothering you guys?"

"I don't know," said Paris. "Maybe the fact that we're undertaking a mission that's incredibly complex."

"Is it?" asked Monty. "Let's break it down and see. Rio, why don't you list off one of the objectives?"

"Objective one, figure out who killed Parker Rutledge," he answered.

"Okay, sounds straightforward," she said. "What's so challenging about that?"

"The fact that he's been dead for six months and there are almost certainly no remaining clues," Paris answered. "Or that when he died, the authorities ruled it a death by natural causes so they didn't look into things when they could."

"Okay, I'll give you that one," Monty conceded. "Who can give me another objective?"

"Objective two, identify Magpie," said Sydney. "That should be easy considering MI6 has been trying to do it for nearly a decade and has come up empty."

"We're also looking for a bird book that was *possibly* hidden by a spy *somewhere* in greater San Francisco," said Kat.

"Oh," said Mother. "Don't forget that we're trying to track down a meeting between Rutledge and Dr. Berliner, you know, who died nearly fifty years ago."

Monty flashed a comical frowny face into the mirror for them to see. "Okay, now I'm convinced. It does sound difficult."

"And we're forgetting the biggest objective of all," said Sydney. "As soon as we land in San Francisco, Mother hops a plane for Australia to go look for Robert and Annie. That's been the main objective from the beginning."

"Let me get this straight," said Monty. "That's five virtually impossible objectives, spread across two continents, three if you count the one we're on, with absolutely no support from MI6."

"That sounds about right," said Brooklyn.

"We're going to have to change our saying," said Monty.

"What do you mean?" asked Kat.

"This operation isn't *hot*," said Monty. "This operation is a *hot mess*!" Everyone laughed, and she let that feeling take hold for a moment. Then with all seriousness she added, "But we are still a go. And there's no team better equipped to pull off this madness than the seven people in this ridiculous blue van."

She reached over and pushed a cassette into the stereo, and the James Bond theme started playing. It was part of her Super Secret Spy mixtape that she liked to use to get everybody fired up. Mother reached over from the passenger seat and turned the volume up all the way, and even though the song didn't have any lyrics, they all still sang along.

When they reached the airport, they followed their normal protocol and split up into separate groups for the flights: first Edinburgh to London and then London to San Francisco before Mother flew by himself to Australia. Rio and Brooklyn sat together, which was a positive sign for the growth of their friendship. They hadn't hit it off at first, but they were slowly getting to know each other. Mother sat them in the same row, hoping that over the course of thirteen hours on a plane, they might find a few new things to talk and bond over. Kat wasn't much of a talker, but like Monty, she found code-breaking thrilling. The two of them sat next to each other working with computer tablets on which they'd copied pages from Rutledge's bird books. The better they understood his symbols, the better chance they'd have of figuring out what he'd learned about Magpie. Mother sat alone in a rear seat that let him keep an eye on everyone. The solitude helped him prepare mentally for the chance that he might see his children for the first time in five years.

That left Sydney with Paris, which was ideal for the mood she was in. Not only were they the oldest, but they were the first two to join the group. They had history, and there were some things that she could say only to him.

She was looking out across the Atlantic when she said, "This operation isn't the only thing that's a hot mess. I've been useless for months."

"That's crazy," he replied. "You've been awesome since the day I met you. I haven't seen any mess."

She turned back toward him and smiled. "Then you're blind. At first I think it was mostly jealousy about Brooklyn. I'm kind of ashamed of that. She's been nothing but great to me. And I love her, but sometimes I get jealous of how good she is at all of this."

"How do you think I felt when you came along?"

"You were jealous of me?" she asked, surprised.

"I don't know if 'jealous' is the right word," he said. "But it sure seemed like you were good at a lot of things that I wasn't."

"But you're amazing at so many things," she said. "You've got crazy good skills."

"Exactly," he said. "As do you. However talented and amazing Brooklyn is, it has no impact on how talented and amazing you are. We're not competing. We're *conspiring*, like the ravens. We're a team. The better each of us is, the better all of us are."

"I know," she said. "But sometimes it feels like a competition."

"Like when you thought Mother had picked Brooklyn for some secret mission and left you out in the cold?" he said. "But you were jealous of something that wasn't real. It wasn't a mission; it was all about the photograph. It was about his kids."

"I know that too," she said. "And that's when it hit me. That's when I realized what the big problem was."

"There's a bigger problem?" he said with a mix of humor and compassion.

She nodded. "Massive."

"What?"

"Robert and Annie," she said. "I mean, I hate myself for even thinking that, much less saying it out loud. It's awful what happened, and I am literally praying that when Mother goes to Australia, he reconnects with them and they get to be a family again."

"So am I," said Paris. "Why is that a problem?"

"What about us? We're the fill-in kids he stumbled across while looking for them. But when he finds them, he won't need us anymore. What's going to happen to us?"

"It's not like that," said Paris. "We're a family."

"I thought that too," said Sydney. "But really we're not. We're *like* a family, but we aren't one. There's a difference. That's what I figured out during that hearing at Parliament. We act like a family, but when that evil cow was attacking me, she made it clear that as far as the rest of the world was concerned, I was an orphan. I was less than."

She sighed and turned back to the window to look at the endless ocean, and the sun setting over a distant horizon. "I never felt so alone in my life."

Chinatown

SAN FRANCISCO WAS COSMOPOLITAN with diverse neighborhoods and a cultural personality built on contradictions. It was a global leader in the development of new technology, but the only city in the world that still used old-fashioned cable cars. Surrounded on three sides by water, it was compact and crowded, yet still home to massive public parks, including one where a small herd of bison roamed. And despite countless breathtaking vistas, its biggest tourist attraction was unwieldy and unattractive: a former prison known as the Rock. Even San Francisco's nickname had an air of uncertainty.

Fog City.

Any questions as to why it was called that were answered the first morning the team was in town. They'd awakened early, their internal clocks out of sync eight time zones from home, and stepped out of their hotel into a hazy cityscape. The visibility was so poor that they heard their first cable car before they saw it, its bell ringing out through the morning mist.

The team split into two groups, hoping to reconstruct the final days of Parker Rutledge's life. Monty, Sydney, Brooklyn, and Kat headed to Muir Woods where Rutledge's body had been discovered, while Paris and Rio went to Chinatown to look for someone named Fay Chie Hong. According to his datebook, Parker met with Hong two days before he died.

"This is so cool," Rio said as they hopped onto the cable car. Rather than sit down, he stood on the running board and hung off the side, one hand holding tight while the other cut through the air like the tip of an eagle's wing.

"Why don't you sit down?" Paris asked nervously. "If you get hurt, Monty will blame me."

"All I'm doing is riding," Rio protested.

"No," said Paris. "I'm riding. You're . . . *dangling*."

"The whole reason this pole is here is so that people can hang on."

Paris wasn't in the mood to debate, so he opted for a surefire technique to get Rio to do what he wanted. "If you sit down, I'll let you pick where we eat lunch."

"Really?"

Paris nodded. "Really."

Rio's love of food trumped everything else, and he instantly sat on the wooden bench right next to Paris. "I'm thinking one of the big three: burgers, burritos, or pizza," he said. "I know good places for all of them."

Paris gave him a look. "You know good places? Here in San Francisco?"

"I've been researching a bunch of restaurant review sites," he answered. "I loaded the best spots onto a mapping app on my phone, so I can always tell which one's closest."

Paris shook his head in amazement. "How is it you can do that, but you never seem to get your homework done?"

"Believe me," Rio said, "if algebra tasted as good as a fajita beef burrito covered in queso, I would never miss an assignment." He paused and savored the thought. "Wow, just saying that out loud makes me hungry."

Paris couldn't believe it. "You had a full breakfast of pancakes and bacon at the hotel not thirty minutes ago, and you're already hungry?"

Rio smiled proudly and said, "I know. It's a gift."

They got off the cable car next to Zee's Bakery and Confectionery. This was where Clementine had taken the photo of Robert and Annie. They looked around to see if there was anything nearby that hinted at a connection to Rutledge but found nothing. Still, Paris took three panoramic shots of the neighborhood so they could examine it later when they were together with everybody else. Kat had proven on many occasions that she noticed things no one else did.

Rio inhaled a lungful of the sweet smell of fortune cookies being baked in industrial quantities. "Do they put the piece of paper with the fortune on it inside the cookie before they bake it or after?"

Paris scoffed as if it was a ridiculous question, but then paused. "You know, I have no idea. You'd think the fortunes would burn if they went in the oven, right?"

"But if you wait until after, how do you slide it in without breaking the cookie?"

Paris did a quick search on his phone. "It's in the middle of the process."

"What do you mean?" asked Rio.

"They bake the cookies as flat circles," Paris answered as he read about it. "Then they put the fortune in and fold the cookie while it's still warm. When it cools, it holds its shape and the fortune is inside."

"Look at us," Rio joked. "It's still early and we're already learning new things. I wonder how Mother had the fortune cookie made when he proposed to Clementine."

"You're talking about a bloke who can have fake passports or fraudulent masterpieces produced on the spot. I'm guessing a proposal hidden inside a fortune cookie is easy compared to those things."

Rio looked at the sidewalk where Robert and Annie had been standing in the photo. He turned to Paris and asked, "You think he's going to find them?"

"Who?"

"Mother," answered Rio. "Do you think he's going to find Robert and Annie?"

Paris had thought about this a lot since his conversation with Sydney on the plane. "I hope so," he answered. "I think Brooklyn did an amazing job locating their school, and I think he's probably going to find them when he gets to Australia." He paused for a moment and considered the questions Sydney had raised about how that would affect them. "What happens after that? I don't know."

Rio read the apprehension in his voice and flashed a smile. "Of course you know. We've got each other. You, me, Brooklyn, Sydney, and Kat are brothers and sisters. We'll work out the rest."

"Yes, we will," Paris responded. "Now let's go find Fay Chie Hong." He checked his phone to look at the picture he'd taken of the entry in Rutledge's datebook:

Fay Chie Hong – 2:30 p.m.

Duncombe + Jackson

Chinatown

There were seven different Fay Hongs who lived in San Francisco, but none had the middle name Chie. Three, however—Fay Lin Hong, Fay Jun Hong, and Fay San Hong—lived in Chinatown. Since that was as close a match as Paris and Rio could find, they started with them.

Although it was a popular destination for visitors, Chinatown wasn't a tourist attraction. It was one of the largest Chinese enclaves outside of Asia—a vibrant, thriving community that stretched for twenty-four blocks. Once they passed through the postcard-perfect Dragon

Gate, it was as if they'd entered a different country. The architecture changed, the signs all featured Chinese characters, and suddenly many of the people were speaking Cantonese. It was also disorienting because in addition to the main streets, there was a maze of narrow alleys and walkways that didn't show up on GPS.

It took them a while to find the apartment belonging to not–Fay Chie Hong number one, but when they knocked on the door, nobody answered. They were luckier with not–Fay Chie Hong number two, but only slightly so. A man answered and said that she'd moved to San Diego.

"That's too bad," Paris replied. "I don't suppose you know when she moved."

He gave Paris an annoyed look and answered, "January seventeenth, around five thirty in the evening."

"Wow," said Paris. "That's really specific."

"Yeah," snapped the man. "I remember because that's when I got home from work and found a note saying she'd left me for the lead guitarist in a band called Sonic Platypus."

Paris and Rio shared a look, unsure how to respond, and after an awkward silence Paris offered, "Guitarists—I hate those guys."

From there, they walked along an alley with murals

on each side and laundry that hung from the fire escapes above. "I feel kind of bad," Paris said.

"Why, because you made him talk about getting dumped?"

"That," he said, "but also because I really want to look up Sonic Platypus to hear what type of music they play."

"I know," said Rio. "I do too. Something about the name."

They both quickly pulled up the group on their phones. Paris pressed play, and the sounds of screaming punk rock filled the alley for about six seconds until he turned it off. They were no longer interested in Sonic Platypus.

"Now I feel really bad," said Rio. "Not only did she dump him, but she dumped him for a guy in a band that's terrible."

Unlike the previous two, they actually met not–Fay Chie Hong number three face-to-face. She lived on Old Chinatown Lane in a warehouse that had been converted into artists' studios. Her business card was taped to the buzzer panel next to the front door and read, FAY SAN HONG ILLUSTRATIONS AND COMICS. Under that, she'd handwritten, "For deliveries press 2."

"She draws comics," Rio said, excited.

"That's pretty cool," said Paris. "I wonder if she's done any that we know."

Fay San Hong's studio was the coolest workplace Paris and Rio had ever seen. Which was saying something considering their "office" was a secret underground room with a supercomputer. There were sketches and illustrations of various characters everywhere. She had tons of action figures in different poses for inspiration. And the bookcases that lined the wall were teeming with comics and graphic novels.

"Is that an actual working classic Spider-Man pinball machine?" Rio asked, amazed.

"Yeah," she said. "I play it to clear my mind when I need to work out a storyline."

While her studio was great, as far as Operation Golden Gate went, Fay San Hong number three was a big miss. She had never heard of Parker Rutledge or R.F. Stroud, and she never had an appointment to meet anyone matching his description.

"You want to look again so you can be sure?" asked Paris, showing her a photo of Parker that he'd gotten from one of the Dodos. "It would've been six months ago."

"I'm positive," she said. "I'm good with faces. It's a necessity of the job."

"Okay, thanks," said Rio. "By the way, I really like your art. Can I get a business card so I can order some of your comics when we get home?"

"Yeah," added Paris. "That would be great."

"I can do better than that," she said with a friendly grin. She walked over to a table and pulled two comic books out of a box. "You can each take one of these. If you want to order more, the info's on the back."

"What's it about?" asked Rio.

"A girl named Molly Wu who's part of a secret society that polices the undead who live in underground tunnels beneath San Francisco."

"There are tunnels underneath San Francisco?" asked Paris.

"Oh, yeah," said Fay San. "There are all kinds of hidden secrets around town. Tunnels, caves, dark alleys. It's that kind of city."

Their eyes lit up as she handed the books to them.

"Thanks so much," said Paris.

"Fog City," Rio said, reading the title off the cover, which featured an image of a girl facing off with a zombie in front of the Dragon Gate. "This looks amazing."

When they got back to the alley, Rio started flipping through the comic as he asked Paris, "Where to next?

We've visited all the Fay Hongs in Chinatown. I say we find a Mexican place, order burritos, and read this awesome-looking comic."

"We're in Chinatown and you're craving Mexican food?" asked Paris. "What would you want if we were in Little Italy? Indian?"

"I can't help it," said Rio. "I suddenly have a craving for burritos, and when it comes to cravings, I have to trust my gut. Literally."

"Now that you mention it, burritos do sound good," Paris agreed. "But in addition to Fay Hong's name, the diary also mentions Duncombe and Jackson, so we should check out that intersection first."

"Okay," Rio said. "But then we eat. I'm starving."

Once again, the GPS had trouble navigating the maze of back alleys. They thought they were near Duncombe Court when they cut through a passageway running behind a row of restaurants. This was not an alley normally visited by tourists. It was dirty and cramped. The path was partially obstructed by trash cans, recycling bins, and stacks of bundled cardboard. Two kitchen workers on their break were sitting on a pair of overturned milk crates.

One was big and burly and wore an apron that

looked like it had once been white but was now dish-water gray. He sat with his back pressed against the wall as he ate from a small metal bowl. The other was lean and drank from a cup as he looked at something on his phone screen.

Between the piles of trash, the workers, and the narrowness of the alley, there was no way for Paris and Rio to pass without intruding into their personal space.

"Excuse me," Paris said as he tried to slip by.

The bigger man barked at him in Cantonese, and Paris gave him a confused look.

"I'm sorry," he said. "We're just trying to pass through."

The man continued speaking.

"I'm sorry, I don't understand," Paris replied. "We're lost. Do you know where Duncombe Court is? *Duncombe Court*?"

The man replied again, getting more animated as he did, and Paris decided to take a long shot and tell him the name of the person they were looking for.

"Fay Chie Hong?"

The man flashed him the universal *What did you just say?* expression, although Paris couldn't tell if it was the positive or the negative usage.

He said it again, trying to pronounce it carefully, but "Fay Chie" was as far as he got.

The man stood up from his makeshift seat and puffed out his chest. He'd gone from confused to angry lightning quick, but luckily for Paris, the other man stepped between them. The two men had a boisterous conversation, all in Cantonese, that ended with the thinner man pointing toward the restaurant and the other man going back inside.

Paris let out a sigh of relief and asked, "Does he know—"

"You called him 'fat boy,'" the thinner man said.

Paris was horrified. "Wait, what? I did? That's terrible. That was a total accident."

"I know it was," said the man. "That was obvious, but he's sensitive about his weight. Are you looking for Fay Chie Hong?"

"Yes," Paris said, excited. "Do you know her?"

"Fay Chie Hong isn't a person. It's a place. It's this place," he said, motioning to the alleyway.

Paris and Rio both looked around confused. "*This* is Fay Chie Hong?"

"I know, it's not much," said the man. "If you want to explore Chinatown, I recommend Grant Avenue."

"We're not really exploring," answered Rio. "We're looking for someone."

Paris had an idea. "Wait a second, this is where you come out for your breaks."

"Twice a day for fifteen minutes," said the man.

"Maybe you can help," Paris responded as he pulled out his phone to show him the picture of Parker Rutledge. "This man met somebody in this alley last October. I know it's a long shot, but I don't suppose you saw him and remember anything about him?"

The man looked at the picture and much to his surprise, he recognized Parker. He'd seen him in the alley the previous October, meeting with a pair of men who were regulars at the restaurant. And while he didn't know anything about Parker, he knew exactly who the two men were. They were from the Ministry of State Security and worked at the Chinese Consulate on Laguna Street. They were secret police, and they did not like people digging into their business, which is why the man handed the phone back to Paris and said, "Sorry, no. I've never seen him before."

Muir Woods

THE MORNING FOG STILL BLANKETED the water, so as Monty and the girls approached the Golden Gate Bridge, it seemed as though its famous orange towers rose magically through the clouds. This was the ultimate symbol of San Francisco and one that exceeded expectations.

"I knew it'd be pretty," Sydney marveled. "But it's absolutely gorgeous."

The bridge marked the division between the Pacific Ocean and San Francisco Bay and connected two peninsulas, one home to the city and the other rich with natural beauty. The transformation was so quick and dramatic that just ten miles north of the soaring skyscrapers was a forest of towering trees hundreds of feet tall, many five to eight hundred years old. This was where Parker Rutledge's life came to an end and where their search for answers would begin.

"Look at that," Kat said, pointing at a rustic wooden sign hanging over the entrance to the forest.

MUIR WOODS

NATIONAL MONUMENT

NATIONAL PARK SERVICE DEPARTMENT OF INTERIOR

"Rutledge took a picture of that sign the morning he died." She pulled up the image on her phone and studied it as she tried to determine where he was standing when he took it.

"I thought he only took pictures of birds," said Sydney.

"Mostly," said Brooklyn. "But there are also lots of them featuring signs for places like national parks, wildlife refuges, city limits, and that sort of thing. It's really quite brilliant."

"How so?" asked Sydney.

"There are thousands of pictures on his cloud account," answered Brooklyn. "It would be difficult to remember where each was taken. But whenever he arrived someplace new, he always took a picture of the sign for that place. So when you scan through the gallery, you always know where you are."

"That *is* smart," said Sydney.

"Here we go," Kat said, still checking the photo against the sign. "This is where he was standing."

"You're kind of creeping me out there," said Brooklyn. "Why do you care where he was standing?"

"Because someone killed him less than two hours after he took this," she said. "These pictures are as close as we'll get to crime scene photos."

"Okay, that makes sense."

Sydney stood behind Kat and looked up at the picture to compare the past with the present. "The sign looks darker in the photo," she said. "I think it's wet. So I'm guessing that means it was a rainy day."

"That's good," said Monty. "Every detail helps."

Next to the entrance was a welcome center with three ticket windows. Monty paid their admission fee and asked the man working there, "Do you know if Ranger Gilson is here today?"

"Kristin?" he said. "Sure. She's at the trading company just down the boardwalk to the right."

"Thank you."

Kristin Gilson had discovered Rutledge's body and filed the report that Brooklyn found online. She was the only person they knew for certain had direct knowledge of what happened that day. Interviewing her was essential, which is why Monty had prepared.

Whenever she had the opportunity, she tried to research someone's past before asking them questions. Usually, you had only one chance with an interview. The right bit of information could mean the difference between someone opening up and someone giving short, useless answers.

With non-spies, or "civilians" as they called them, research was usually as simple as a quick scan through social media. For example, Gilson had active accounts on multiple platforms as well as a travel and adventure blog. Within twenty minutes, Monty knew that she was a native Californian who had a career in the army before joining the National Park Service. She was an avid rock climber who loved camping and Labrador retrievers.

It was her love of dogs that Monty planned to exploit.

Like a great number of buildings in national parks, the Muir Woods Trading Company was painted dark brown to give it a rustic, natural feel. It was located a hundred yards into the park and featured a small store, a café, and an information desk staffed by a park ranger.

This is where they found Kristin Gilson. She was tall and fit with long black hair, her love of rock climbing evidenced by lean, strong arms. She wore the standard park ranger's uniform of tan shirt, dark green pants, and a wide-brimmed tan hat.

Monty went straight to the information desk while the others continued into the store to get out of the way. People tended to talk more when there were fewer people around.

"Good morning," Monty said. "Are you Ranger Gilson?"

"Yes, I am," said the woman. "How can I help you?"

"I was hoping you could give me some information," said Monty.

"That's why I'm here. Do you want to know about the park? The redwoods?"

"Actually, it's about something that happened here around six or seven months ago." Monty subtly added a hint of emotion to her voice. "A family friend passed away in the park. He had a heart attack."

The ranger's demeanor changed instantly from

cheerful to practiced. "I'm sorry to hear that, but I'm not authorized to discuss—"

Monty managed to create the hint of oncoming tears as she interrupted. "I mean, he was more than a friend. He was like family. He lived down the street and was best friends with my father. He traveled a lot, and when I was growing up, I would always watch his dogs for him when he'd go on trips."

At the mention of a dog, Gilson leaned forward slightly. Monty's strategy was working, but she still had a way to go. She was careful not to rush her story.

"In fact, my father was taking care of his dogs when he came on that last trip to California," Monty continued. "Dad still has them. He took them in of course. But even though it's been half a year, I get the sense the dogs keep expecting him to come home and walk through the door."

The ranger cleared her throat and asked, "What kind of dogs are they?"

"Labradors," answered Monty. "He always had Labs. He loved the outdoors and said that they were the best kind of dog to take camping or hiking."

"He was absolutely right," said Gilson. "I have two Labs myself."

And Monty knew that she had her. But she still didn't push. She waited and let the conversation pause until the ranger filled it in. Gilson looked both ways to make sure no one could hear and said, "Was it a Mr. Rutledge?"

"That's him," said Monty. "Parker Rutledge. Good memory."

"Well, of course I remember. It's not the kind of thing that happens every day. I'm so sorry for your loss. How can I help you?"

"I'm not even sure that you can," said Monty. "I'm a teacher on a school trip, and I came to pay my respects. I guess I was wondering if you could just tell me what happened. That way, when I get home, I might be able to fill in some gaps for my father. Put him at ease a little bit."

"Of course," said Gilson. "He was up in the Cathedral Grove. I can show you where on a map." She opened a guide map and circled a spot. "If it's any consolation, the grove is peaceful and spiritual. It got its name because it feels like you're in a grand church when you're standing there. You should tell your father that the last images his friend saw were among God's most beautiful creations."

Monty was touched by the ranger's sensitivity. She even felt guilty for putting her through the emotional toll of it. "Are there any specific details you remember about that day that I can pass along to my father?"

"It was kind of drizzly, if I recall. Personally, I think that's when the forest is its prettiest. I opened up the park that day, and I remember Mr. Rutledge was the first one in. For some reason that stuck out to me. I don't think I said anything more than 'Welcome to Muir Woods.' But I do remember him being first."

"He was an avid bird-watcher," prompted Monty. "Is there part of the forest that's particularly good for doing that?"

"Not really," said Gilson. "There are spotted owls and pileated woodpeckers, but truthfully, redwood forests aren't great for birding. There aren't a lot of bugs, and birds go where the bugs are. I see a lot more birders when I'm working the Marin Headlands."

"You have another job?" said Monty.

"Same job, different location," said the ranger. "The park service manages more than twenty sites in the Golden Gate National Recreation Area. I rotate between three of them, although I'm primarily here at Muir Woods."

Monty paused as she led into a tender question. "Do you know who found him?"

Gilson nodded solemnly. "I did. He was in the grove, near the FDR plaque. He wasn't breathing, so I called for help on the radio and started performing CPR to resuscitate him. But it didn't work. I'm sorry about that. It kind of haunts you. Someone dying right in front of you. I've wondered what might have happened if I'd found him just a few minutes earlier. I wonder if I would have been able to save him."

"You can't think that way," said Monty. "What you did was great. Heroic, even."

"Thank you. Is there anything else?"

"One more thing. He usually carried a camera with him when he traveled. Do you remember if he had that?"

The woman shook her head. "No, I don't. But any personal property would've been loaded onto the ambulance with him. You'd have to check with the hospital about that."

"That's what I figured," said Monty. "Thank you so very much."

"Here," the woman said, pulling a business card out of her breast pocket. "This has the number of the office here at Muir Woods. If your dad would like to ask me anything, I'm more than happy to discuss it with him."

"That's very kind," Monty said, taking the card. "I really appreciate you talking about this with me. And I really appreciate everything you did to try to help Parker. Have a nice day."

"You too."

Monty slipped the card into her pocket and walked over to the store where the girls were looking at T-shirts and various redwood-themed knickknacks.

"Check this out," Sydney said excitedly when she saw Monty.

She led her past the souvenirs to a section for campers and hikers visiting the park. There were camping supplies, canned goods, hiking gear, and other everyday items you might need away from home.

"Do you see it?" asked Sydney, gesturing toward a shelf.

It took Monty a moment, but when she did, she smiled. "The envelope."

"That's right," said Sydney. "He bought it here."

On the shelf, next to pens and pads of paper, were envelopes identical to the distinctive padded one Parker used to mail his pocket calendar back to Oxford.

"So he gets here, buys the envelope, and mails his calendar back home," she said. "Why? He obviously didn't plan to do that. What happened here?"

"Something must've spooked him," said Sydney. "Or someone."

Monty turned to a man working at the checkout counter. "Excuse me. If I wanted to mail a letter, could I do it from the park?"

"Absolutely," answered the man. "We sell stamps, and there's a mailbox right in front of the trading company. A lot of people like to send their postcards from there. I think they expect it to have some sort of special postmark, but it doesn't. Still, it's convenient."

"Thank you," said Monty.

She tried to piece together what happened. She thought Sydney might be onto something. He got here and then he got spooked. By what?

They started out the door, but had to wait for Brooklyn, who was buying something.

"What are you getting?" asked Sydney.

"A new addition to my collection," Brooklyn answered, holding up a snow globe with a redwood scene inside it. "Only this one doesn't make snow."

"A snow globe that doesn't make snow?" said Sydney. "What does it make?"

"Fog," said Brooklyn. She gave it a vigorous shake and a mist filled the ball. "Isn't it great?"

"I love it," said Monty.

Monty always wanted the kids to enjoy the amazing

places they went, even when they were on a mission. That's why she didn't rush as they walked the half mile from the trading company to the Cathedral Grove. She wanted them to soak up the natural beauty of the redwoods.

"The colors are so vivid," Brooklyn said. "Such deep greens and browns."

"I like the way the sunlight breaks through the trees every now and then," said Sydney. "It looks like they're almost glowing."

Kat sucked in a deep breath. "I like the smell. It reminds me of Nepal."

Monty took a picture of the three of them sitting on a small wooden bridge spanning a creek that ran through the park, and another of them next to a giant cross section of a fallen redwood that had lived for more than a thousand years. In the cross section they could see all the rings that marked each year of the tree's life. Little arrows matched historic events to the ring from that year.

"That is so cool," Brooklyn said as she traced her finger along the rings. "This is what a thousand years looks like."

They reached the Cathedral Grove where a wooden sign read, ENTER QUIETLY.

It was a place of reflection for park visitors, so Monty talked in hushed tones as she laid out the scene as described by the ranger.

"His body was right here," she whispered. "Next to this plaque."

Alongside the pathway, in the center of a grove, was a bronze plaque commemorating a gathering held in 1945. Delegates to the newly forming United Nations came for a memorial service honoring President Franklin Roosevelt, who'd died just a month earlier. The UN held its first meetings in San Francisco's Grand Opera House, and it seemed fitting to honor the president who'd played such an important role in creating the organization.

They looked around the grove for about ten minutes, taking pictures and searching for even the barest hint of what could be a clue. When they were done, they went back down the path and sat on a row of wooden benches. Here, away from the quiet of the grove, they could talk more openly.

"What do we know?" said Brooklyn, asking the question that often started these types of conversations.

"We know that Parker Rutledge was the first to enter the woods when it opened at eight o'clock and that according to her report, Ranger Gilson found his body at ten forty-seven," said Monty.

"So something happened during those three hours that led to him being murdered," said Brooklyn.

"We know that he got spooked," said Sydney. "Or at least we think he did. Something happened that made him buy an envelope and send his datebook back to Oxford. Why would he do that?"

"Because he wanted to make sure no one saw it?" said Brooklyn.

"Or maybe to make sure someone specific didn't see it," said Sydney. "Maybe he saw someone here and was worried they'd get their hands on it."

"Who?" asked Brooklyn.

Sydney said, "Check the 'crime scene' photos. Let's look at the pictures he took to see if there's any hint in those."

Kat had all the pictures loaded up on her phone and scanned through them. "He took eleven pictures that morning," she said. "The first one is of the sign. He's got a bunch with this owl. There are a few just of the redwoods. And then there's this." She held it up for them to see.

The photograph was shot from across the creek, looking back toward the trading company. In the picture, a park ranger was talking to three people whose backs were turned to the camera.

"Is that ranger the same woman you just spoke to?" asked Kat.

"I think so," Monty answered as she used her fingers to zoom in on the image. "It would make sense. We know she was the ranger who opened the park that day."

"Then who is she talking to?" asked Kat. "He takes pictures of birds and signs. Sometimes trees. But never people. Who was so interesting that he decided to take this picture?"

"You mean, who scared him enough that he decided to mail home his datebook?" asked Brooklyn.

Something clicked for Sydney, and she grabbed the phone. "Let me see that," she said excitedly.

"What is it?" asked Brooklyn. "What do you see?"

"Mo Salah! Mo Salah!"

"Who's Mo Salah?" asked Brooklyn.

"He's a footballer," said Kat. "Even I know that and I don't know anything about football."

"I don't understand," said Brooklyn.

"Neither do I," added Monty.

"The boy in the picture is wearing a number eleven

Mo Salah Liverpool jersey," Sydney explained. "It's Robert. And this girl is wearing the same shirt she did in the picture from in front of the fortune cookie bakery. It's Robert and Annie."

Kat looked at the woman standing between them and said, "Which means that's Clementine."

Sydney nodded. "So he saw Clementine and he panicked."

Rose Hill

ANNIE

ANNIE WAS SUCH A GOOD WATER POLO player that her coach gave her a key to the aquatic center so she could do some extra training whenever she wanted. She liked the quiet of the pool at times like this when she had it all to herself. She walked to the edge of the water, tucked her hair into her swim cap, and dove in.

It had been almost six years since she'd last seen her father. Six years, seven countries, nine schools, and ten different names. She'd changed identities so often that she'd become highly skilled at filling in the gaps of newly created biographies. She was likable and friendly, but she avoided making friends. Not real ones at least. She'd made that mistake before and regretted it when the abrupt but inevitable announcement came that they were moving yet again. Other than swimming, the only continuity in her life was her brother.

They were close, and even though their mother told them not to, when they were alone they still called each other by their real names. It was their only true act of rebellion in what was an impossible situation. They didn't know why their lives had turned upside down when they did. They knew their mother had worked for MI6 and that something had gone terribly wrong. They'd been told they were hiding from very bad people, which seemed the only logical explanation for their current lifestyle. They'd also been told their father had died, and while they both acted as if they believed this, they secretly prayed that it wasn't true. They both dreamed that one day a door would open and he would walk back into their lives.

MOTHER

In the nearly six years since he'd last seen his children, Mother had searched for them tirelessly. He'd so often imagined what it would be like to reunite with them that he had several variations completely scripted out and memorized.

There'd been a half dozen times when he'd thought he was close to finding them, but none had been as promising as this. Still, he tried to temper his expectations as he walked up to the main office of Rose Hill Academy. He'd been disappointed too often. He took a deep breath before he entered and reminded himself to look sharp and act happy—traits in keeping with the role he was playing. He was posing as the father of a prospective student and had arranged for a tour of the campus.

ANNIE

Despite her nomadic existence, Annie considered herself happy. Somehow, she'd managed to detach the oddness of her circumstance from the day-to-day existence of being a teenager. Besides, all the other kids at her prep school were away from their homes and parents too. And many of them had families they described as "freak shows." She loved her mom and truly looked up to her. No matter what the real story was, something bad had happened and her mom had kept the family safe. And while Annie didn't always *believe* her, she did always *believe in* her.

MOTHER

"It's a gorgeous campus," Mother said as the headmaster showed him around the school. "Do you have a strong sports program?"

"It's very vigorous," he said. "Athletics aren't compulsory, but virtually all of our students participate in a sport no matter their skill level. And our girls compete in the top division across the board in basketball, footy, netball, you name it."

"What about water polo?" asked Mother. "My daughter loves water polo and competes on a travel team."

"Then she's in luck," the headmaster said with a big grin. "Our water polo team is one of the best in New South Wales."

Mother smiled. "She'll love hearing that. I don't suppose I can get a few minutes with the coach."

"I don't see why not. She should be in her office at the aquatic center."

"Wonderful."

Mother's heart raced as they headed toward the pool. And while he was thrilled at the possibility of being reunited with his kids, he did have one nagging concern. *What if they don't recognize me?* he thought. Not only had it been years since they'd seen him, but Mother had survived a terrible fire. In the reconstructive surgery afterward, MI6 had seen to it to change his appearance. This was to make sure no one in Umbra could recognize him. But what about his own family? Would they?

ANNIE

Annie's muscles burned as she put in lap after lap in the water. It was the off-season, and she was working on increasing her endurance. When she touched the wall for the last lap, she reached up and rested her arms on the edge of the pool as she took deep, full breaths.

That's when the door opened. She looked up expecting to see her coach, but instead it was a family member. She smiled the instant she saw him.

He looked both ways to make sure they were alone. "Hello, Annie."

"Hello, Robert. What brings you to the pool?"

"Looking for my favorite sister," he answered. "If you're almost done, we can eat some dinner while you try to explain my maths homework to me."

MOTHER

Meanwhile, 4,859 miles away, Mother tried to mask his emotions as the Rose Hill water polo coach gave him the disappointing news.

"Chloe was our star player," she said, referring to Annie by the cover name that Clementine had selected for her. "It's a shame she moved. You say your daughter played with her?"

"They met at a summer camp," he replied. "They'd kept in touch online. I hadn't realized she'd moved."

"About two or three months ago," said the coach.

"Do you know where she went?" he asked.

"Actually, no," she answered. "It was kind of all of a sudden. But her leaving opens up a spot on the offense, so maybe your daughter will be the one to fill it."

Mother forced a smile. "That would be great."

ANNIE

It had been three months since they'd suddenly left Rose Hill and Australia. It was a shame, because she'd really liked the school and loved being part of the water polo team. The team at her new school wasn't nearly as good, but other than that she was adjusting well.

New country. New school. New name. Same old routine.

32.

Fisherman's Wharf

THE TEAM PICKED UP DINNER AT A SEA-food stand on Fisherman's Wharf and ate it at the end of one of the nearby piers. With souvenir shops, sight-seeing boats, and street performers, the wharf was definitely more for tourists than locals. But the clam chowder was delicious, and the sunset view was impossible to beat. They found a pair of benches away from everybody so they could talk about what they'd learned during the day.

"So, Clementine was at Muir Woods when Parker

Rutledge was killed?" Paris said, turning it over in his head. "What do you think that means?"

"I think seeing her spooked him," said Sydney. "First, he took her picture, and he never took photographs of people. Then he bought an envelope and used it to mail his datebook home. I think he was worried she might get her hands on it."

"And what?" asked Rio skeptically. "You think Clementine killed Rutledge?"

"We don't want to think she'd do that, but it's definitely a possibility," said Brooklyn.

"Wow, a few months ago she saved your life, and now you think she's a killer," said Rio. "I don't buy it. No way."

Sydney had just swallowed a bite of her crab sandwich and asked, "Why not?"

"Two reasons," said Rio. "First of all, we think Magpie killed Rutledge, right?"

"Right," said Sydney. "And Clementine could be Magpie."

"No she couldn't," said Rio. "Magpie's a double agent stealing information from MI6 and giving it to Umbra. Clementine can't do that because she left MI6 five years ago. It would have to be someone who can still easily come and go at Vauxhall Cross. If Clemmie showed up there, they'd have her cuffed before she made it to the metal detectors."

"But she still could've killed him," said Brooklyn.

"No she couldn't have," said Rio.

"And you know this because?" asked Brooklyn.

Rio gave her an incredulous look. "Because she's the one who gave us the clue. If it weren't for Clementine giving you the picture and putting the photo of the three ravens on Rutledge's cloud account, no one would think he'd been murdered. She would've gotten away with it. So why would she have given us the clues to incriminate herself?"

"Okay," Sydney said. "That makes a lot of sense. But still, she was there and he took a picture of her. Why?"

"That, I don't know," said Rio. "I'd figure it out, but I just burned off a bunch of energy with all that deductive reasoning. I think I need some more clam chowder to recharge my batteries."

He gave Monty a hopeful look, but she didn't bite.

"I think you've had enough food today, mate," said Paris. "We practically ate our way across the city."

"Was it only eating?" asked Brooklyn. "Or did you manage to find anything useful?"

"We most certainly did," he answered proudly. "We figured out something about the datebook. Or more to the point, we figured out something about the names in the datebook."

"What?" asked Kat, her interest piqued.

Paris pulled out Rutledge's pocket calendar from his backpack and opened it to the last week. "Check this out. Fay Chie Hong; Bernhard Berliner, MD; and Charles Blyth are all appointments from that week."

"Right," said Kat. "We knew that. We just haven't been able to figure out who they are."

"Because they're not people," said Paris.

The girls each gave him a confused look.

"They're places," answered Paris. "Each one is a specific location. Fay Chie Hong is an alley in Chinatown, and a kind of sketchy one at that. By the way, it literally translates into 'fat boy alley,' so you have to be careful who you ask about it."

"And Bernhard Berliner, MD?" said Kat. "How is that a place?"

"That's the best one," said Rio.

"He says that because he's the one who figured it out," Paris joked.

"This is my story to tell and I'll tell it the way I want,"

said Rio. He turned to the others. "After Chinatown, we went across town to Golden Gate Park."

"Why?" asked Sydney.

Paris laughed. "Why do you think?"

"Of course," she said, rolling her eyes. "Food."

"Yes, food was involved. But it wasn't just food," Rio said. "There's also an excellent magic shop there, and we went to check out the latest tricks. And the food wasn't *just* food. They were the greatest burritos I've ever eaten."

"They were really good," Paris agreed.

"Anyway, after we ate, Paris suggested we check out the botanical garden, which was just down the street."

"I'd remembered that Rutledge had taken a picture of the sign there and then of some birds in the garden," said Paris. "So I went back and looked to see which day he'd taken them. Then I checked that against the calendar. He took them the same day he was supposed to meet Bernhard Berliner."

"Who's been dead for forty-four years," said Sydney.

"And then the most amazing thing happened. . . ." Paris paused dramatically.

"What?" asked Monty, enjoying this. "We're on tenterhooks."

Paris laughed and said, "Rio's eating finally caught up with him. He was actually full."

The others reacted comically. "That can't be."

"Unbelievable."

"Impossible."

"I may have eaten a few too many burritos," Rio admitted.

"Burritos with an *S*, as in plural?" asked Sydney. "How many did you have?"

"The number's not important," said Rio. "What's important is what happened next. I could feel the carne asada and chorizo churning around in my stomach, and I told Paris that I needed to take a break, so I sat on one of the benches. I thought I'd look at the flowers and let things settle. But while I was sitting there, I noticed there was a plaque on the bench dedicated to a woman named Blanche Thebom."

"Who's Blanche Thebom?" asked Kat.

"I have no idea," said Rio. "But it got me thinking about the names on the benches. So—and this was my idea—we started checking the names on *all* the benches."

"Just for the record," Paris interjected, "the botanical garden is made up of fifty-five acres and features hundreds of benches."

"After we'd checked thirty, Paris wanted to stop," said Rio. "But I insisted we keep going."

"And?" asked Brooklyn.

"Number forty-two," Paris said, holding up his phone for them to see the picture. It was a photograph of a wooden bench with a commemorative plaque that read:

BERNHARD BERLINER, MD

1885–1976

"Unbelievable," marveled Monty. She reached into her pocket, pulled out a ten-dollar-bill, and offered it to Rio.

"What's this for?" he asked.

"Go buy yourself another clam chowder in a sourdough bread bowl," she said. "You're a rock star."

Rio swiped the money with a huge grin and raced down the pier toward the seafood stands.

"So the names aren't the people he's meeting," said Brooklyn. "They're the places where he's meeting them."

"Classic spycraft, if you think about it," said Monty. "You'd never want to risk giving up an asset, so you wouldn't write down their name. Not even a code name or an alias. But if these are meeting spots, then the person still stays anonymous."

"So who's he meeting in these places?" asked Kat.

As Monty considered the answer, she stared out

toward the sun setting beyond the Golden Gate Bridge. The sky was on fire with color.

"Let's think it through," said Monty. "He's trying to figure out Magpie's identity. To do that, he'd have to go anyplace where there's any inkling that Magpie's been. Every city has old spies skulking around. Especially the cities he'd been visiting, like Moscow, Berlin, Beijing, and Tokyo. So he had to go to these places and meet with local assets to try to dig up anything on Magpie. But that's very dangerous."

"How so?" asked Brooklyn.

"Because those old spies and agents are probably some of the same people Magpie's using to pass along secrets and help Umbra with all their criminal activity. It's not always easy to tell who's on which side. So if he came across the wrong one, that could be bad."

"Worse than bad," said Sydney. "It could be deadly."

"Okay," said Kat. "If the names are places and not people, then what other places did he visit?"

Paris smiled. "I got a weird one for you." He opened up the datebook and said, "'October twelfth: Charles Blyth, four fifteen.' Then under it he wrote the initials SV."

"Are those the initials of the asset's name?" suggested Brooklyn.

"No, I don't think he'd do that," said Monty. "You've got to protect those names. Even initials."

"Silicon Valley," said Kat.

"You're quick," Paris said, impressed. "That's exactly what I thought too, although it took me a lot longer to come up with it. It makes total sense. Silicon Valley is the biggest tech center in the world. Which makes it a giant candy store for any cyber spies out there. Plus, it's just thirty miles south of San Francisco."

"But . . . ," Sydney said, sensing a problem with the logic.

"But there's nothing to do with Charles Blyth in Silicon Valley," Paris answered. "There are a few of people with that name who live down there, but we're no longer looking for people. We're looking for places."

"Did you find one?" asked Brooklyn. "A place, I mean."

"Yes," he said, beaming. "Two hundred miles northeast of here is a little ski resort named Squaw Valley. Also SV." He went to his phone and opened up Rutledge's cloud account. "So I double-checked against his photos, and sure enough, he shot a bunch of pictures of birds in the mountains that day. And the sign at the beginning of those pictures was this."

On the phone was a photo of a giant sign eighty feet tall and thirty feet wide. It was curved and featured the crests of various countries as well as the words SQUAW VALLEY, USA. At the very top were the Olympic rings.

"It's called the Tower of Nations," said Paris. "And it was the centerpiece of the 1960 Winter Olympics. This is where the Olympic torch was situated and where the medals were presented."

"And what does Charles Blyth have to do with the Olympics?" asked Brooklyn. "Did he win a medal there?"

"No, but he was the key person to bring the Olympics to Squaw Valley and so they named the ice-skating rink after him," he said. "The rink's gone, but there's a plaque commemorating it, and I was able to find a picture of it online."

"Let's get this straight," said Sydney. "All week he's meeting spies and assets in San Francisco. Then, two days before he's murdered, he drives four hours to meet someone in Squaw Valley, California. I mean, it's one thing to find spies in Moscow and Beijing. But a little town none of us have ever heard of?"

"I can think of worse places to retire than a ski resort," said Monty.

Rio returned with his new bread bowl full of clam chowder. "This is so delicious," he mumbled with his mouth full. "How far did you get?"

"Squaw Valley Olympics," said Paris.

"Cool, isn't it?" said Rio. "It totally makes sense."

"Except it doesn't," said Kat. "Let me see that," she said as she took the datebook from Paris.

"Hey, just because you're not the one who solved the riddle this time doesn't mean that we're wrong," said Rio.

"I don't think you're wrong at all," said Kat. "Quite the contrary. I think you're exactly right. This solution is brilliant."

At the mention of brilliance, Rio smiled proudly and then ate another spoonful of clam chowder.

"I have no doubt that you're right," she said. "Which makes this entry even more confusing."

She opened the datebook. "Here, the day before he died, he had an appointment for R.F. Stroud at nine thirty a.m."

"But *he's* R.F. Stroud," said Rio.

"Exactly," answered Kat. "And when I thought the entries were all people, I convinced myself that it was his little way of reserving time to be by himself. I didn't really believe that, but I ignored the problem. Well, now I can't ignore it."

"What do you mean?" asked Paris.

"I believe in patterns. Patterns are everything," she said. "And you have convinced me that these entries are places, not people. That's a pattern, except this one doesn't fit. How could he think of himself as a place to visit?"

Monty's phone rang and she looked down at the caller ID. "It's Mother," she said. Then she walked off so she could talk with a bit of privacy.

Everyone watched closely, trying to read her reaction. This was the call they'd been waiting for. They were dying to know if he'd found Annie and Robert. The conversation was quick, and when Monty walked back to the group, the lack of a smile was telling.

"They weren't there," she said.

"Oh no," said Brooklyn. "I was wrong. I can't believe I made such a big mistake and got his hopes up."

"You weren't wrong, honey," said Monty. "They'd been at the school. You nailed it. But Clementine withdrew them a few months ago."

"Any idea where they went?" Sydney asked hopefully.

Monty shook her head. "None," she said. "They've disappeared."

The lively mood of team problem-solving quickly turned somber as they weighed the news. They sat quietly and imagined what Mother was going through.

Sydney was near tears, so she walked over to the end of the dock and looked out at the water, her face turned away from the others.

Monty moved over next to her. She knew Sydney blamed herself and would take this hardest of all. She could've made a thousand arguments for why none of it was her fault, but she knew Sydney didn't want to hear any of those. At least not now. So she just reached over and put her arm around her.

The sun had set, and there was a chill in the air as the wind blew off the bay. Soon everybody was at the railing except Kat, who stayed on the bench looking at her phone.

During the hour they'd been at the wharf, the entire view from the waterfront had transformed. When the sun was setting, attention naturally fell on the Golden Gate Bridge and the Pacific Ocean beyond it. But now that night had fallen and the sky was black, the focus shifted to the island just a mile offshore.

It was Alcatraz, a notorious prison that was now the city's most popular tourist attraction. At night it was all lit up, and the group silently stared at it for a few minutes. No one wanted to talk, until Kat let out a yelp.

"What is it?" Monty asked.

Kat looked up from her phone and answered uncertainly, "I don't know if I should say."

"What do you mean?" asked Monty.

Kat scrunched up her face. "I'm not great at reading social cues. And I don't always know what's appropriate."

Monty chuckled at Kat's blunt honesty.

"I feel really sad for Mother," Kat continued. "And when I feel sad, I like to solve problems. It helps distract my brain."

"That's good," said Monty.

"And before the call came, we were trying to solve a problem . . . so I did. I solved it. But I don't know if I should wait until later to tell you the solution."

"What problem?" asked Paris. "R.F. Stroud?"

Kat nodded.

"You figured it out?" said Rio, impressed.

She nodded again.

"Please," Monty said, "tell us."

"Yeah," added Brooklyn. "It would be nice to hear something positive."

They turned to face Kat, although Sydney still had a

hangdog expression as she wiped away some tears with the arm of her hoodie.

"Like I said earlier, I believe in patterns," said Kat. "And this pattern didn't make sense to me. But it's not the only one. Another pattern has been nagging at me for days. When Mother first joined MI6 and was on Rutledge's spy team, what alias did Rutledge give him?"

"Swift," said Paris. "Gordon Swift."

"Yes. And what was Clementine's?"

"Robin something," said Brooklyn.

"Right, Swift and Robin," said Kat. "Both birds. That's a pattern, and it makes sense because Rutledge loves birds."

"So what doesn't fit about the pattern?" asked Rio.

"He doesn't," said Kat. "His alias is R.F. Stroud, which doesn't have anything to do with birds. Or at least I didn't think it did. But the entry in the datebook got me thinking, so I searched for something and found this."

She looked down at her phone and read what was on it. "Robert Franklin Stroud was a notorious criminal who spent most of his adult life in prisons across the United States. While in solitary confinement at one, he discovered a nest of injured birds and cared for them. He became fascinated with birds, studied them, and turned into a noted ornithologist. From prison he wrote scholarly papers about various species, primarily canaries."

"Wow," said Paris. "That's quite a transition from criminal to scientist."

"But it explains why Rutledge would use that as an alias," said Brooklyn.

"There's more," said Kat. "Stroud became so famous that a movie was made about his life. The film was even nominated for four Academy Awards."

"Really?" said Brooklyn. "That's kind of amazing."

"What was the movie called?" asked Rio.

Kat looked out across the water as she said, *"Birdman of Alcatraz."*

SFO

ELEVEN HOURS AND FIFTEEN MINUTES
after taking off from London, British Airways flight 287
landed at San Francisco International Airport just before
midnight. Among those seated in the elite business class
was a passenger named Jordan Pope.

Or at least that was the name on the phony passport.

Pope's real name had been buried under so many
aliases and fake identities that it had long since lost any
meaning. That was the price of being a spy. At some

point, you stopped being the person you once were and just became a temporary identity.

"Welcome to San Francisco," said the immigration officer. "Passport, please."

Pope slid the passport to the man and waited. As far as forgeries went, this one was as good as there was. There was no doubt it would pass inspection. The officer scanned it through a reader, looked up, and asked, "So, what brings you to the United States? Business or pleasure?"

Magpie smiled and said, "Actually, I think a little bit of both."

The Rock

IT WAS A CHILLY MORNING, AND WITH A brisk wind blowing off the water, most of the passengers stayed inside and enjoyed the view through the panorama windows for the fifteen-minute ferry ride from Pier 33 to Alcatraz. Sydney was an exception. She stood at the front of the *Alcatraz Clipper* with the sea spray against her face, her cheeks turning pink and tender. She loved it all: the smell, the taste of salt in the air, the Golden Gate Bridge soaring to her left.

"Aren't you cold?" Brooklyn asked, tugging the ends

of her sweatshirt over her hands as she joined Sydney along the front rail.

"Nah," said Sydney. "This is nothing compared to cruising the North Sea on the *Sylvia Earle*. *That* was cold."

"And yet you still went scuba diving," kidded Brooklyn.

They both laughed, and it felt good. It was the first time they'd joked about what had happened on the *Sylvia Earle*.

"Can you believe that was only a month ago?" asked Sydney.

"Really?" said Brooklyn. "It seems so much longer."

"I know," said Sydney. "Hopefully, not too long for me to apologize."

"Apologize for what?" asked Brooklyn.

Sydney gave her a look. "For what I said. For the way I acted. For . . . *everything*."

Brooklyn looked at her friend and gave her a wink. "Best mates."

Sydney nodded. "Best mates." She took a deep breath of salt air and added, "And as your best mate, I need to ask a favor."

"Wow, that was quick," joked Brooklyn.

"When we get back to the FARM, I need you to show me how I can help look for Annie and Robert," she said. "I feel terrible for Mother. I'm obviously not as good with a computer as you are, but there has to be something I can do."

"Absolutely," said Brooklyn. "I'm determined that we will find them. Yesterday was a dead end, but it wasn't *the* end."

"You know," joked Sydney, "there's a Motherism for that."

"Of course there is."

"*Dead ends are only course corrections to help you find the right direction.*"

Brooklyn laughed. "God, he is so corny with those things."

"I know," said Sydney. "But they really work."

Alcatraz was a rocky island with little vegetation that stood tall out of the water a mile and a half offshore in San Francisco Bay. Over its history it had been home to a lighthouse, a fort, a military prison, and a bird sanctuary. For one nineteen-month period, it was occupied by activists protesting for better treatment of Native Americans. But it was most famous for its history as a federal penitentiary.

From 1934 through 1963, Alcatraz was home to some of the country's most dangerous and notorious criminals, including Al Capone, Machine Gun Kelly, Mickey Cohen, and Robert Stroud, the famed Birdman. Now it was a historic landmark run by the National Park Service that welcomed nearly one and a half million visitors a year.

One of those visitors had been Parker Rutledge, who came to the island the day before he was murdered. Now Sydney, Brooklyn, Paris, Rio, and Kat were retracing his footsteps to see if they could find any significance in his scheduled "meeting" with R.F. Stroud. Monty was still in the city, following up on a few other appointments they'd found in his datebook. Normally, they would've broken up into teams, but Monty didn't want any of the kids to miss out on visiting Alcatraz, so she went alone.

"You'll have a lot of fun," she'd said that morning in the hotel. "Certainly more fun than if you were driving around with me all day."

Meanwhile, Mother was on a marathon thirteen-and-a-half-hour flight from Australia and was due to arrive in San Francisco at seven that evening. They were all going to have dinner together and figure out their next steps.

"Welcome to the Rock!" a park ranger said over a loudspeaker as the passengers disembarked from the *Clipper*. She gave a brief orientation talk at the same spot where prisoners once arrived to begin their sentences. Above her a weathered sign proclaimed:

UNITED STATES

PENITENTIARY

ALCATRAZ ISLAND AREA 12 ACRES

1 1/2 MILES TO TRANSPORT DOCK

ONLY GOVERNMENT BOATS PERMITTED

OTHERS MUST KEEP OFF 200 YARDS

NO ONE ALLOWED ASHORE

WITHOUT A PASS

"Imagine how chilling it was to come here and see that sign," Paris said. "All you had to do was look across the water and you could see civilization and freedom, but you realized that even though you could see it, you could never go there."

The elevation change from the dock to the prison was one hundred and thirty feet, and the team had to climb a series of steep paths and stairways. Once they made it, they joined a tour being led by another park ranger. It was fascinating. They walked along the different cellblocks on concrete pathways named after famous American streets like Broadway and Michigan Avenue. They toured cells, went through the cafeteria and laundry, and walked across the exercise yard. The highlight was at the end when they were looking into one of the cells and the ranger asked, "Does anybody want to know what it's like to hear that door shut behind you?"

There were fifteen people in the group, but the only one to raise a hand was Rio.

"I'll do it," he said.

"Are you sure?" asked the man. "It's kind of scary in there."

"No problem," Rio claimed.

"Well, then, let's lock you up," the ranger said playfully. "By the power vested in me by the National Park Service, I sentence you to serve time in Alcatraz."

Rio entered the cramped cell as the ranger continued.

"It's five feet wide and nine feet deep," he said. "So I hope you're not claustrophobic."

"I'll be okay," Rio said confidently.

"You say that now, but how does this change things?" replied the ranger.

He closed the door, and it made a loud metal-against-metal clanging that sent a shiver up Rio's spine.

"It's nothing," Rio said, determined not to show any fear. "I could stay here all day."

"I'm glad you said that," replied the ranger. "Because my supervisor's not going to be by here with the key for at least another hour."

"Wait, what?" Rio said, suddenly panicked.

The man smiled and pulled a key ring out of his pocket, and everybody laughed.

"Let's hear it for our inmate," the ranger said as he freed Rio, and everyone in the group clapped.

"How was it?" Paris asked Rio when he returned to the group.

"You couldn't pay me to go back in," said Rio. "Not even with food."

The ranger asked if anyone had any questions, and Paris raised his hand and asked, "Can you tell us which cell Robert Stroud was in?"

"Ah, the Birdman," said the ranger. "He spent most of his time in solitary in a cell on the hospital wing, which you can't see. But when he was out here among the population, he was on Dog Block—that's cellblock D, the very last cell at the end."

After the tour, the team headed straight for cellblock D and Robert Stroud's cell. It was much like the one Rio had just been locked in. It was painted light green along the bottom half and white on the top. There was a cot with a blanket, a small sink and toilet, and a desktop that folded down from one wall. Along the back was a window with two layers of caged bars, and a pair of shelves that held some of Stroud's personal books. The cell was open, but a Plexiglas door kept visitors from entering and disturbing it.

"Is this where we think Rutledge came?" asked Sydney.

"It makes sense," said Kat. "Whenever there was a name in his datebook, it stood for a place. This is the most logical *place* for R.F. Stroud."

"Yeah," said Sydney looking at an information poster. "According to this he was almost always in solitary confinement, so he rarely left this cell."

"So this has to be the place," said Paris. "But who was he meeting?"

"Another spy?" said Rio.

"I'm having trouble seeing that," said Paris.

"Why?"

"It completely makes sense for two spies to meet in an alley in Chinatown or on a bench in the park," he answered. "Both of those places are kind of anonymous and easy to get into and out of. But to come to Alcatraz you have to buy tickets, take a ferry, climb up the hill, and find cellblock D. And then, when you meet, you're surrounded by tourists walking around taking photographs, and if anything goes wrong, you're stuck on an island."

"I agree," said Sydney. "It doesn't feel like a meetup with a spy."

"Then who?" asked Brooklyn.

"I think he came to meet Stroud," Kat said, pointing at the cell. "Think about it. The two of them couldn't have been more different. One's a terrible criminal and the other's an MI6 spy. One's a villain and one's a hero. But they both love birds. They *really* love birds. So I think he came because he was curious and wanted to get a sense of Stroud. See his cell. Look at which ornithology books he had. Look at the—"

She stopped midsentence as something caught her eye and a smile slowly formed on her face.

"And?" asked Paris.

"And what?" said Kat, still looking at the shelf.

"You were in the middle of saying something, and then you just kind of stopped."

Kat turned to Rio. "Can you pick this lock?" she said motioning to the lock on the Plexiglas door.

"Sure, I can pick any lock," he said. "But I am not going into the cell, if that's what you're thinking."

"I don't need you to go in," she said. "I only need you to pick it. Just like Rutledge did."

"How do you know Rutledge picked the lock?" asked Paris.

"Top shelf, third book from the right," she said. "It's his bird book."

"They're all his bird books," said Rio, confused.

"Not Stroud's," said Kat. "Rutledge's. The missing one."

The others looked and saw what Kat was talking about. Alongside Stroud's books on canaries, pelicans, and others was a volume with a distinctive blue spine with red horizontal stripes. It matched the spines of the books Sydney and Paris had stolen from the Bodleian. It was the final one of Rutledge's handwritten field journals.

"Here?" asked Paris. "Why would he leave it? Was he trying to hide it?"

"Maybe he was done with it," suggested Kat. "Maybe he didn't need it anymore and thought it'd be cheeky to leave it with the Birdman's books."

"If that's true and he was done with it," said Brooklyn,

"then maybe he solved the case, figured out who Magpie was."

It took Rio only thirty-five seconds to pick the lock, and because the cell was so small, Sydney had to take only two steps in to reach the shelf. She grabbed the book, and without even looking at it hid it under her sweatshirt and started walking toward an exit. Rio locked the Plexiglas door again, and everyone followed.

Sydney led them to the far end of the exercise yard, and they formed a semicircle alongside the fence. This was as much privacy as they could get.

"We don't know for sure that it's Rutledge's," Sydney said, the book still hidden under her sweatshirt.

"Let's find out," said Brooklyn.

Sydney pulled it out and handed it to Kat, who'd been doing most of the work decoding the other bird books. She opened it to the first page and smiled.

"This is it."

"Wow!" said Paris. "Just wow."

"With this we can find out everything that happened the last six months of his life," Sydney said. "We can compare it to his datebook and photographs and pick up his trail."

"We can do better than that," said Kat. "Brooklyn

was right. Here on the last page it says that he's figured out who Magpie is."

"Are you serious?" said Rio. "What does it say?"

"It's the drawing of a magpie in a birdcage," she answered. "Underneath it says, 'October twelfth.' And next to that, 'Magpie: life list number eight three seven.'"

"Does it say who it is?" asked Rio.

"Not that I can tell," she said. "At least not yet. But give me a little time."

"October twelfth?" said Sydney. "But he was here on the thirteenth. Where was he on the twelfth?"

"Squaw Valley," answered Paris. "We've got to get out of here and call Monty," he continued as he pulled out his phone. "We'll meet up at the hotel and figure it out."

"Oh no," said Brooklyn. "This is bad."

"What are you talking about?" said Kat. "This is great."

"No, it is very, very bad!"

Brooklyn took a deep and nervous breath.

"What are you talking about?" asked Sydney.

The recreation yard overlooked the steep path that led to the prison. While the others were focused on the bird book, someone had caught Brooklyn's eye. It was a man, and he stood out because, unlike the other tourists, who were looking around at the prison and surrounding area, he was walking fast, his eyes studying his phone. There was a distinctive quality about the way he walked that she recognized. She couldn't place it at first, but the path wound back and forth all the way up, and when he turned, she knew exactly who it was.

He'd shaved his beard and dyed his hair blond, but she still recognized his face and spied the tattoo on his neck.

"That's Emil Blix."

35.

Fort Point

"HOW DO THEY PUT UP WITH THIS BLOODY traffic?" Monty exclaimed in frustration as she looked through the windshield toward an endless line of taillights. It had been hard enough for her to transition from driving on the left side of the road, as they did in the UK, to the right. But San Francisco's endless steep hills and its notorious gridlock were making a frustrating day even worse.

She'd already run into two dead ends trying to track

down locations listed in Rutledge's datebook and then struck out at the hospital checking to see if any of his possessions had made it into lost and found.

"'I'm sorry, but we have no record of a Mr. Stroud ever being admitted to this hospital,'" she said, doing a mocking impression of the administrator who'd been exceedingly unhelpful.

She'd tried to be patient with the woman. She'd even showed her a copy of the park service report that Kristin Gilson had filed saying that an ambulance took him "to the UCSF Medical Center."

"'Well, he's not listed on the computer, which means he never got here,'" Monty said, doing another scathing impression. "'Maybe whoever wrote the report got it wrong.'"

Monty wondered if that had been the case. Could the ranger have made a mistake? She pulled over and dug through her purse until she found Ranger Gilson's business card. She grabbed her phone and dialed.

"Muir Woods ranger office," answered a man's voice.

"Yes, hello," said Monty. "I'm looking for Ranger Gilson. Is she available?"

"Sorry, Kris isn't here," said the man. "She's working at Fort Point today."

"Fort Point?" asked Monty. "Where's that?"

"At the base of the Golden Gate Bridge," he answered. "On the city side."

Monty could see the bridge from the car. She was close. Finally, a lucky break today.

"Great," Monty said. "Thank you."

"Do you want to leave a message?"

"No thank you," she said. "I'll catch up with her another time."

She ended the call and programmed Fort Point into her GPS.

Even though she was only a few miles away, it took a little more than thirty minutes to get there. The ranger on the phone hadn't been exaggerating. Fort Point was a four-story redbrick fort that was literally at the southern anchorage of the Golden Gate Bridge. One of the bridge's support arches spanned directly over it, much like the roof of a domed stadium.

A sign at the entrance notified visitors that the entire top floor and parts of the second and third floors were closed to guests because a project was underway to restore the brickwork.

"Excuse me," Monty asked a ranger. "I'm looking for Ranger Gilson. Is she available?"

"She's in the office," said the man. "Is she expecting you?"

"No, but yesterday she was helping me, and there are a few more questions I need to ask her."

The ranger got his walkie-talkie and turned to Monty. "What's your name?"

"Alexandra Montgomery."

"Hey, Kris," the ranger called into his walkie-talkie. "I have an Alexandra Montgomery here to see you."

"I don't know an Alexandra Montgomery," came the reply.

"Of course," Monty said. "I probably never told her my name. Just tell her that it's the woman from England she was helping yesterday. The one with the family friend who loved Labradors."

He passed the message along, and Gilson replied that he should send her right up.

The man gave her directions to the ranger's office, which was on the third level.

"That part of the fort is closed to guests," he explained. "So please don't disturb any of the areas where they're doing the repairs."

"Of course not," she said. "Thank you so much."

The fort had five sides ringing an open courtyard.

Monty followed the directions to the third floor and knocked on the door marked RANGER'S OFFICE.

"Come in," called a voice.

Monty entered to find Gilson sitting at a desk. She'd obviously been working on her computer.

"Hi," Monty said. "So sorry to bother you. I called Muir Woods, but the ranger said you were here, and since I was nearby, I just dropped by rather than called. This will just take a second."

"Okay," she said. "How can I help you?"

"Well, first, I was wondering if perhaps our conversation yesterday jogged your memory at all. Did you happen to remember anything after I left?"

"No," she replied. "I told you everything I remember."

"And the hospital," said Monty. "I went to UCSF Medical Center today, and they had no record of him ever being there. Could he have gone somewhere else?"

Gilson thought about it. "He could have," she said. "I was there when they loaded him onto the ambulance, but it's ultimately up to the paramedics to decide where to take him. I assumed it was UCSF, but I could've gotten that wrong."

Monty mentally ran through everything from the day before. She pictured the Cathedral Grove.

"And at the Cathedral Grove, you found him by the plaque for President Roosevelt, right?"

At this point the ranger was getting perturbed. "Yes, as I told you yesterday. Now, I'm really sorry about Mr. Rutledge, but I don't have anything else to tell you, and I have a ton of paperwork I have to take care of."

"Yes, of course," Monty said, chastened. "I apologize for taking so much of your time."

She stood up to leave, and that's when she realized what had been nagging her. The part that didn't fit.

"One more thing," she said.

"What is it?" Gilson asked, exasperated.

"How did you know his name was Rutledge?"

The ranger gave her a quizzical look. "What?"

"You said it yesterday and you said it again just now. You called him Rutledge. How did you know that was his name?"

"I'm sure I read it on his identification from his wallet."

"But on your report you wrote Stroud."

"I'm sorry, what?" asked Gilson.

Monty opened the picture on her phone and looked right at it. She couldn't believe that she hadn't noticed it before. "Right here you wrote, 'The man was later identified as R.F. Stroud of Watlington, United Kingdom.'"

She looked up at Gilson and said, "Yet, you told me it was Rutledge."

The two of them stared at each other for a moment, and then a woman's voice spoke up from the adjoining office.

"Seriously, can't you get anything right?" said the woman. "This is why I hate to work with ex-CIA. You all are so sloppy."

Monty turned toward the voice and saw a gun pointed directly at her.

"Hello, Monty," said Magpie.

36.

Escape from Alcatraz

"EMIL BLIX IS HERE?" PARIS ASKED Brooklyn. "The scary dude who hijacked the *Sylvia Earle*?"

"The one and only," she replied.

"That doesn't make sense. Why would he be here?"

"That's a great question," Brooklyn said, annoyed. "Unfortunately, I don't know the answer. I just know that I don't want to see him again."

"Are you positive it's him?" asked Kat. "He's pretty far away."

"Yeah," said Brooklyn. "He shaved his beard and dyed his hair, but I totally recognize him, and I can see the tattoo on his neck."

They observed him for a moment as he continued up the path. He was moving at a fast pace and barely watching where he was going. Instead, his eyes were glued to the screen on his phone.

"What's he looking at?" asked Rio.

"Uh-oh," said Paris. "It may be a tracker."

"What makes you say that?" asked Brooklyn.

"You can tell he's not reading text," said Paris. "It's like he's looking at a map. That's why he's walking so quickly. I think he may be tracking you."

"How could he even do that?" Brooklyn asked.

"It's actually not that hard," he said. "Did he ever have access to your phone?"

"Yes," Brooklyn said sarcastically. "In the middle of the hijacking we stopped for a moment and compared phones and mobile plans."

"I think Paris is right," said Sydney. "I think he's tracking you. Or me. Or us."

Just then Blix looked up from the screen and in their direction. They quickly stepped back and out of view.

"This is not good," said Paris. "We have to think."

Blix was actually tracking both Brooklyn and Sydney using a device Magpie attached to their phones while they were testifying in Parliament. On his screen, they appeared as two dots on a map. As he got closer the dots got brighter, and the beeping he could hear in his earbuds got faster.

Beep. Beep.

He entered the prison and walked along the cellblocks following the dots.

Beep. Beep. Beep.

The dots were brighter when he turned down the corridor known as Michigan Avenue and walked along cellblock B.

Beep. Beep. Beep. Beep.

He was almost to them.

Beep. Beep. Beep. Beep. Beep. Beep.

The beeping intensified as he approached a cell. He turned to look and—

There was no sign of them. Just an empty cell. Still, the dots were practically glowing and the beeping was lightning fast. He stepped into the cell and looked to see that both phones had been placed on the bookshelf. He had no idea what was going on until he heard a loud noise behind him.

CLANG!

It was metal on metal. He spun around to see that the cell door had been shut behind him. He grabbed at it and tried to open it, but it was locked.

Brooklyn stepped out from around the corner and looked through the bars at him.

"You better get used to this," she said. "Turns out your daughters are going to have to visit you in prison."

Just then Sydney and Rio came running up with the park ranger who'd given them the tour.

"There he is," Sydney said breathlessly, pointing at Blix. "I've seen him on the news—that's the man who hijacked that boat in Scotland!"

37.

The Aftermath

EMIL BLIX WAS NO LONGER ON DISPLAY on cellblock B. He'd been moved to an actual holding cell that the National Park Service used for anyone breaking the law while visiting Alcatraz. He'd been identified, the FBI had agents rushing to the scene, and a few videos that tourists shot on their phones had already begun to go viral.

News was quickly spreading that the notorious Emil Blix had been captured. Although how he was captured was fuzzy, even among park rangers who'd supposedly done the capturing. In the midst of it all, the five City Spies gave performances that were worthy of any acting award. It was the way the story bounced from person to person that made it both believable and impossible to pin down at the same time.

"We were walking along cellblock B when I noticed this guy who was acting strange," Sydney said.

"She pointed it out and I said, 'You're right, he is acting strange,'" added Brooklyn.

"But it was Kat who recognized him," said Rio.

Kat nodded. "I watch the news a lot and was fascinated by the hijacking. I've seen all the shows about it. One of them showed pictures of Blix without his beard and that's how I recognized him."

"And the tattoo," added Brooklyn. "My cousin is a tattoo artist and I study them, and I noticed his and recognized it from a special report I'd seen online."

"We didn't know what to do," said Paris. "We didn't want to spook him and let on that we knew it was him."

"And then I remembered you and how nice you were on the tour," Rio said, buttering up the ranger. "So I ran to look for you."

"And then Blix walked in front of the same cell where you'd played the joke," said Paris. "And I don't know what came over me, but I just pushed him into the cell and slammed the door shut."

"And then you guys showed up to save the day," Sydney said, pointing to the rangers. "Thank goodness for you."

"But we really don't want to be part of the story," Brooklyn said. "He's a member of a dangerous criminal organization, and if they found out about us, we could be in trouble."

"Although we would like to get our phones back," Sydney said.

The explanation was dizzying and confusing. But what wasn't confusing was that a notorious criminal had literally been caught at Alcatraz, and the rangers were well positioned to be hailed as the heroes who'd captured him. They didn't really need to confuse the issue with a story about five kids that didn't make much sense to begin with.

Each of the five filled out a personal statement, and signed it with a fake name and address.

As soon as they were done, they hopped on the *Alcatraz Clipper* for the ferry ride back to Pier 33. This time they all stood on the front deck to plot their next steps. Brooklyn started taking apart Sydney's and her phones to look for the trackers, while Paris called Monty to tell her the news. The instant the call went through, he started blurting out what happened.

"Monty, you won't believe it," he said breathlessly. "We found the bird book on Alcatraz and Emil Blix showed up and has been arrested. Oh yeah, according to the bird book, Rutledge figured out Magpie's identity, but we don't know who it is."

There was a pause as Paris waited for an answer. But Monty didn't speak. Instead, a woman whose voice he did not recognize said, "Well, haven't you all been busy."

Double Rogue

THREE HOURS.

That's how much time they had to save Monty.

Magpie had laid it out for them. She had Monty and said she would trade her for the bird book straight up. The swap would happen at eight o'clock. One of them would bring the book to the location, and Magpie would deliver Monty. She'd call and give them the location twenty minutes before the swap.

Sydney demanded proof that she really had Monty, and ten minutes after the phone call a five-second video clip arrived that showed Monty gagged and tied in front of a brick wall.

The kids were at their hotel not far from Fisherman's Wharf.

"What do we do?" asked Paris. "Call the police?"

"And tell them what?" said Sydney. "That we're really young MI6 agents who need help capturing a mole and rescuing the cryptographer who's like a mother to us? I'm guessing that by the time they believe us, it's too late."

"How soon does Mother's flight land?" asked Kat.

"Two hours," said Paris. "If it's on time."

"What about alerting MI6?" suggested Brooklyn.

"Who can we call?" Sydney asked. "Tru gave only verbal approval and said that MI6 would disavow the operation should anything go wrong. We are in the middle of a rogue mission."

"Then we go double rogue," said Paris.

"What's double rogue?" asked Kat.

"That's one rogue op on top of another," he said. "We figure out the mission. We save the day."

"Absolutely," said Sydney.

"So what's our plan?" he asked her.

"Why are you asking me?" she said.

He smiled. "I don't know. Double rogue rebellious stuff sounds right up your alley. I'm thinking you've got to be the alpha on this."

"Me?" she said, confused. "Why would you want me? I've been a total screwup for months."

Paris nodded and said, "So I guess it's time to get your act together."

"Yeah," said Brooklyn. "We need you."

"I agree," said Kat.

"We know that you can do it; just tell us the plan," added Rio.

Sydney looked at their faces and realized they weren't just saying this. They meant it. They believed in her, and that gave her strength and confidence. There were a million things to consider and everything was moving at light speed. So she decided to slow down and break it all into smaller parts.

"What's Magpie's greatest advantage?" she asked.

"Anonymity," said Paris.

"Right," Sydney said. "So let's take that away from her." She turned to Kat and Brooklyn. "Take the bird book, the datebook, and Rutledge's pictures, and figure out Magpie's identity. He figured it out, which means the answer's in there somewhere."

The two of them took the books over to a table and started working.

"What's our greatest weakness?" she asked Paris and Rio. "What's keeping us from rescuing Monty?"

"We have no idea where she is."

"Then find her," she said. "Both of you."

"How?" asked Paris.

"Use those big brains," she said. "Start with the video and work from there."

"And what are you going to be doing?" asked Rio.

Sydney smiled and answered, "I've got some shopping to do."

She left and the two teams got to work.

"What can you see in the video?" Paris asked.

They played it a couple of times.

"Bricks," said Rio.

"Yes," Paris said. "But in a very distinct pattern. Like an arch."

Meanwhile, across the room Kat and Brooklyn were digging around in the bird book, looking for information.

"He really solved it in Squaw Valley?" said Brooklyn.

"That's what the book says," answered Kat.

Brooklyn laughed. "With all the exotic places he went,

he found the answer in Squaw Valley, California. Talk about your patterns that don't work: Berlin, Moscow, Beijing, Tokyo, Mexico City, and Squaw Valley."

Even though he was across the room, working on the other team, it was Paris who figured it out.

He overheard her and said, "That pattern works perfectly."

"It does?" asked Kat. "How?"

"The Olympics!" he said.

"Right," answered Brooklyn. "Squaw Valley hosted the Winter Olympics."

"No," he said. "All of those cities hosted the Olympics. That's what they have in common. That's the pattern."

"Okay," said Kat. "But how does the Olympics help us?"

"Let's look at it completely differently," said Paris. "We assumed that Rutledge was traveling around the world in Magpie's footsteps and that Magpie was traveling around the world to meet with spies."

"Right," said Kat. "So how do we turn that upside down?"

Paris smiled. "What if Magpie was traveling around the world for something else, and the spies were coming to wherever they were?"

"Then we need to identify why someone would go to

the cities where the Olympics were held," reasoned Kat.

"Exactly," said Paris.

Brooklyn gasped and excitedly started bouncing up and down. "I know who Magpie is! I know who Magpie is!" She took a calming breath and said, "It's Virginia Wescott."

"Who's Virginia Wescott?" asked Rio.

"She was on the *Sylvia Earle* with us," she answered. "She's a documentary filmmaker with the BBC. She made a huge series on the Olympics. She had to travel to those cities over and over."

"And if she's a double agent, that means that's where Umbra would send their people to talk with her."

"You know, a documentary filmmaker is a brilliant cover for a spy," said Paris. "They travel all over. They get access to places most people won't. They have the best recording equipment."

"She was the other MI6 agent on the boat," said Brooklyn, shaking her head.

"So we've got that figured out," said Rio. "Why don't you come over here and help us find Monty?"

Operation Golden Gate

SAN FRANCISCO INTERNATIONAL AIRPORT

MOTHER'S FLIGHT LANDED SIXTEEN MIN-utes late, and the moment he touched down, he turned on his phone and it instantly lit up. There were several messages from Paris, each more urgent than the last. He checked the time, and even before he tried calling him, he called Tru. She'd given him her personal number to use in case of emergency.

This more than qualified.

It was just after three in the morning in London, and Tru was not happy.

"Is this Harrison Marcus?" he asked, using the cover name for the number.

"Do you have any idea what time it is?" Tru asked.

"Of course I do," said Mother. "I'm about to tell you some things that are unexpected to say the least. I need you to listen and believe. And then I need you to act upon them. We can talk later about the whys and hows."

He waited for her to protest, but she remained quiet.

"Good," he said. "I've just arrived in San Francisco from Sydney, where I tracked Annie and Robert to their most recent school. While I was in flight, my team initiated the arrest of Emil Blix, located Parker Rutledge's final bird book, and uncovered the identity of Magpie. While they were doing that, Magpie captured Monty and is holding her to exchange for the book. The exchange is scheduled to happen in minutes at a place called Fort Point at the base of the Golden Gate Bridge. I need the CIA and FBI to arrive at the scene. And I need a car to be waiting for me the instant I get through passport control to take me to the location."

After she waited to make sure he was done, Tru responded, "Well, you sure do know how to wake someone up."

FORT POINT

There were two key elements that enabled them to figure out where Monty was being held. The first was the brickwork in the background of the picture. It was distinctive but impossible to search. But then Kat made a keen observation while they were still at the hotel.

"We all assumed that Rutledge was surprised to see Clementine at Muir Woods, and that's why he took the picture. That's what spooked him," she said. "But Clementine, Annie, and Robert weren't the only ones in the picture. The park ranger was in the picture too. *She* might have been the one who spooked him."

This changed everything. The idea that the park ranger might be a villain altered their search. They looked at National Park locations in the San Francisco area and quickly stumbled across Fort Point. The brickwork matched perfectly. That's why Paris and Sydney were climbing up the building's exterior wall when the phone call came from Magpie telling them that the swap would happen right at the fort's entrance in twenty minutes.

Magpie knew twenty minutes wasn't enough time to plan anything. But what she didn't know was that the

City Spies had already been there for more than an hour. The position of the fort in relation to the Golden Gate Bridge acted as a screen hiding their ascent.

"We need to be up there in fifteen," Paris said to Sydney.

"We've got it," she replied. "By the way, you were right on the plane."

"What do you mean?"

"When you said it wasn't a competition," she answered. "It's true. The better any of us are, the better all of us are."

"I know," said Paris. "That's part of what makes us family."

KING'S CROSS, LONDON, UK

Even though she was still in her pajamas, Tru stood up while talking to the chief of MI6. It was an official call and standing felt right.

"Yes, C, I am aware of the time," she said. "But two years ago you asked Parker Rutledge to come out of retirement and find Magpie. It cost him his life. Well, now one of my teams has not only found Magpie, but also the person who murdered Rutledge. And I'll be blunt, sir, they need help right away."

FORT POINT

It was ten minutes to eight, and Brooklyn was in position. She stood near the entrance to the fort, holding Rutledge's bird book. They'd debated whether or not to use the actual book. They knew it would be important evidence in proving that Virginia Wescott was Magpie, so they didn't want to risk her getting it. But they also knew they needed to play along in order to save Monty, and that was more important.

Brooklyn kept her position and focused her attention on the roof. She saw a light flash twice. Then there was a pause and it flashed two more times. That was the signal. Sydney and Paris had reached their positions. Everything was on schedule.

Even though no one could hear her, Brooklyn knew the mission wasn't real until someone said the magic words. So she said them aloud and assumed her teammates were doing the same.

"This operation is hot. We are a go."

SAN FRANCISCO INTERNATIONAL AIRPORT

As soon as he'd cleared immigration, Mother sprinted through the airport. Just as he reached the curb, a black sedan with US government license plates pulled up. A power window lowered and the driver asked, "Mother?"

FORT POINT—ROOF

Once they reached the roof, Paris and Sydney tied off a rope and lowered the other end down to the ground. Rio and Kat both climbed quickly, just as they had in a recent Saturday Match Day competition. Sydney checked her watch.

"Hurry up," she said as she reached out and helped Rio up the last bit. "We've got to stay on schedule or we're going to leave Brooklyn high and dry."

FORT POINT—ENTRANCE

Brooklyn approached the fort carefully and waited near a door marked STAFF ONLY, just as Magpie had instructed. Although it wasn't Magpie who came to the door. It was Gilson.

"Where's the book?" asked the ranger.

Brooklyn pulled it out of her backpack and showed it to her. "Where's Monty?"

"Oh, about that. There's been a change of plans," she

said. "You give me the book and you get out of here."

"What about Monty?"

"Don't you worry about Monty," said the woman.

"Then the deal's off," Brooklyn replied. "No Monty, no book." She put the journal back in the backpack and zipped it shut.

Gilson wasn't pleased. "Give me the book."

"Or what?" asked Brooklyn. "Are you going to do to me what you did to that agent in Manila?"

Gilson gave her an angry look. "What are you talking about?"

"Or will it be like the time in Kuala Lumpur?" Brooklyn asked. "You got in a lot of trouble for that. That's why they kicked you out of the army. Or rather, the CIA pretending you were in the army."

Gilson was about to explode.

"You see, I hacked your records," said Brooklyn. "And what I think is interesting is that the deal in Kuala Lumpur really hurt Umbra. It cost them millions. I wonder if they know that you're the one who was responsible for that."

"Who are you?"

"I'm the twelve-year-old girl who's running circles around you."

Gilson grabbed her by the arm and dragged her back toward the office. Just as Sydney had laid out in her plan.

FORT POINT—ROOF

"She's on the move," Sydney said, checking the read-out on her smartwatch. It was hooked up to a Find My Friends app on Brooklyn's phone. "She should lead us right to Monty. You're up, Kat."

Kat pulled out her phone and accessed a bogus e-mail account she'd just set up at the hotel. She hit send and then turned to the others and said, "It's amazing how easy it is to send 3,797 e-mails. All I had to do was press one button."

"Three thousand, seven hundred, and ninety-seven?" asked Paris. "That seems kind of random."

"Nothing I do is random," replied Kat. "It's a left-and-right-truncatable prime number. Primes do for me what carne asada burritos do for Rio."

FORT POINT—RANGER OFFICE

Magpie paced the floor of the ranger's office, anxiously awaiting Gilson's return with the bird book. Suddenly her phone started vibrating incessantly as her in-box blew up. She looked to see hundreds of e-mails arriving. The subject line for each one was "Magpie." And when she opened one, it revealed an animation of a squawking black bird.

"What on Earth?" she said, trying to make sense of it.

Gilson arrived with Brooklyn.

"Why did you bring her?" she demanded

"She knows too much," said Gilson.

Magpie did a quick pat-down on Brooklyn and discovered her phone. She swiped a couple of screens until she found the Find My Friends app.

"You idiot!" screamed Magpie. "Now they know exactly where we are."

"They're just kids," said Gilson.

Magpie slammed the phone on the floor and stomped on it until it was destroyed. "They are very much not *just* kids."

FORT POINT—ROOF

Sydney looked at her screen and watched as the signal suddenly went dead. "Magpie found the phone," she told the others. "We need to pick up the pace."

"Were you able to lock on the location?" asked Rio.

"You bet I was," replied Sydney. "Now, let's go get the rest of our family."

That word resonated with Paris, and he smiled at her as they started racing across the roof.

FORT POINT—STORAGE ROOM

Monty was bound and gagged in a darkened storage room. Suddenly the door opened and Brooklyn was shoved into the room. Her hands were duct-taped, and when Gilson pushed her, she fell onto the floor and landed alongside Monty, their faces right next to each other. Gilson slammed the door and locked it, but there was still enough light for the two to look at each other.

Monty had a panicked look and mumbled something worried.

"Don't worry," said Brooklyn, who hadn't been gagged. "I'm here to rescue you."

She flashed a smile.

That's when the first explosion went off.

CALIFORNIA HIGHWAY 1—NORTHBOUND—SAN FRANCISCO

Mother was impressed by the agent's driving skill as he zipped through traffic, dodging cars and racing to the scene. A call came over the radio.

"We just had a report of an explosion at Fort Point," said the voice.

The driver looked worried, but Mother smiled.

"Sydney!"

FORT POINT—RANGER OFFICE

Magpie's world was falling apart. A second burst of e-mails started filling her in-box, but these were also being sent to governments and news agencies around the world. They detailed some of the ops she had run. Just some recent highlights that Kat had been able to decipher. It was enough to blow her cover everywhere. In the language of spies she was burned.

A second explosion went off on the roof. It was designed for minimal damage and maximum visuals. It looked like a fireworks show outside of the fort and was sure to attract tons of attention.

FORT POINT—STORAGE ROOM

Despite Magpie's protestations, Ranger Gilson didn't quite grasp that Brooklyn was anything more than a smart kid who knew some damaging information. If she realized that Brooklyn had gone through extensive MI6 training, she might've been more careful when she duct-taped her wrists together.

As Gilson bound her, Brooklyn held her elbows and forearms tight against each other and made fists with her hands, just as she'd been taught in a hostage survival course. This had the effect of creating a seal between her arms. Once Brooklyn was certain Gilson was gone, she stood up, held her arms above her head, and quickly pulled them down and apart at the same time. The tape ripped open, and her hands were free. She ungagged Monty and started untying the rope that bound her.

FORT POINT—COURTYARD

Sydney had no intention of damaging the fort. Her explosions were designed to disrupt, not destroy, just as they had been on the *Sylvia Earle*. Only here she didn't have any plastic explosives to work with. Luckily, Chinatown was famous for fireworks, and even though they were against the law, there were plenty of black market dealers working out of souvenir shops. She found more than enough material to make some "bangers," as she liked to call them. She was about to set a third one out on the parade ground of the courtyard when Magpie came running toward the exit.

Magpie was simply trying to escape, but when she saw Sydney, her urge to run became one to fight. They'd spent a week together on the *Sylvia Earle* and had become friendly. Now they were mortal enemies. Magpie moved toward Sydney, her eyes filled with rage, and she started charging.

Sydney wanted nothing to do with that. She tossed her final banger and sprinted toward the fort's exit, hoping to disappear into the darkness of night.

Magpie was gaining, and it was only a matter of seconds before she would've caught up.

Sydney tripped over the curb when she reached the parking lot and crashed against the pavement, cutting the palms of her hands and gashing her left knee.

She looked up at Magpie, who had almost reached her, and braced for the impact.

Then a blur came from the side, and just like that,

Magpie was gone from Sydney's frame of vision. She heard two loud thuds and looked to see what had happened.

There, lying on the ground in a pile, Mother lay on top of Magpie. A perfect flying tackle that had taken the air out of both of them.

As a pair of FBI agents swarmed to cuff Magpie, Sydney saw a veritable army of them charge into the fort.

"Watch out for—" she called out, but Mother cut her off.

"They will," he said. "They know who all the good guys are."

Mother and Sydney shared a look, and after a couple of deep breaths, Sydney smiled and said, "Took you long enough."

Bertie and Jimmy

IT WAS A SATURDAY, TWO WEEKS AFTER the team had returned from San Francisco, and the FARM smelled like a bakery. For the second time in six weeks, Monty was on a baking binge. Only now she was making everybody's favorites. The trip to San Francisco had been a huge success and it was time to celebrate. In addition to lamingtons, pineapple upside-down cake, and millionaire's shortbread, she was also making *queijadinha*, chocolate layer cake, and macarons. Brooklyn was in the kitchen helping, although it really seemed more like she was there for any emergency tasting, when the doorbell rang.

"Weather weirdo," Brooklyn guessed.

"Probably," Monty said. "Can you get that?"

"Absolutely." She headed for the door, but along the way managed to swipe a finger full of chocolate frosting.

"I saw that," Monty said.

"Don't know what you're talking about," Brooklyn mumbled, her mouth full.

She answered the door to find a rather tall, well-dressed man. He looked familiar, although she couldn't quite place the face. "Good day," he said. "Is Bertie home?"

"I'm sorry," answered Brooklyn. "There's no one by that name who lives here."

"Right, right," he replied. "I believe you call him Mother."

"Wait a second. Mother's real name is Bertie?"

"Was I not supposed to say that?" he asked with a cringe.

"Come on in, I'll get him," she said.

"Thank you."

As he walked in, Brooklyn realized why he seemed familiar. "Has anyone ever told you that you look like the Prince of Wales?"

"Tragically, yes," said the man. "Although I think his hair is even more ridiculous than mine. Don't you agree?"

Brooklyn's eyes opened wide as she realized. "Wait a second," she gasped. "*Are* you the Prince of Wales?"

Just then Mother came down the stairs wearing his best suit.

"Ah, there's the man of the hour," said the prince. "How are you, Bertie?"

The other kids came in from watching television and were stunned by the scene unfolding before them.

"Seriously, Jimmy," Mother said. "How many times do I have to tell you not to call me that?"

"You know the Prince of Wales and you call him Jimmy?" asked Sydney.

"Well, I'm certainly not going to call him Your Highness or some such nonsense."

Mother got to the bottom of the stairs, and the two men greeted each other with a bear hug.

"Good to see you, mate," said the prince.

"Thanks for coming," replied Mother.

"Hold on a second!" exclaimed Paris. "What is going on here?"

Before Mother could answer, Monty came in from

the kitchen. Her hair was piled on top of her head in no particular fashion. She was wearing a T-shirt; sweatpants; and an apron covered in flour, chocolate, and coconut. Upon seeing her future king, she quickly tried to comport herself. She stood up straight, brushed her hair out of her face (streaking flour across her forehead as she did), and smiled totally unaware of the chocolate frosting on her front tooth.

"Good afternoon, Your Royal Highness."

"You must be Monty!" the prince said.

"Yes," Monty answered, baffled but still maintaining proper etiquette. "I must."

The prince turned to Mother and said, "She's just how you described her."

Monty stared daggers at Mother, and he turned to see the others.

"Great, we're all here," he said. "I'd like to introduce you to a friend from uni, who I believe you've all recognized by this point. This is James, Prince of Wales."

"So nice to meet you," said the prince.

"He's actually here on a bit of official business," Mother said. "So if you all would be so kind as to give him a little tour, I need to speak to Monty for a moment. Let's say we'll meet up in the priest hole in precisely ten minutes."

"Lovely," said James. "Now, which one of you is Sydney?"

"I am," she said meekly.

"How's the leg?" he asked. "I heard you took a nasty fall in San Francisco."

Sydney couldn't believe that the Prince of Wales not only knew her name, but that he also knew about her injured leg.

"Good," she said. "Thank you."

Sydney and the others led them around while Mother walked over to Monty.

"I noticed you're dressed in your best," Monty said.

"What, this old thing?" he joked. "Wanted to present well. After all, the Prince of Wales is here."

"So you knew he was coming?" she asked.

"Yes," he said.

"And it never occurred to you to let me know?"

"What?" he said. "And miss this?" He motioned to her mid-baking wardrobe.

"So are you going to tell me what's up?" she asked.

Mother nodded and started to explain the situation.

Seven minutes later, everybody was down in the priest hole. The initial shock of royalty arriving had begun to wear off. The prince was highly skilled at putting others at ease, and when Paris found out he was a Liverpool fan, he was in heaven.

"Okay," Sydney said. "Now that we're all down here, explain how it is that you know each other."

"We met at Freshers Week at St. Andrews," said the prince. "Everybody treated me the way you'd treat a prince. But Bertie treated me the way you'd treat a mate. And that's what I needed more than anything. We've been friends ever since."

"But you're here on official business?" asked Rio.

"Yes," he said. "In my position, I am aware of who you are and what you do. And whilst we can never talk about such things out in public, down here, amongst ourselves, let me give you the grandest thanks from everyone at Buckingham Palace. And I mean *everyone*."

They beamed.

"Your accomplishments in San Francisco are staggering," he continued. "You are, in my estimation, the best of Britain."

They thanked him, and Mother added, "You'd think the least you could do is give them a medal or something."

"I also understand that two of you are responsible for saving the *Sylvia Earle* and in the process saving the very annoying girl that is my cousin Alice. So thank you for that. I think."

"You're welcome," said Sydney and Brooklyn, laughing.

They were all clustered together congratulating one another when the prince spoke again.

"There is something else," he said. "Bertie came to me some time ago with a request. This was long before this most recent mission or the events of the *Sylvia Earle*. He asked me to do him a favor and I was happy to oblige, although even with my position it took some time, not to mention quite a bit of arm twisting and string pulling."

He turned to Sydney and Brooklyn and said, "The final hurdle was cleared after the two of you testified at Parliament. Bloody Mary Somersby was rightly embarrassed by her actions, and I offered her a chance to make up for them."

"What is it?" Sydney asked, totally confused.

"You see, along with my role as the Prince of Wales, I have various positions and patronages that are quite dear to me. The one that's the most important is that I am the royal patron for children's welfare. Although this is a responsibility I share with Parliament, which is why I needed the help of Mary Somersby."

"I don't understand," said Sydney.

"Maybe Mother should explain this part," he said.

Mother tried to find the words to express what he was feeling.

"What we have here—our team—is very unusual," he said. "But it means the world to me. Just as *you* mean the world to me. And by every definition that matters, *we* . . . are a family." He had to pause for a moment to keep tears from coming. "I know you're used to calling me Mother, but I would be honored if the five of you would also call me father."

Sydney was stunned. All of them were stunned.

"Are you saying you're adopting us?" she asked. "Legally?"

Mother looked at them, and he could no longer fight the tears.

"If you'll have me."

The first one to reach him was Sydney, and she wrapped him tight in a hug and held on as if she might never let go.

UK EYES ONLY

Secret Intelligence Service/MI6

Vauxhall Cross, London, UK

Project City Spies (aka Project Neverland)

Dossier prepared by A. Montgomery

CONFIDENTIAL

BROOKLYN

NAME: ~~Sara Maria~~
~~Martinez~~

COVER IDENTITY:
Christina Diaz

AGE: 12

BIRTHPLACE: Vega Alta, Puerto Rico

SKILL SET: A computer virtuoso. She was secretly tasked with hacking into the personal computers of several members of MI6 senior staff when a software glitch altered their passwords. As payment, ten pizzas were specially delivered from her favorite New York pizzeria.

FAVES: Likes the combo of art and technology and started studying graphic design for fun.

HAPPY PLACE: Since moving to the UK, she has become addicted to watching Bollywood movies on late-night telly. She usually watches with Kat while munching on a massive bowl of masala popcorn. They dance along with the characters when they think no one else is watching.

PARIS

NAME: ~~Salomon Omborenga~~

COVER IDENTITY: Lucas Doinel

AGE: 15

BIRTHPLACE: Kigali, Rwanda

SKILL SET: Has a lucky cricket bat named Charlie that he's used to fend off a masked intruder, break into an Indonesian railway station, and help pull Sydney to safety after she'd fallen through the ice on a frozen pond. Oddly, he's never used it to play cricket, which he considers mind-numbingly dull.

FAVES: Not spiders! They terrify him. He once extracted a key hidden in a tank filled with snakes without breaking a sweat only to return to the hotel, where he saw a harmless house spider and almost fainted.

HAPPY PLACE: Watching Liverpool FC on the widescreen with a full array of snacks. Warning: He wears the same red socks for every game and only washes them once the season's over.

SYDNEY

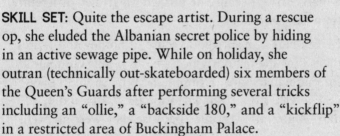

NAME: ~~Olivia Rose~~

COVER IDENTITY: Eleanor King

AGE: 14

BIRTHPLACE: Bondi Beach, New South Wales, Australia

SKILL SET: Quite the escape artist. During a rescue op, she eluded the Albanian secret police by hiding in an active sewage pipe. While on holiday, she outran (technically out-skateboarded) six members of the Queen's Guards after performing several tricks including an "ollie," a "backside 180," and a "kickflip" in a restricted area of Buckingham Palace.

FAVES: Rule-breaking. (See skateboard story above.)

HAPPY PLACE: The ocean. She regularly surfs in the frigid waters of the North Sea on a stretch of beach the others have christened "Sydney Surf."

KAT

NAME: ~~Amita Bishwakarma~~

COVER IDENTITY: Supriya Rai

AGE: 13

BIRTHPLACE: Monjo, Nepal

SKILL SET: Sees patterns where others see randomness. This helped her identify an undercover spy posing as a mail carrier because he pushed his trolley differently than his coworkers.

FAVES: Has a sneaky good sense of humor and writes jokes that she regularly posts in an online community for mathematicians. Examples: "Why shouldn't you take advice from pi? It's irrational." "Why did 4, 12, and 34 go into overtime? Because they were all even."

HAPPY PLACE: Life goals include constructing a crossword puzzle that gets printed in the *Times*, studying at Trinity College like Isaac Newton, and attending Comic-Con in San Diego dressed as Chewbacca (despite her petite size).

RIO

NAME: ~~João Cardozo~~

COVER IDENTITY: Rafael Rocha

AGE: 12

BIRTHPLACE: Copacabana, Rio de Janeiro, Brazil

SKILL SET: An accomplished magician, he's used sleight of hand and deception countless times during operations. He also puts on a magic show every December for patients at the Royal Aberdeen Children's Hospital.

FAVES: Has a lovely singing voice and is a soloist in the Kinloch Abbey boys' choir.

HAPPY PLACE: He's obsessed with eating and keeps a journal in which he rates food on a scale from one to one hundred according to a secret formula that he will not share. Kat and Brooklyn are competing to see who can crack the code first.

Acknowledgments

The City Spies team that comes together to publish these books is every bit as wonderful and impressive as the team featured on the pages. And like their secret agent counterparts, most of their essential work is done behind the scenes and without recognition. That said, I'd like to acknowledge some of the ones who helped bring *Golden Gate* to life.

First and foremost is the amazing Kristin Gilson, who edited the book and helped turn it into much more than it would've been without her. She demonstrated great patience, clear thinking, and best of all, laugh-out-loud humor. This is the first of what I hope will be many collaborations to come. I'm also thrilled to work with publisher extraordinaire Valerie Garfield. We've only just begun, but I feel like we're off to a wonderful start and can't wait to see where we go from here.

This is my eighth novel with Aladdin, and I'm constantly wowed by the creativity and hard work everyone there puts in to bring a book to life. Huge thanks to Cassie Malmo, Lauren Hoffman, Rebecca Vitkus, Sarah Woodruff, Emily Hutton, Nicole Russo, Caitlin Sweeny,

Amy Beaudoin, Anna Jarzab, Alissa Nigro, Savannah Breckenridge, Tiara Iandiorio, Erin Toller, Beth Parker, Beth Adelman, Jeannie Ng, Chelsea Morgan, and Amanda Livingston. Also, I am in love with the artwork created by Yaoyao Ma Van As.

I am beyond fortunate to call Rosemary Stimola my agent and my friend, although not in that order. The entire Stimola family (both literal and professional) is as good as it gets. Special thanks to Alli Hellegers, Peter Ryan, and Nick Croce. I'd also like to give a huge shout-out to Jason Dravis of the Dravis Agency.

While the idea of tween and teen superspies may stretch the imagination, I do aim for accuracy in almost everything else. Much of this means calling (and probably annoying) experts and friends with random questions about minute details.

For their expertise on Oxford University, I relied on Clementine Gaisman and Justin Graham. For all things nautical, I reached out to Hannah Delapp and Jay Coles. Ed Marsh is a font of knowledge across the spectrum and has been a wonderful friend ever since film school. Alex Rocha provided both culinary and cultural support, while Chris Graham answered no fewer than two hundred questions about cameras and photographic metadata. Ranger Maja Follin of the San Francisco Department of Recreation and Parks provided both wonderful insight and information. I'd also like to thank Shannon George for her numerous contributions for all my books.

I am beholden to young readers everywhere, and particularly to a handful who read while I'm writing to give me vital feedback. This includes Chloe, Jack, Madeline, Harrison, and Liz.

Most of all, I am thankful for the incredible love and support I get from my family.

Keep reading for a sneak peek at the City Spies' next mission!

CITY SPIES

FORBIDDEN CITY

New York Times Bestselling Author
JAMES PONTI

Billionaires' Row

IT WAS DARK, AND AS PARIS LOOKED OUT at the traffic, he caught a glimpse of his own reflection in the window. There was nothing remarkable about his face. No feature or quirk someone would notice or remember. He'd been born in Rwanda, grew up in Paris, lived in Scotland, and was now in London. And in each of those locations, he'd learned to blend in and disappear. This was an important quality because Paris wasn't just a schoolboy. He was also a spy. Blending in was essential.

Unlike spies in movies, whose modes of transportation ranged from jet packs and mini-submarines to bullet-proof Aston Martins tricked out with rocket launchers, he was headed to his latest mission on a city bus. The number seventy to South Kensington to be precise. That was the problem with being undercover *and* underage, you always needed somebody else to give you a ride.

"This is pathetic," he said, turning to Kat, who was sitting next to him. "Absolutely pathetic."

"What is?" she asked.

He looked around to make sure no one was listening and then leaned in to whisper, "We're about to break into one of the most expensive homes in London to steal a priceless work of art, and our getaway car is a bright red double-decker bus that does a max speed of five miles an hour."

Kat laughed, which only frustrated him more.

"First of all, we're not *stealing* it, we're *returning* it," she answered in an equally hushed tone. "Or have you forgotten about the little treasure that's been sewn into the lining of your jacket? Secondly, once you've put it back, why would anyone bother to chase us? Logic dictates that our *getaway* vehicle is irrelevant."

He nodded reluctantly and admitted, "Okay . . . you may have a point there."

"Of course I do," she replied. "Your problem is that you think being a spy is like being in an action movie."

"It's not?"

"No. It's like eating in the lunch hall at school."

"How do you figure that?" Paris asked.

"You pretend you belong and hope nobody notices you while you figure things out," she said. "Not to mention there's a decent chance the food's been poisoned."

He chuckled and saw that they were nearing their stop at Notting Hill Gate. "Finally, this is us."

He stood up to leave, but she stayed put, blocking his way.

"I'm not moving until you say it," she said firmly.

Paris was the alpha, which meant he was in charge now that they were in the field. It also meant he was the one who was supposed to say the phrase that officially started the mission. It was as much a good-luck ritual as it was an operational command.

"Here?" he replied. "On the bus?"

"Don't knock the bus," she said. "James Bond was named after one just like this."

"What do you mean?"

"When Ian Fleming was writing the first Bond book, he lived out in Kent and had to ride the bus back and forth to London," she explained.

"And?" he replied, not getting the connection.

"The bus from Kent to Victoria was number double oh seven."

"You're joking," he said.

"No. That's where he got the name. And, if it's good enough for Ian and James, it's good enough for you and me."

"Well, if you put it that way." He flashed a sly smile and said, "This operation is hot. We are a go."

Paris and Kat were part of the City Spies, an experimental team of five undercover agents, aged twelve to fifteen, who MI6 used when they had a mission in which adult agents would stand out. In this instance, they were about to crash the sweet sixteen party of a London socialite named Tabitha Banks.

The Secret Intelligence Service wasn't really interested in the birthday girl, but they were fascinated by her father. Reginald Banks was a multibillionaire whose business dealings sometimes involved nefarious underworld characters and shadowy figures from foreign intelligence agencies. MI6 desperately needed to get an agent into his home, and this party offered a rare opportunity to access the highly secure mansion located on Kensington Palace Gardens, one of the most exclusive neighborhoods in the world.

"Testing comms, one, two, three," Paris said as they walked away from the bus stop. "Can you hear me?"

He was using a covert communication device that looked like an everyday earbud to speak with team members monitoring the situation from a nearby safe house.

"Roger that, we hear you loud and clear," replied Mother, the MI6 agent in charge of the team.

"How about me?" asked Kat, testing her comms device.

"Perfect," Mother replied. "We are ready to rock and roll. We've got Brooklyn on the computer, and Sydney is . . ." There was a pause as Mother turned to Sydney. "What exactly are you doing?"

She gave him a look as if the answer were obvious. "I'm standing by just in case," she replied.

"We have Sydney standing by . . . just in case," Mother continued. "Although, technically, she's pacing more than standing."

"Relax, Syd," Paris said confidently. "We've got this."

"She's not pacing because she's worried about the mission," Brooklyn pointed out. "She's pacing because she's jealous that she's not the one doing it."

This brought a round of laughs, and Sydney didn't even bother to disagree. She always wanted to be the alpha and hated it when she missed out on the action.

"Just remember that I'm here if you need me," she offered. "Ready and willing."

"Good to know," said Paris.

"We've almost reached the guard gate at the end of the street," Kat said. "Any last words of wisdom?"

"Yes," answered Mother, who cleared his throat and paused dramatically before saying, *"This mission is fraught, so don't get caught."*

He liked to use rhyming couplets, nicknamed *Motherisms*, to remind the team of important elements of spy craft. This one left Kat and Paris completely uninspired.

"Seriously?" Kat replied.

"Is that the best you've got?" asked Paris.

"Well, I could've pointed out that if you get caught it will not only involve the Metropolitan Police, but quite likely the prime minister, the head of MI6, the Foreign Secretary, the French ambassador, and the president of Nepal," said Mother. "But I didn't want to overwhelm you, and it's exceedingly difficult to make all that rhyme."

"Fair points all," said Paris.

"Oh, there is one more thing, Paris," interjected Brooklyn.

"What's that?" he replied.

"Try to remember that your microphone is very sensitive," she said.

"Okay, but why am I remembering that?"

"Because it will blow out our headsets if you squeal too loudly when KB5 take the stage," she said, eliciting more laughter.

"You are so very funny," Paris replied. "Trust me, if I scream, it will be because I'm in musical agony. Although, calling what they do *music* is an offense to everyone from Beethoven to the Beatles."

KB5 was a British boy band whose heartthrob members had their pictures plastered on bedroom walls around the globe. Despite Paris's opinion of their musical ability, they regularly performed in sold-out arenas bursting with screaming fans. Tonight, however, they were playing a private concert for Tabitha's birthday. This was an advantage of having Reginald Banks for a father. Not only was he one of the richest people in the

United Kingdom, but he also created KB5 and owned the record label that produced their albums.

"I like their music," Sydney offered. "It's not too late if you want to swap roles."

"I would gladly do so," said Paris, "if only Australia had built their embassy on Kensington Palace Gardens."

Nicknamed Billionaires' Row, Kensington Palace Gardens was home to business tycoons, royal family members, foreign embassies, and the residences of several ambassadors. It was a half-mile long and protected at both ends by guard gates with armed police officers. For any outsiders who still didn't get the hint, there were even signs that read NO PHOTOGRAPHY.

Sir Reg, as he was known in the tabloids, couldn't just hold a concert in his backyard without the approval of his very powerful and extremely private neighbors. So, he'd come up with a brilliant solution and opened up the celebration to all the young people who lived on the street. Since no parent wanted to face the wrath of a furious teen or tween who'd missed out on the party of the decade, permission was granted.

Invitations were also extended to the children of embassy workers, which is when MI6 saw an opportunity.

As good fortune would have it, Kensington Palace Gardens was home to the ambassador of France and the embassy of Nepal, Paris and Kat's home countries. Some favors were called in and their names were added to the guest list.

For Paris, this meant swapping identities yet again, something he'd done countless times during his five years with MI6. As he approached the guardhouse, he flipped a mental switch and became someone else, like an actor stepping onto the stage in a West End play. Until the curtain fell on this little drama, he'd be Antoine Tremblay, the fifteen-year-old son of the second secretary for cultural affairs.

"Which embassy?" asked a guard.

"France," replied Paris.

The guard motioned him to a row of tables marked with flags representing the different countries. Here, the young guests were screened to make sure no overzealous KB5 fans were able to sneak into the party. Paris went to the table with the French tricolor and smiled at the man dressed in a sharp black suit.

"Invitation and identification," said the man.

Paris handed him two flawless forgeries: an official-looking invitation to the party, complete with a security hologram, and a French diplomatic ID for Antoine Tremblay.

"*Bonsoir, Antoine,*" the man said, slipping into French to test him. "*Ça va?*"

"*Oui, ça va bien,*" Paris replied naturally.

The guard checked his name off a list on a clipboard.

"*Comment vous aimez KB Cinq?*" asked the guard to see if he was excited about seeing KB5.

One of the keys to being undercover was not lying when it wasn't necessary. The more honest you were about specific things, the more believable you were overall. So rather than pretending to be excited about a boy band he detested, Paris answered truthfully. "*Disons, j'aime beaucoup mieux le gâteau d'anniversaire.*" I'm more excited about the birthday cake.

The man laughed and handed him a red wristband. "Put this on now and don't take it off until you leave for the night."

"*Merci beaucoup,*" replied Paris.

At a nearby table, Kat answered similar questions in a mix of Nepali and English.

Unlike the other kids who eagerly hurried toward the party, Paris and Kat took their time as they walked down the street. They'd been trained to study the landscape surrounding any mission and made mental notes of key details like the locations of security cameras and the fact that one of the streetlights was out. They looked for escape routes and potential hiding places. They also marveled at the mansions.

"Wow!" Paris said when they reached the one belonging to Sir Reg. "It looks even bigger than I imagined. The pictures don't do it justice."

"No kidding," said Kat. "You're going to need GPS just to find your way around in there."

The two of them had studied everything they could about the house including photographs, blueprints, and video from a BBC show about London's finest estates. The building was three stories tall and a showcase of Italian Renaissance architecture with thirty-eight rooms, including an indoor swimming pool, home cinema, and gymnasium.

It was also home to museum-quality art. There was a large Picasso that hung in the entryway, a pair of Van Gogh sketches in the living room, a Rodin statue in the garden, and an ornate Fabergé egg, known as the *Pearl of Russia*, that sat on the mantel above the fireplace in Sir Reg's private office.

Or at least that's what he thought.

In reality, it was a high-quality fake that contained a tiny hidden microphone British Intelligence had used to eavesdrop on his business meetings for nearly three years. The actual Fabergé egg worth nearly five million pounds was currently nestled inside a secret pocket sewn into Paris's jacket.

The *Pearl of Russia* was one of fifty-two jeweled eggs hand-crafted over a period of three decades for Tsars Alexander III and Nicholas II. Each year they'd given them as Easter presents to their wives and mothers. Paris's assignment was to sneak the real egg back into the office and replace it before the fake was exposed. This was necessary because Sir Reg had recently announced that he was loaning it to a museum in Moscow, where it would no doubt be examined by experts who would uncover the microphone. MI6 couldn't let that happen.

"We've arrived," Paris announced to the others in the safe house.

"How are the access points?" asked Mother.

"The walkway gate is manned by staff directing everyone to go around the house to the party in back," answered Paris. "But the gate for the driveway is wide open. The tour bus and equipment trucks for KB5 have blocked it so it can't shut."

"What about the house?" asked Mother.

"Two guards at each door," said Kat. "Judging by the holster bulges underneath their jackets, I'd say they're all armed."

"If there was only one per door, you might be able to pull off a diversion and distract the guard long enough to slip in," said Mother. "But with two, the main floor is a no-go. That means you'll need to enter the house through the alternate route."

Paris and Kat both turned their attention to the roof.

"Looks like someone's going to be playing Santa Claus," said Kat.

Paris gave her a raised eyebrow and replied, "Ho, ho, ho."

Middle school is hard.

Solving cases for the FBI is even harder. Doing both at the same time—well, that's just crazy. But that doesn't stop Florian Bates! Get to know the only kid who hangs out with FBI agents *and* international criminals.